PENGUIN CLASSICS

THE EUROPEANS

SERIES ADVISOR: PHILIP HORNE

HENRY JAMES was born in 1843 in Washington Place, New York, of Scottish and Irish ancestry. His father was a prominent theologian and philosopher and his elder brother, William, also became famous as a philosopher. James attended schools in New York and later in London, Paris and Geneva, before briefly entering the Law School at Harvard in 1862. In 1865 he began to contribute reviews and short stories to American journals. He visited Europe twice as an adult before moving to Paris in 1875, where he met Flaubert, Turgenev and other literary figures. However, after a year he moved to London, where he met with such success in society that he confessed to accepting 107 invitations in the winter of 1878–9 alone. In 1898 he left London and went to live at Lamb House, Rye, Sussex. Henry James became a naturalized British citizen in 1915, and was awarded the Order of Merit in 1916, shortly before his death in February of that year.

In addition to many short stories, plays, books of criticism, biography and autobiography, and much travel writing, he wrote some twenty novels, the first of which, *Watch and Ward*, appeared serially in the *Atlantic Monthly* in 1871. His novella 'Daisy Miller' (1878) established him as a literary figure on both sides of the Atlantic. Other novels include *Roderick Hudson* (1875), *The American* (1877), *The Europeans* (1878), *Washington Square* (1880), *The Portrait of a Lady* (1881), *The Bostonians* (1886), *The Princess Casamassima* (1886), *The Tragic Muse* (1890), *The Spoils of Poynton* (1897), *What Maisie Knew* (1897), *The Awkward Age* (1899), *The Wings of the Dove* (1902), *The Ambassadors* (1903) and *The Golden Bowl* (1904).

ANDREW TAYLOR is a senior lecturer in English Literature at the University of Edinburgh. He is the author of *Henry James and the Father Question* (2002) and co-editor of *The Afterlife of John Brown* (2005) and *Transatlantic Literary Studies: A Reader*

(2007). He is also co-editor of the *Edinburgh Series in Transatlantic Studies*, published by Edinburgh University Press.

PHILIP HORNE is a Professor of English at University College London. He is the author of *Henry James and Revision: The New York Edition* (1990); editor of *Henry James: A Life in Letters* (1999); and co-editor of *Thorold Dickinson: A World of Film* (2008). He has also edited Henry James, *A London Life & The Reverberator*; and for Penguin, Henry James, *The Tragic Muse*, and Charles Dickens, *Oliver Twist*. He has written articles on Henry James, and on a wide range of other subjects, including telephones and literature, zombies and consumer culture, the films of Powell and Pressburger and Martin Scorsese, the texts of Emily Dickinson, and the criticism of F. R. Leavis.

HENRY JAMES

The Europeans

A Sketch

Edited with an Introduction and Notes by
ANDREW TAYLOR

PENGUIN BOOKS

PENGUIN CLASSICS

Published by the Penguin Group
Penguin Books Ltd, 80 Strand, London WC2R ORL, England
Penguin Group (USA) Inc., 375 Hudson Street, New York, New York 10014, USA
Penguin Group (Canada), 90 Eglinton Avenue East, Suite 700, Toronto, Ontario, Canada M4P 2Y3
(a division of Pearson Penguin Canada Inc.)
Penguin Ireland, 25 St Stephen's Green, Dublin 2, Ireland
(a division of Penguin Books Ltd)
Penguin Group (Australia), 250 Camberwell Road, Camberwell, Victoria 3124, Australia
(a division of Pearson Australia Group Pty Ltd)
Penguin Books India Pvt Ltd, 11 Community Centre, Panchsheel Park, New Delhi – 110 017, India
Penguin Group (NZ), 67 Apollo Drive, Rosedale, North Shore 0632, New Zealand
(a division of Pearson New Zealand Ltd)
Penguin Books (South Africa) (Pty) Ltd, 24 Sturdee Avenue, Rosebank, Johannesburg 2196, South Africa

Penguin Books Ltd, Registered Offices: 80 Strand, London WC2R ORL, England

www.penguin.com

First published 1878
Published in Penguin Classics 2008

3

Introduction and editorial material copyright © Andrew Taylor, 2008
Chronology copyright © Philip Horne, 2008
All rights reserved

The moral right of the editors has been asserted

Set in 10.25/12.25 pt PostScript Adobe Sabon
Typeset by Rowland Phototypesetting Ltd, Bury St Edmunds, Suffolk
Printed in Great Britain by Clays Ltd, St Ives plc

ISBN: 978-0-141-44140-5

Contents

Chronology

1843 *15 April*: HJ born at 21 Washington Place in New York City, second of five children of Henry James (1811–82), speculative theologian and social thinker, whose strict entrepreneur father had amassed wealth estimated at $3 million, one of the top ten American fortunes of his time, and his wife Mary (1810–82), daughter of James Walsh, a New York cotton merchant of Scottish origin.

1843–5 Accompanies parents to Paris and London.

1845–7 James family returns to USA and settles in Albany, New York.

1847–55 Family settles in New York City; HJ taught by tutors and in private schools.

1855–8 Family travels in Europe: Geneva, London, Paris, Boulogne-sur-Mer. Returns to USA and settles in Newport, Rhode Island.

1859–60 Family in Europe again: HJ attends scientific school, then the Academy (later the University) in Geneva. Learns German in Bonn.

September 1860: Family returns to Newport. HJ makes friends with future critic T. S. Perry (who records that HJ 'was continually writing stories, mainly of a romantic kind') and artist John La Farge.

1861–3 Injures his back helping to extinguish a fire in Newport and is exempted from military service in American Civil War (1861–5).

Autumn 1862: Enters Harvard Law School for a term. Begins to send stories to magazines.

1864 *February*: First short story, 'A Tragedy of Error', published anonymously in *Continental Monthly*.

May: Family moves to 13 Ashburton Place, Boston, Massachusetts.

October: Unsigned review published in *North American Review*.

1865 *March*: First signed tale, 'The Story of a Year', appears in *Atlantic Monthly*. HJ's criticism published in first number of the *Nation* (New York).

1866–8 Continues reviewing and writing stories.

Summer 1866: W. D. Howells, novelist, critic and influential editor, becomes a friend.

November 1866: Family moves to 20 Quincy Street, beside Harvard Yard, in Cambridge, Massachusetts.

1869 Travels for his health to England, where he meets John Ruskin, William Morris, Charles Darwin and George Eliot; also visits Switzerland and Italy.

1870 *March*: Death in USA of his much-loved cousin Minny Temple.

May: HJ, still unwell, is reluctantly back in Cambridge.

1871 *August–December*: First short novel, *Watch and Ward*, serialized in *Atlantic Monthly*.

1872–4 Accompanies invalid sister Alice and aunt Catherine Walsh ('Aunt Kate') to Europe in May. Writes travel pieces for the *Nation*. Between October 1872 and September 1874 spends periods of time in Paris, Rome, Switzerland, Homburg and Italy without his family.

Spring 1874: Begins first long novel, *Roderick Hudson*, in Florence.

September 1874: Returns to USA.

1875 *January*: Publishes *A Passionate Pilgrim, and Other Tales*, his first work to appear in book form. It is followed by *Transatlantic Sketches* (travel pieces) and then by *Roderick Hudson* in November. Spends six months in New York City (111 East 25th Street), then three in Cambridge.

11 November: Arrives at 29 rue de Luxembourg, Paris as correspondent for the *New York Tribune*.

    December: Begins new novel, *The American*.

1876 Meets Gustave Flaubert, Ivan Turgenev, Edmond de Goncourt, Alphonse Daudet, Guy de Maupassant and Émile Zola.

    December: Moves to London and settles at 3 Bolton Street, just off Piccadilly.

1877 Visits Paris, Florence and Rome.

    May: *The American* is published.

1878 Meets William Gladstone, Alfred Tennyson, and Robert Browning.

    February: Collection of essays, *French Poets and Novelists*, is the first book HJ publishes in London.

    July: Novella 'Daisy Miller' serialized in *The Cornhill Magazine*; in November Harper's publish it in the USA, establishing HJ's reputation on both sides of the Atlantic.

    September: Publishes novel *The Europeans*.

1879 *December*: Publishes novel *Confidence* and *Hawthorne* (critical study).

1880 *December*: Publishes novel *Washington Square*.

1881 *October*: Returns to USA; visits Cambridge.

    November: Publishes novel *The Portrait of a Lady*.

1882 *January*: Death of mother. Visits New York and Washington D.C.

    May: Travels back to England but returns to USA on death of father in December.

1883 *Summer*: Returns to London.

    November: Fourteen-volume collected edition of fiction published by Macmillan.

    December: Publishes *Portraits of Places* (travel writings).

1884 Sister Alice moves to London and settles near HJ.

    September: Publishes *A Little Tour in France* (travel writings) and *Tales of Three Cities*; his important artistic statement 'The Art of Fiction' appears in *Longman's Magazine*.

    Becomes a friend of R. L. Stevenson and Edmund Gosse. Writes to his American friend Grace Norton: 'I shall never marry . . . I am both happy enough and miserable enough, as it is.'

1885–6 Publishes two serial novels, *The Bostonians* and *The Princess Casamassima*.

    6 March 1886: Moves into flat at 34 de Vere Gardens.

1887 *Spring and summer*: Visits Florence and Venice. Continues friendship (begun in 1880) with American novelist Constance Fenimore Woolson.

1888 Publishes novel *The Reverberator*, novella 'The Aspern Papers' and *Partial Portraits* (criticism).

1889 Collection of tales *A London Life* published.

1890 Novel *The Tragic Muse* published.

1891 Play version of *The American* has a short run in the provinces and London.

1892 *February*: Publishes *The Lesson of the Master* (story collection).

    March: Death of Alice James in London.

1893 Three volumes of tales published: *The Real Thing* (March), *The Private Life* (June), *The Wheel of Time* (September).

1894 Deaths of Constance Fenimore Woolson and R. L. Stevenson.

1895 *5 January*: Play *Guy Domville* is greeted by boos and applause on its premiere at St James's Theatre; HJ abandons playwriting for many years.

    Visits Ireland. Takes up cycling. Publishes two volumes of tales, *Terminations* (May) and *Embarrassments* (June).

1896 Publishes novel *The Other House*.

1897 Two novels, *The Spoils of Poynton* and *What Maisie Knew*, published.

    February: Starts dictating, due to wrist problems.

    September: Takes lease on Lamb House, Rye, Sussex.

1898 *June*: Moves into Lamb House. Sussex neighbours include the writers Joseph Conrad, H. G. Wells and Ford Madox Hueffer (Ford).

    August: Publishes *In the Cage* (short novel).

    October: 'The Turn of the Screw', ghost story included in *The Two Magics*, proves his most popular work since 'Daisy Miller'.

1899 *April*: Novel *The Awkward Age* published.

August: Buys the freehold of Lamb House.

1900 Shaves off his beard.

August: Publishes collection of tales *The Soft Side*.

Friendship with American novelist Edith Wharton develops.

1901 *February*: Publishes novel *The Sacred Fount*.

1902 *August*: Publishes novel *The Wings of the Dove*.

1903 *February*: Publishes collection of tales *The Better Sort*.

September: Publishes novel *The Ambassadors*.

October: Publishes memoir *William Wetmore Story and his Friends*.

1904 *August*: Sails to USA, his first visit for twenty-one years. Travels to New England, New York, Philadelphia, Washington, the South, St Louis, Chicago, Los Angeles and San Francisco.

November: Publishes novel *The Golden Bowl*.

1905 *January*: Is President Theodore Roosevelt's guest at the White House. Elected to the American Academy of Arts and Letters.

July: Back in Lamb House, begins revising works for the New York Edition of *The Novels and Tales of Henry James*.

October: Publishes *English Hours* (travel essays).

1906–8 Selects, arranges, writes prefaces and has illustrations made for New York Edition (published 1907–9, twenty-four volumes).

1907 *January*: Publishes *The American Scene* (travel essays).

1908 *March*: Play *The High Bid* produced at Edinburgh.

1909 *October*: Publishes *Italian Hours* (travel essays).

Health problems.

1910 *August*: Travels to USA with brother William, who dies a week after their return.

October: Publishes *The Finer Grain* (tales).

1911 *August*: Returns to England.

October: Publishes *The Outcry* (novel adapted from play).

Begins work on autobiography.

1912 *June*: Receives honorary doctorate from Oxford University.

October: Takes flat at 21 Carlyle Mansions, Cheyne Walk, Chelsea; suffers from shingles.

1913 *March*: Publishes *A Small Boy and Others* (first volume of autobiography). Portrait painted by John Singer Sargent for seventieth birthday.

1914 *March*: Publishes *Notes of a Son and Brother* (second volume of autobiography).

August: Outbreak of World War One; HJ becomes passionately engaged with the British cause and helps Belgian refugees and wounded soldiers.

October: Publishes *Notes on Novelists*.

1915 Is made honorary president of the American Volunteer Motor Ambulance Corps.

July: Becomes a British citizen.

Writes essays about the war (collected in *Within the Rim* (1919)) and the Preface to *Letters from America* (1916) by the poet Rupert Brooke, who had died the previous year.

2 December: Suffers a stroke.

1916 Awarded the Order of Merit in New Year Honours.

28 February: Dies. After his funeral in Chelsea Old Church, his ashes are smuggled back to America by sister-in-law and buried in the family plot in Cambridge.

Philip Horne

Introduction

First-time readers should be aware that details of the plot are revealed in this Introduction.

In 1878, the same year that he published *The Europeans* with the British publishers Macmillan, Henry James was commissioned by them to contribute a volume on the American writer Nathaniel Hawthorne (1804–64) to their *English Men of Letters* series, a characteristically Victorian enterprise that aimed to unite biographical detail with cultural and moral analysis. The thirty-nine volumes of the initial series, of which James's was one, were the introductory guides of their day, written to provide brisk accounts of the life and works of the chosen subjects, and designed for the general reader and for use in schools. The series was successful, both critically and commercially, and included volumes on Walter Scott, Percy Bysshe Shelley and John Milton. Of the first twenty-two titles published, only one, James's, treated an American author, an indication of the degree to which, in the eyes of the British publishing world at least, literary culture in the United States was felt to be lacking in substance and quality.

James was a new author to Macmillan, and the publishers were keen to make use of him. As well as *The Europeans*, his collection of essays *French Poets and Novelists* appeared under its imprint in 1878. In turn, it made sense for James to maintain his relationship with the company founded in 1843 by the brothers Alexander and Frederick Macmillan, for it was a powerful presence in the British book market, with the potential to bring a wider readership to his work than it had hitherto enjoyed. Writing to Frederick Macmillan before the publication of *The Europeans*, James humorously revealed his enlarged ambitions: 'it will be the beginning of my appearance before the British public as a novelist – as *the* novelist of the future, destined to extract from the B.P. eventually (both for himself & his publishers) a colossal fortune!'[1] It seems, though, that James accepted the Hawthorne commission with reservations, confessing to his friend Grace Norton in December 1879 that he had written it 'sadly, against my will. I wanted to let him [Hawthorne] alone.'[2] Despite the evidence of such retrospective qualms, James's *Hawthorne* is anything but a reluctant work. It was his most important piece of criticism to date, and remains the only book in the *English Men of Letters* series that is still regarded as required reading on its subject. As a significant intervention in transatlantic literary culture, *Hawthorne* delineated many of the conceptual parameters that informed James's writing career, although, as we will see, these parameters were continually open to contestation and revision.

To read *The Europeans* alongside the Hawthorne biography sets up a number of intriguing questions about Henry James's attitude to national identity, artistic possibility, and the form that fiction might take if it is to escape the dangers of provincial irrelevance. *The Europeans* establishes contrast and difference as its organizing narrative impulse: New England is visited by Europe, and the ensuing story of understanding and misreading, of connection and dislocation, propels the plot. The novel is an early example of James's so-called 'international theme', that is to say, his interest in the fictional possibilities of transatlantic exchange and migration as a means of exploring various forms of identity, personal and national. With *Roderick Hudson* (1875) and *The American* (1877), two earlier novels structured around the comparison between the Old and New Worlds, James had already announced the cosmopolitan nature of his subject matter. With *Hawthorne* and *The Europeans*, though, the international theme is treated differently. Whereas in his previous work James was writing about contemporary European and American societies, *these* two books establish chronological as well as geographical distance. *Hawthorne* is a biography of a writer and of a culture both now surpassed; *The Europeans* is written in the 1870s about a transatlantic encounter in the

1840s. In both, James is looking back to what he regards as a thinner, less complex era, one in which a residual Puritanism might be too narrowly restrictive for the free play of the imagination.

By the time James came to write *Hawthorne*, he was living in London and seeking to establish himself as part of a wider, European literary scene. He is therefore doubly displaced, temporally remote from the world of his celebrated literary precursor and also voluntarily exiled from the nation that produced them both. The biography allows James to write about Hawthorne – the New England writer was a 'beautiful, natural, original genius' whose life was 'as pure, as simple, as unsophisticated as his work' – *and* to position his own claims for artistic importance in opposition to his subject.[3] By inference, James is the practitioner of modern literary expression, working in the European realist tradition of the novel rather than in the romance form that he identifies as Hawthorne's provincial limitation. It is to Hawthorne's credit that he was able to produce the works that he did, but finally, for James, he was defeated by the aridness of a culture that could not sustain serious art. 'The moral,' writes James, 'is that the flower of art blooms only where the soil is deep, that it takes a great deal of history to produce a little literature, that it needs a complex social machinery to set a writer in motion' (*Hawthorne*, p. 320). Such conditions, for James, were missing from the New England world of the 1840s. Indeed he chooses to define this earlier American society by its absences, those elisions in the political and cultural fabric that are indicative of shallowness and arrested forms of pre-modernity, 'the negative side of the spectacle on which Hawthorne looked out' (*Hawthorne*, p. 351). The list is extensive – James is making his point as much through excess as through the pertinence of the list's specific elements – and is selectively quoted here:

[O]ne might enumerate the items of high civilization, as it exists in other countries, which are absent from the texture of American life . . . No State, in the European sense of the word, and indeed barely a specific national name. No sovereign, no court, no clergy, no army, no manors, nor old country-houses, nor parsonages, nor thatched cottages nor ivied ruins ... no great Universities nor public schools ... no literature, no novels, no museums, no pictures, no political society, no sporting class – no Epsom nor Ascot! (*Hawthorne*, pp. 351–2)

The present tense of this passage clearly suggests that James regards this as a *current* American situation; the narrowness of a pre-Civil War culture seems to have persisted into the present. The list veers between the obvious, the plausible and the highly contentious (is there *really* no 'political society' in the United States?); and the qualified notion of a State ('in the European sense') is suggestive of the degree to which James is writing for his British publisher and his new British audience. Such a reading constituency enables him to adopt a critical persona of Europeanized sophistication; he can present his version of a denuded United States from the vantage point of one who recognizes the superiority of Old World forms, even when some of those forms are being gently mocked ('no Epsom nor Ascot!'). Before embarking on his litany of gaps, James acknowledges that such a listing might seem 'almost ludicrous', but that word 'almost' prevents us from being able to read this passage as merely a type of satire, of humour generated by exaggeration. It is 'almost ludicrous' to regard the United States in this way, but not entirely so.

As John Carlos Rowe has noted, the importance of *Hawthorne* lies in its assertion of an international literary tradition within which James wants to place his own and America's writing. 'James mythologized Hawthorne as the last American innocent,' Rowe comments, 'alienated by the provinciality of young America, precisely to establish for himself a local and native American tradition that could be taken up in order to be denationalized.' What we are presented with is an 'international James, free from the boundaries he invents to trap his Hawthorne'.[4] From his self-identified perspective of cosmopolitan modernity, the look back to a simpler time allows James to impose a framework of difference that might be historically questionable (are cultures ever that simple?), but one that is nevertheless highly productive as a way of organizing narrative. The double perspective of the 1840s and the 1870s establishes a generative contrast built around ideas of innocence and experience, narrowness and expansion, rigidity and flexibility. At the age of thirty-six, the author of *Hawthorne* appears to be participating in that conventional gesture of Romantic rebellion, the necessary disavowal of his place of origin as a means of establishing artistic independence.

The expression of national identity in James's fictional work is more complex, however, than the polemical condescension to be found in *Hawthorne* might suggest. James's barely disguised rejection of narrow nationalism in that book is one position among many that his writing explores. As a manifesto of authorial intent, *Hawthorne* makes its claims with verve and conviction; but in the more conflicted world of James's stories we are introduced to numerous nuanced expressions of affiliation, where often the distinctions between European and American identities are less clearly defined. If the United States is indicative of innocence and provinciality, it also produces individuals who possess astonishing vivacity and freshness; if Europe is the valued repository of tradition and history, it is also the location for corruption and sexual intrigue. James's characters negotiate their way around and through these often hidden markers of representation, aspiring to a form of cosmopolitanism that, in the process, finds selfhood confronted with often unfamiliar cultural signs. In an 1877 essay 'Occasional Paris', James describes the 'cosmopolite spirit' as one which tries 'to convince you that national virtues are numerous, though they may be different, and to make downright preference really very hard'.[5] Many of the central characters in his fiction – one thinks of Roderick Hudson in the novel of that name (1875), Isabel Archer in *The Portrait of a Lady* (1881) and Lambert Strether in *The Ambassadors* (1903) – find themselves having to read strange forms of international culture in order to acquire the appropriate language and codes of behaviour.

The kind of openness to experience that James suggests is essential to cosmopolitanism has its own risks, however, especially when it is faced with an inflexibility of attitude that resists all attempts at interaction. That such a notion of narrow rigidity could be located *anywhere* – not just in Hawthorne's New England – is evident in James's early review (1866) of the nineteenth-century French diarist Eugénie de Guérin. Here he reverses the conventional hemispheric demarcations of innocence and experience. For de Guérin, James writes, 'there existed but two objects – the church and the world, of neither of which did it occur to her to attempt an analysis. One was all good, the other all evil.'[6] De Guérin's French provinciality – 'the social vacuity of her life' – is contrasted with a very different conception of American (and specifically New England) identity from that to be found in *Hawthorne* in 1879. In the earlier essay James acknowledges the 'moral rectitude' of his American scene (something that *The Europeans* also conveys), but he goes on to complicate any straightforward analogy that might be made between this form of high-minded morality and a state of intellectual simplicity:

> [T]o a certain extent, virtue and piety seem to be nourished by vice and scepticism. A very good man or a very good woman in New England is an extremely complex being. They are as innocent as you please, but they are anything but ignorant. They travel; they hold political opinions; they are accomplished Abolitionists; they read magazines and newspapers, and write for them; they read novels and police reports; they subscribe to lyceum lectures and to great libraries; in a word, they are enlightened. The result of this freedom of enquiry is that they become profoundly self-conscious. They obtain a notion of the relation of their virtues to a thousand objects ... and, owing to their relations with these objects, they present a myriad of reflected lights and shadows. (*Literary Criticism*, vol. II, pp. 434–5)

Against the roll-call of negatives that describe his later version of the United States, this assessment of New England, written in the year after the Civil War ended but still reflecting its antebellum character, is remarkable for its listing of attributes and qualities: here there *is* a political and literary culture at work. Central to the passage is the word 'relation', a key

Jamesian term that emerges here in a context suggesting that Americans have learned the idea of connection, of the possibility of writing narrative itself (the story of the relationship between oneself and others). In *Hawthorne* he wrote of the 'certain sense of proportion and relation' that characterized post-Civil War America, a time of post-lapsarian complexity in which selfhood had to be renegotiated in the light of the national trauma (*Hawthorne*, pp. 427–8). In the first chapter of *The Ambassadors*, like *The Europeans* another tale of transatlantic exchange but this time in the reverse direction, the narrator describes the situation of Lambert Strether. He is sent on his ambassadorial mission to Paris to reclaim for New England one of its sons, Chad Newsome, who might or might not be having a sexual relationship with a French woman. Strether, we are told, will find 'that his relation to his actual errand might prove none of the simplest'.[7]

Such an idea of 'relation' introduces into narrative the kinds of ambiguity and indeterminacy that drive James's fiction, where to exist in a relationship with something outside of the secure parameters of the self might threaten the very foundations upon which that self is built. The 'virtue and piety' of the New England character are dependent upon a relation with 'vice and scepticism'. This is not so that virtue can be thrown into clearer relief when placed alongside its opposite; instead James is more concerned to show the extent to which identity incorporates seemingly conflicting attributes that are, in fact, mutually reinforcing. Virtue is 'nourished' by vice, it provides an essential ingredient that both allows for its growth but also, more worryingly perhaps, might compromise its moral effectiveness. This undermining of positions of absolute interpretative authority – something that will concern James's brother, the philosopher and psychologist William James, as he begins to think through a philosophy of pragmatism – is present in the notion of the 'thousand objects' with which the New Englander has 'relations'. What is acknowledged here is the potential plurality of meaning and definition that guards against inflexible assertions. The acquisition of self-consciousness does not imply secure foundations for clear understanding – the

'myriad . . . reflected lights and shadows' may distort as much
as they reveal. As Ian Bell has remarked, 'Lights and shadows
are attractively but simultaneously deceptive: their reflections
belong above all to the realm of appearance, performance,
mirror, surface, and social gambit.'[8] Only superficially do artifice and performativity stand opposed to naturalness and sincerity. As James's response to Eugénie de Guérin makes clear
(and as *The Europeans* also explores), what might constitute
an idea of the 'natural', and where it might reside, is inevitably
more complex than any assertion of American provinciality
and European sophistication assumes.

Like the New England world that it portrays, the plot of *The
Europeans* is deceptively simple. Two arrivals from Europe,
Eugenia, the Baroness Münster, and her brother, Felix Young,
appear in Boston in search of family cousins. Eugenia is 'morganatically' married (see Notes, chapter II, note 4) to a member
of the German aristocracy who wishes to end the relationship;
her motives for visiting these American relatives are therefore
partly mercenary ('I insist upon their being rich,' she declares
(9)). Felix is an eternally optimistic artist, contracted to repro-
duce scenes of New England life for a newspaper. For both
characters, then, the New World is in part treated as a resource,
a means for economic advancement where the production of
commodities is linked to the tourist gaze. For Felix, the landscape offers itself for mass reproduction; Eugenia, as we will
see, offers herself as the consumable item and represents the
most troubling manifestation of cultural difference in the book.
Introductions are made with the American branch of the family,
and Eugenia and Felix are invited to stay with their uncle, Mr
Wentworth, his daughters, Charlotte and Gertrude, and his
son, Clifford, seven and a half miles outside the city. In this
intensely pastoral and domestic space, various romantic pair-
ings are entertained, attempted or achieved. Felix falls in love
with Gertrude, who is the focus of attention from Mr Brand,
the Unitarian minister, who is, in turn, the object of Charlotte's
desires. Robert Acton, a cousin and neighbour, finds himself
attracted to the exotic Eugenia. While such a summary may

suggest a transplanted version of Jane Austen, with her characteristic orchestration of relationships of misunderstanding that
culminate in marriage resolutions, James is less inclined to
conclude his work with such reassurances of social harmony.
While there is certainly something magically enclosed and protected about the world of the book (indeed something that
might remind us of James's own criticisms of Hawthorne's
'want of reality' (*Hawthorne*, p. 404)), *The Europeans* does
more than simply perpetuate an environment of fanciful
artistry. At the end of the novel, Eugenia's marriage plans
remain unachieved and she returns to Europe, her self-willed
expulsion from the American Garden of Eden suggestive of
how her identity is, finally, incommensurate with the norms
and parameters of 1840s New England.

In an important study of the cultural and social codes of
bourgeois nineteenth-century America, Karen Halttunen argues
that, from the 1850s onwards, a fundamental shift in con-
ceptualizations of identity took place. Values of sincerity and
transparency gave way to an acceptance of performance and
consumption as constitutive elements of selfhood. The 'sentimental demand for a transparent display of feeling', in a rapidly
expanding urban environment, was succeeded by 'a new view
of character as a theatrical part to be played by respectable men
and women'.[9] James's novel, we read on the first page, is set in
a past of 'upwards of thirty years', in the era of Hawthorne and
the provincial simplicity James discusses in his biography of
that writer. But while *Hawthorne* offers a cultural critique from
the vantage point of the late 1870s as a means of creating
temporal and artistic distance from the earlier period, *The
Europeans* dramatizes an encounter in which Eugenia, a figure
steeped in the rituals of performance and surface, meets the
apparent simplicity of antebellum America; it is as if she steps
out of the 1870s and back into a pre-Civil War culture of
authenticity. In so doing, James takes a very familiar feature of
his own time – the dominance of spectacle and artifice – and
places it in an earlier cultural moment in which those attributes
are regarded with more suspicion.

Readings of James that turn upon the relationship between

identity and capitalist consumption have tended to focus on his later writings such as *The Sacred Fount* (1901) and *The Golden Bowl* (1904), which address this connection explicitly. Jean-Christophe Agnew, for one, has written of how, in the late James, 'social life approximates a traffic in effects, the social selves generated therein acquire the durable and resilient feature of goods'. Furthermore, he notes that 'theatricality and commerce mix themselves in James's writing so as to suggest that conspicuousness itself – the exposure of stage or shop window – burnishes its human objects'.[10] Such a judgement can be extended back into James's earlier literary career too, to take into account the effect that Eugenia exerts in *The Europeans*. Walking around a sunny Boston 'gilded as with gold that was fresh from the mine' (11), the marriage of economics and theatricality is made explicit. Revelling in the 'much admiring observation' she has provoked, Eugenia's status as commodity is willingly embraced in the expectation of a reciprocal economic gain: she 'could not be an object of indifference . . . If she had come to seek her fortune, it seemed to her that her fortune would be easy to find' (11–12). One reaction to the performative style of Eugenia – her self-advertisement as an exotic consumable – is the retrenchment of sincerity as a normative, proscribed aspect of behaviour; an alternative is the emancipation of behaviour into possibilities of feeling and attachment triggered by such liberating theatricality. James's book explores both options, and a range of possible shades in between.

With consummate economy of style, the opening chapter of the novel introduces Eugenia's restless, ultimately unassimilable character. Waiting in a Boston hotel with her brother for the weather to clear, we first meet her 'looking out of one of the windows' at an unpropitious view. James's narrative voice here appears to endorse Eugenia's dismal opinion of America: the 'gloomy-looking inn', 'the mouldy tombstones and funereal umbrage' receiving 'ineffectual refreshment' from 'a dull, moist snow-fall' (1) announce an unimpressive landscape even before Eugenia states her dislike of it. Rather than offering the reader a distinctive register, one that is clearly separated from others in the book and so able to guide us reliably, the narrative voice inhabits a perspective that anticipates the point of view of the novel's most forceful character. Appropriately enough, a tale that is so preoccupied with different types of performativity, with the possibility of inhabiting a variety of roles, begins with an act of ventriloquism. We soon realize that this is just one of many tones that James's narrating sensibility will voice during the course of the story. As Kenneth Graham has remarked, there is a 'ubiquity' of narrative presence in *The Europeans*, 'sometimes adopting purely decorative postures, frequently outlining and evaluating action or character by irony, comparison, or straightforward commentary'. Such narrative mobility is perfectly in tune with James's desire to test the categories of artifice and authenticity as they are articulated in the book. What Graham calls the book's 'dynamic narrative mode'[11] anticipates the rapid and subtle changes in mood, tone and evaluation that will come to characterize James's later writing.

Immediately the reader is made aware of Eugenia's preoccupation with appearance and posture, with exaggeration and stance. She stands in front of a mirror, her hands adjusting her hair 'with a movement half caressing, half corrective', lost in a moment of 'desultory self-inspection [when] her face forgot its melancholy' (2). Her speech and actions are affected with an air of excessive gesture: ' "It's too horrible!" she exclaimed. "I shall go back – I shall go back!" And she flung herself into a chair before the fire' (3). Such theatricality of response, in which surface impression dominates, inevitably makes Eugenia a complex, inscrutable figure for her American cousins more used to an unshakeable alliance of appearance and truth. She is a potentially unstable combination of alternatives and possibilities: 'not pretty' but with a face that it is 'interesting and agreeable'; 'slender, [yet] with a great deal of extremely well-fashioned roundness of contour'; 'a suggestion both of maturity and flexibility' (3). Eugenia's is an indeterminate, fluxional identity that occupies a number of positions simultaneously. Her 'morganatic' marriage to the Prince of Silberstadt-Schreckenstein signifies a status that is neither proudly single nor conventionally wedded. Difficult to locate, her strangeness is emphasized by her hair being 'braided in a manner that suggested

some Southern or Eastern, some remotely foreign, woman' (3).
National affiliation becomes increasingly uncertain under these
conditions: Eugenia's original American self, already compro-
mised by her European marriage, is here further reduced to
make way for an appearance of exotic strangeness. But James
immediately works to undermine the opposition he seems to be
establishing here between New World stability and foreign
performance. Remarking on the 'violent blue of the [New Eng-
land] sky', Felix observes: 'It shows how extremes meet . . .
Instead of coming to the West we seem to have gone to the
East. The way the sky touches the house-tops is just like Cairo;
and the red and blue sign-boards patched over the face of
everything remind one of Mahometan decorations' (10). West
meets East, as if the signs that might suggest cultural difference
can no longer be located securely. New England itself seems to
be performing another, unfamiliar identity.

The difficulty of establishing a national identity in a context
of increased migration and cosmopolitan travel is deployed to
comic effect early on in the book, when Gertrude and Felix
meet for the first time. Talking about his father, Felix says:

'. . . My poor father was born in Sicily, but his parents were
American.'

'In Sicily?' Gertrude murmured.

'It is true,' said Felix Young, 'that they had spent their lives in
Europe. But they were very patriotic. And so are we.'

'And you are Sicilian,' said Gertrude.

'Sicilian, no! Let's see. I was born at a little place – a dear little
place – in France. My sister was born at Vienna.'

'So you are French,' said Gertrude.

'Heaven forbid!' cried the young man. Gertrude's eyes were
fixed upon him almost insistently. He began to laugh again. 'I
can easily be French, if that will please you.'

'You are a foreigner of some sort,' said Gertrude.

'Of some sort – yes; I suppose so. But who can say of what sort?
I don't think we have ever had occasion to settle the question.
You know there are people like that. About their country, their
religion, their profession, they can't tell.' (22–3)

Gertrude's desire to place Felix within secure geographical parameters is continually confounded by his playful resistance to identification. The combination of European residence *and* American patriotism creates an unfamiliar mix in the mind of James's daughter of Puritan simplicity. Instead of regarding national belonging as secure or fixed, Felix shares his sister's sense of play and performance: 'I can easily be French, if that will please you' suggests an embrace of identity not confined by birth or ancestry. Felix and Eugenia are early embodiments of the kind of borderless, cosmopolitan identity that is such a feature of our own time, with its globalized economy and permeable boundaries. Many of James's characters display the migratory ease of transnational worldliness that sees rigid definition as limiting. Felix cannot 'settle' on matters that, to the Wentworths at least, seem unproblematic. Rowe has argued that, from the end of the nineteenth century onwards, James's idea of cosmopolitanism was associated 'not only with understanding different cultures' achievements but also with a certain latitude in regard to social, sexual, and personal identities'.[12] While it is true that there is a marked preoccupation in James's post-1890 writing with destabilizing these forms of selfhood, with its cross-cultural, transatlantic framework *The Europeans* anticipates exactly this loosening of character. The degree of 'latitude' may not be as marked as in later works, but the response of the New England community to its European visitors is one of James's early considerations of America's potential for inhabiting a precious cosmopolitan identity.

Mr Wentworth, the 'very rigid and grave' (31) American patriarch, lives in a house, described at the beginning of chapter II, with 'large, clear-coloured rooms, with white wainscots' (19) whose doors and windows are 'all wide open, to admit the purifying sunshine' (14). The apparent lack of privacy, the absence of a space in which difference might be nurtured, is suggestive of a culture that avers all notions of deception and hidden identity. Architectural features – the house is 'painted a clean, clear, faded grey' – seem to correspond to the New England self, offering referential suggestions about the nature of the building's inhabitants. A 'well-ordered consciousness'

(40) regulates the Wentworth home. But even here James includes an unexpected element that unsettles this neat affinity between design and sensibility: 'half a dozen of those small cylindrical stools in green and blue porcelain ... suggest an affiliation between the residents and the Eastern trade' (15). At the heart of this scene of provinciality, then, are objects that remind us of contexts and environments outside and beyond its narrow confines. Although it is the book's worldly narrator who draws our attention to the stools, the inclusion of this detail infers the permeability of cultures by larger systems of exchange and circulation, even if only conjectured ones. At the same time as James is tracing the effects of a cultural Puritanism on mid-century New England, he is beginning to write of a world in which networks of travel will be central. Eugenia decorates her pastoral cottage, lent her by her uncle, with the kind of glimmering strangeness that is a wonder to her hosts: 'There were pink silk blinds in the windows, by which the room was strangely bedimmed; and along the chimney-piece was disposed a remarkable band of velvet, covered with coarse, dirty-looking lace' (48). Charlotte Wentworth, the more conventional of the two sisters (her 'imagination took no journeys whatever' (45)), is so confused by the aesthetic impropriety of the scene that she almost offers to help Eugenia 'put her superfluous draperies away'. 'Superfluous' is the telling word here, drawing our attention to a Puritan distrust of self-display and exaggerated visibility. The paraphernalia of Eugenia's performance exceeds the aesthetic (and one might add cultural, emotional and social) decorum of the cousins' world. The narrator tells us that 'The Baroness had brought with her to the New World a copious provision of the element of costume' (48): central to this idea of role-playing is a view of the self as heterogeneous, de-centred and implicated with other subjects, rather than unified and autonomous. In his influential account of James's writing, Ross Posnock observes that James 'is less concerned with role playing organized by a centred self than with putting in question the notion of this anchoring self'. The idea of a 'core self', 'static and homogenous', is replaced by a 'theatrical self [that] "bristles" with the

mobility and impurity of internal difference, of something not wholly itself'.[13]

Eugenia's appearance, manner and language work to disrupt the stabilities of the largely untravelled Americans. Mr Wentworth confesses to feeling 'perplexed and weighed upon' by the way she looks at him. His anxious response to the news of her morganatic marriage indicates a desire to resolve the interpretative questions such a concept has provoked in his mind. 'Was it right, was it just, was it acceptable?' (31) reveal the criteria by which judgements get settled in a culture where ambivalence is required to harden into forms of certainty. The narrator gently mocks Wentworth, who, in the face of 'The strange word "morganatic"' is reminded 'of a certain Mrs. Morgan whom he had once known and who had been a bold, unpleasant woman' (32). 'Bold' and 'unpleasant' are clearly Wentworth's opinions – at this point the narrative inhabits his point of view as he struggles to connect the strangeness of European vocabulary to his own provincial experience. Yet such is the flexibility of the narrative voice that the following sentence takes us immediately outside of the character's linguistic register: 'He had a feeling that it was his duty, so long as the Baroness looked at him, smiling in that way, to meet her glance with his own scrupulously adjusted, consciously frigid organs of vision.' The 'feeling' may be Wentworth's, but the precision of these adjectives is the work of the narrator. Vision that is frigid, for James, is no vision at all. What the book is asking us to consider is the way in which value becomes assigned to the natural at the expense of the artificial. The Wentworths may represent pastoral naturalness, but what kind of naturalness is it that depends upon an oppressive belief that pleasure is always subservient to responsibility? Much of James's early writing, in particular, revolves around patterns of opposites (innocence/experience; New World/Old World; provincialism/cosmopolitanism), and a large part of the work that we as readers do is to watch the play of these terms and locate our evaluations within and around them. James is careful to draw our attention to the performative nature of Mr Wentworth's response to the foreignness of Eugenia's stare. The patriarch's returning look is *as* crafted and posed ('scrupulously', 'consciously') as he perceives her gestures to be. If the manners of the visitors are a form of deception, then so, at times, is the simplicity of the New Englanders. In other words, while performance can point to paths of emancipation (what Richard Poirier has called its ability to keep us 'from being smothered by the inherited structuring of things'[14]), it can also be deployed in the maintenance of forms of orthodoxy. Self-fashioning of this kind may promote imaginative expansion, but it can just as easily betray that possibility.

The Europeans is alive to this kind of shifting exchange: James establishes his conceptual binaries but then works to show how they become translated through the narrative impetus of a transatlantic encounter. Late in the book Gertrude Wentworth, the one member of the family who is positioned by the text at a remove from the perspective of her father (we first meet her, on a Sunday, 'not dressed for church' (14)), has a conversation with Mr Brand, the Unitarian minister who believes himself to be in love with her:

> '. . . I think I ought to advise you.'
>   'To advise me?'
>   'I think I know your nature.'
>   'I think you don't,' said Gertrude, with a soft laugh . . .
>   'You are trying, as I said just now, to lower yourself.'
>   'I am trying for once to be natural!' cried Gertrude passionately. 'I have been pretending, all my life; I have been dishonest; it is you that have made me so!' Mr. Brand stood gazing at her, and she went on, 'Why shouldn't I be frivolous, if I want? One has a right to be frivolous, if it's one's nature. No, I don't care for the great questions. I care for pleasure – for amusement. Perhaps I am fond of wicked things; it is very possible!' (99–100)

Just as the distinctions between Old World and New are carefully blurred in the novel, the categories of 'natural' and 'artificial' have become detached from their conventional associations. Brand's assumptions here about Gertrude's 'nature' are refuted by her assertion that naturalness and honesty are synonymous with being frivolous. For Gertrude, her genuine self lies in the playfulness and possibility of artifice, and her declaration in favour of enjoyment places her beyond the narrowly conceived morality of the rest of her family. Mr Brand's first two statements here are important: his assertion of the right to advise, followed by his claim to the kind of omniscient knowledge of human nature that is reserved only for James's cosmopolitan narrator, clearly signal a belief in a readable and correctable self. Gertrude's response to such presumption confounds Brand's interpretative framework, one that is derived from a Puritan belief in transparent communication and unadorned immediacy. At a fundamental level, definitions of words become strange through Gertrude's deployment of them here.

Standards of honesty and truthfulness, as maintained through correct language use, are at the centre of one of the novel's key episodes. Eugenia makes a social call on the elderly Mrs Acton, mother of Robert Acton, the Baroness's potential suitor. Robert is a fascinating mixture of the worldly and the prim. His New World identity has been sufficiently disturbed by overseas travel, yet his lingering attachment to American probity deters him from an uninhibited embrace of difference. His 'national consciousness,' we learn, 'had been complicated by a residence in foreign lands, and ... yet [he] disliked to hear Americans abused' (76). Acton is regularly depicted with his hands in his pockets, anticipating the imaginative cowardice that marks his reluctance to commit unequivocally to the possibilities that Eugenia might offer. Initially though, with his cosmopolitan background, Acton appears promising as someone located slightly askance of the reigning values of New England society. Yet the meeting that he supervises between his mother and Eugenia plays out an important incompatibility between New and Old World perspectives on language. Tellingly, Mrs Acton ('very modest, very timid, and very ill' (80)) has a book of Ralph Waldo Emerson's essays at her bedside. Emerson (1803–82), the Transcendentalist philosopher and poet, was a close friend of James's father, and the subject of some critical attention by James himself. As with his reading of Hawthorne,

James's estimation of Emerson is predicated upon a sense of temporal distance: writing in the *Century Magazine* in 1883 he notes that Emerson's letters 'are especially interesting for the impression they give us of what we may call the thinness of the New England atmosphere in those days'. What James describes as its 'lightness, sparseness, transparency' reflects Emerson's romantic belief in the possibility of a transcendent self, unfettered by the contingencies of the everyday.[15]

In such a realm, where language can be attached securely to its referent, lies the apotheosis of 'sincerity' as a guiding principle, both of character-formation and of interpretative enquiry. Emerson believed that all languages were developments from a single originary language, and that it might be possible to reform linguistic structures in such a way that the lost relationship between word and thing could be re-established. An environment in which ambiguity is removed from communication, where the idea of performance becomes redundant, is the New World ideal against which all forms of social interaction are judged. Mrs Acton's meeting with Eugenia (who she regards as 'a clever foreign lady' (80)) is the occasion of Emersonian transparency confronted by its apparent opposite:

'I have heard a great deal about you,' she said, softly, to the Baroness.

'From your son, eh?' Eugenia asked. 'He has talked to me immensely of you. Oh, he talks of you as you would like,' the Baroness declared; 'as such a son *must* talk of such a mother!'

Mrs. Acton sat gazing; this was part of Madame Münster's 'manner'. (80–81)

When faced with such unusual social etiquette, Mrs Acton is at a loss as to how to respond to a 'manner' that marks itself out as performance (James's use of inverted commas to highlight this word emphasizes its accentuated visibility). Robert Acton, despite his pretensions to cosmopolitan breadth, recoils from the implications of Eugenia's speech, 'in vivid consciousness that he had barely mentioned his mother to their brilliant guest'. His mother's identity, we learn, has become distilled for him 'simply into the subjective emotion of gratitude'. Cleverly James manipulates the point-of-view in this scene. Acton's subjective position in relation to his mother abruptly switches to Eugenia's perception of this triangular encounter: 'The Baroness turned her smile toward him, and she instantly felt that she had been observed to be fibbing. She had struck a false note. But who were these people to whom fibbing was not pleasing?' The free indirect style locates us momentarily in Eugenia's sense of confusion, followed by indignation. What kind of society is it, she wonders, in which 'fibbing' – even, as here, for the sake of a smooth sociability – is deemed to be fundamentally transgressive? Acton's combination of the 'homely and the liberal' (79) is a construction that unravels at the slightest pressure, one that masks the fact that the primness of his cousins and neighbours is also his own. 'He believed', we are told, 'in the doctrine of wild oats', although the narrator slyly adds that 'he had not quite the courage to declare it' (104). Acton is ironically named, given his habitual inclination *against* action in the novel, and his hesitancy paralyses him in a state of arrested development. Failing to rise to the challenge of the dangerous opportunity that Eugenia presents, our last view of him is contained in the novel's pointed final line: 'Robert Acton, after his mother's death, married a particularly nice young girl.' The charade of his cosmopolitan difference can only be maintained by a relationship that will not challenge it – the blandness of 'nice' telling us all we need to know about Acton's wife.

In a letter of 1878 to his friend Lizzie Boot, James offered his own opinion on his recently published novel: 'The off-hand marrying in the end was *commandé* [ordered] – likewise the length of the tale. I *do* incline to melancholy endings – but it had been part of the bargain with Howells that *this* termination should be cheerful and that there should be distinct matrimony. So I did it off mechanically in the closing paragraphs.'[16] William Dean Howells was the editor of the *Atlantic Monthly*, which published *The Europeans* in serial form between July and October 1878. The reference to him here is a reminder of a commitment James had given that the story would be 'the brightest possible sun-spot'.[17] Indeed, the final paragraph of the story does present a tying up of strands almost in the manner of Jane Austen. Felix and Gertrude, once married, leave the United States, indicative of New England's unhomeliness for at least one of the Wentworth children.[18] Gertrude's more conventional siblings marry more conventionally: Clifford's bride is Lizzie Acton (they find 'their felicity in a narrower circle' (168)), and Charlotte weds the Unitarian Mr Brand. However, James's acknowledgement to Lizzie Boot that he deliberately resisted his usual disposition for the melancholy is only half the story. We have already seen how Robert Acton's marriage is held up for gentle disdain; the sunny mood is further clouded by the final image of Wentworth, who is listening out for 'the echo of [Gertrude's] gaiety' that 'often came back to the home of her earlier years' (169). Unable to generate his own playful environment, Wentworth relies on the recollection of ghosts from the past to remind him of a cosmopolitan American future for which he is fundamentally unsuited. Behind the apparent mechanical neatness of the narrative resolution, James allows shadows to intrude that belie his own apologetic dismissal.

By the time James came to re-read his fiction for what would comprise the collected New York Edition of his writing career (published in twenty-four volumes between 1907 and 1909), he decided quite quickly that *The Europeans* would be one of seven of his novels not to make the final selection. Although we have no definitive account of his reasons for excluding them, it is clear that James's carefully cultivated self-image as a modernist Master of nuanced complexity did not sit easily with his estimation that some of the earlier works (such as *The Europeans*, if his letter to Lizzie Boot is anything to go by) failed to display sufficient artistry.[19] But as I have been suggesting here, this underestimates the controlled sophistication of the novel. To be sure, the story does not display the intense interiority of much of the later works' often claustrophobic focus on the subtle interplay of different consciousnesses. *The Europeans* is lighter in its tone, more airy in its narrative perspective. Yet its qualities of characterization and flexible point-of-view, its concern with the relationship between national identity and selfhood, all look forward to the writing still to come. An unsigned review of the novel in the Boston-based *Atlantic Monthly* (February 1879) unwittingly recognized its prescience. Towards the end of a detailed but lukewarm account, the reviewer objected to the comparative, transatlantic shape of James's book: 'In general, one cannot help wishing that our native authors would have done with this incessant drawing of comparisons between ourselves and the folk in Europe, and our respective ways of living, thinking, and talking.' Instead of looking back at the Old World, 'we have our own life to live, our own resources to unfold, our own crude and complex conditions finally to compel into some sort of symmetry, our youth to train'.[20] As a country still to be narrated properly, the reviewer felt that America's writers should concern themselves with the work of national self-definition rather than worrying about European models.

To the extent that the review successfully hits its target, literary nationalism of this kind is indeed an authorial role alien to James. As we have seen, identifying him as a 'native author' is itself problematic, given his biographical and intellectual cosmopolitanism. But where *The Europeans* reveals its nascent modernity is in its realization that a genuinely transatlantic literature involves more than merely the comparison of discrete differences, and more than the establishment of a hierarchy between those differences. Whereas the reviewer in the *Atlantic Monthly* objected to James's apparent neglect of an authentic American culture, *The Europeans* is more concerned with showing how a mid-nineteenth-century environment of international exchange and mobility has *already* started to question the integrity of national demarcations and the literary characteristics that accompany them. Rather than trying to identify what constitutes a 'natural' New World identity, one untainted by the 'artifice' of Europe, James's novel works to undermine those binaries by showing how implicated they are in each other. In our current globalized world, where peoples and ideas circulate and percolate with apparent ease, James's historical tale of transatlantic misreading writes of and in a time of accelerating modernity. Although the story's subtitle, 'A

Sketch', does justice to the generally open and relaxed structure of the book, the great skill of *The Europeans* lies in its concern with the effects, both psychological and social, of unexpected encounters. It is an early example of James's lifelong project of internationalizing the novel and his prescient anticipation of what is now a familiar world of permeable borders and pluralized identities.

NOTES

If not given here, full details of the publications cited below will be found in Further Reading.

1. Rayburn S. Moore, ed., *The Correspondence of Henry James and the House of Macmillan, 1877–1914: 'All the Links in the Chain'* (Baton Rouge: Louisiana State University Press, 1993), p. 16.

2. *Henry James: Letters*, ed. Leon Edel, vol. II, *1875–83*, p. 262.

3. Henry James, *Hawthorne* (1879), in *Literary Criticism*, vol. II, *Essays, American & English Writers*, p. 457. Further references are given within brackets in the text.

4. John Carlos Rowe, *The Theoretical Dimensions of Henry James*, pp. 46, 47.

5. Henry James, *Portraits of Places* (London: Macmillan, 1883), p. 76.

6. *Literary Criticism*, vol. II, *French Writers, Other European Writers, the Prefaces to the New York Edition*, p. 435.

7. Henry James, *The Ambassadors* (London: Penguin Books, 2008), p. xx.

8. Ian F. A. Bell, 'Sincerity and Performance in *The Europeans*', p. 127.

9. Karen Halttunen, *Confidence Men and Painted Women: A Study of Middle-Class Culture in America, 1830–1870* (New Haven, CN: Yale University Press, 1982), pp. 193, 167.

10. Jean-Christophe Agnew, 'The Consuming Vision of Henry James', in Richard Wightman Fox and T. J. Jackson Lears, eds., *The Culture of Consumption: Critical Essays in American History 1880–1980* (New York: Pantheon Books, 1983), pp. 84, 85.

11. Kenneth Graham, *Indirections of the Novel: James, Conrad, and Forster*, pp. 19, 30.

12. John Carlos Rowe, 'Henry James and Globalization', *Henry James Review* 24 (2003), p. 212.

13. Ross Posnock, *The Trial of Curiosity*, p. 58.

14. Richard Poirier, *The Performing Self: Compositions and Decompositions in the Languages of Contemporary Life* (New York: Oxford University Press, 1971), p. xiii.

15. *Literary Criticism*, vol. II, pp. 244–5.

16. *Letters*, vol. II, p. 190.

17. *Letters*, vol. II, p. 104.

18. Paul Giles in *Virtual Americas: Transnational Fictions and the Transatlantic Imaginary* (Durham, NC: Duke University Press, 2002) notes that the experience of feeling estranged within one's own inherited cultural or national space is characteristic of Jamesian cosmopolitanism: 'James's personae . . . resist the comforts of cultural assimilation and take a more perverse pleasure in being strangers everywhere' (p. 117).

19. For an account of the genesis and development of the New York Edition, see Michael Anesko, *'Friction with the Market'*. Martha Banta, in her essay 'The Excluded Seven: Practice of Omission, Aesthetics of Refusal', suggests some of the aesthetic and literary reasons that might have influenced James in his selection. See David McWhirter, ed., *Henry James's New York Edition: The Construction of Authorship* (Stanford, CA: Stanford University Press, 1995), pp. 240–60.

20. Kevin J. Hayes, ed., *Henry James: The Contemporary Reviews*, p. 63.

Further Reading

BY HENRY JAMES

Autobiography, ed. Frederick V. Dupee (Princeton, NJ: Princeton University Press, 1983).

The Complete Letters of Henry James, ed. Pierre A. Walker and Greg Zacharias (Lincoln, NE: University of Nebraska Press, 2006–).

The Complete Notebooks, ed. Leon Edel and Lyall H. Powers (New York and Oxford: Oxford University Press, 1987).

The Complete Plays of Henry James, ed. Leon Edel (London: Rupert Hart-Davis, 1949).

Complete Stories, 5 vols. (New York and Cambridge: Library of America, 1996–9).

Henry James: Letters, ed. Leon Edel, 4 vols. (Cambridge, MA: Belknap Press, 1974–84).

Henry James: A Life in Letters, ed. Philip Horne (London: Penguin, 1999).

The Letters of Henry James, ed. Percy Lubbock, 2 vols. (London: Macmillan, 1920).

Literary Criticism, ed. Leon Edel and Mark Wilson, 2 vols. (New York and Cambridge: Library of America, 1984).

BIOGRAPHY, CRITICISM AND REFERENCE

Edel, Leon, *Henry James: A Life* (New York: Harper & Row, 1985).

—, and Dan H. Laurence, *A Bibliography of Henry James*,

third edn. revised with the assistance of James Rambeau (Oxford: Oxford University Press, 1982).

Gard, Roger, ed., *Henry James: The Critical Heritage* (London: Routledge & Kegan Paul, 1968). Contains a very full selection of contemporary reviews and comments.

Graham, Kenneth, *Henry James: A Literary Life* (Basingstoke: Macmillan, 1995).

Kaplan, Fred, *Henry James: The Imagination of Genius* (London: Hodder & Stoughton, 1992).

Nowell-Smith, Simon (compiler), *The Legend of the Master* (London: Constable, 1947).

P.H.

CRITICAL WORKS RELATING TO *THE EUROPEANS*

Anesko, Michael, *'Friction with the Market': Henry James and the Profession of Authorship* (New York: Oxford University Press, 1986).

Bell, Ian F. A., *Henry James and the Past: Readings into Time* (Basingstoke: Macmillan, 1991).

—, 'Sincerity and Performance in *The Europeans*', *Modern Philology* 88:2 (1990), pp. 126–46.

Bell, Millicent, *Meaning in Henry James* (Cambridge, MA: Harvard University Press, 1991).

Buitenhuis, Peter, *The Grasping Imagination: The American Writings of Henry James* (Toronto: University of Toronto Press, 1970).

Eakin, Paul John, *The New England Girl: Cultural Ideas in Hawthorne, Stowe, Howells, and James* (Athens, GA: University of Georgia Press, 1976).

Freedman, Jonathan (ed.), *The Cambridge Companion to Henry James* (Cambridge: Cambridge University Press, 1998).

Geary, Edward A., '*The Europeans*: A Centennial Essay', *Henry James Review* 4:1 (1982), pp. 31–49.

Graham, Kenneth, *Indirections of the Novel: James, Conrad, and Forster* (Cambridge: Cambridge University Press, 1988).

Hayes, Kevin J., ed., *Henry James: The Contemporary Reviews* (Cambridge: Cambridge University Press, 1996).

Leavis, F. R., *The Great Tradition* (London: Chatto and Windus, 1948).

Lee, Brian, *The Novels of Henry James: A Study of Culture and Consciousness* (London: Edward Arnold, 1978).

Poirier, Richard, *The Comic Sense of Henry James: A Study of the Early Novels* (London: Chatto and Windus, 1960).

Posnock, Ross, *The Trial of Curiosity: Henry James, William James, and the Challenge of Modernity* (New York: Oxford University Press, 1991).

Rowe, John Carlos, *The Theoretical Dimensions of Henry James* (London: Methuen, 1985).

Sicker, Philip, *Love and the Quest for Identity* (Princeton NJ: Princeton University Press, 1980).

Tanner, Tony, *Henry James: The Writer and his Work* (Amherst: University of Massachusetts Press, 1985).

Tuttleton, James W., 'Propriety and Fine Perception: James's *The Europeans*', *Modern Language Review* 73 (1978), pp. 481–95.

Ward, J. A., 'James's *The Europeans* and the Structure of Comedy', *Nineteenth-Century Fiction* 19 (1964), pp. 1–16.

Woolf, Judith, *Henry James: The Major Novels* (Cambridge: Cambridge University Press, 1991).

A.T.

A Note on the Text

The Europeans is the first novel by Henry James for which there is a surviving, and almost complete, manuscript. A facsimile of all but the final three chapters of the manuscript, with an introduction by Leon Edel, was published in 1979 (New York: Howard Fertig). The novel first appeared in serial form in the *Atlantic Monthly*, with four instalments published between July and October 1878. Macmillan and Company of London published it as a two-volume book on 18 September 1878. Less than a month later (on 12 October), the Boston publisher Houghton, Osgood and Company issued the first American book edition, this time in one volume. When, in 1883, Macmillan published a fourteen-volume edition of James's principal novels and tales, *The Europeans* appeared in volume nine alongside *Confidence* (first published 1879). *The Europeans* was not included in the New York Edition (1907–9). The text used here is the Osgood first American printing. As the editor of the authoritative 1983 Library of America edition has noted, this represents the most accurate reproduction of James's manuscript. For this edition, English forms of spelling have been used and some minor adjustments have been made to punctuation including the substitution of spaced n-dashes for long ones, the closing up of contractions ('wasn't' for 'was n't'), and single quotation marks instead of double ones. There has been no attempt to regularize James's inconsistent use of italics for French words and expressions.

A.T.

THE EUROPEANS

A Sketch

I

A narrow grave-yard in the heart of a bustling, indifferent city, seen from the windows of a gloomy-looking inn, is at no time an object of enlivening suggestion; and the spectacle is not at its best when the mouldy tombstones and funereal umbrage have received the ineffectual refreshment of a dull, moist snow-fall. If, while the air is thickened by this frosty drizzle, the calendar should happen to indicate that the blessed vernal season is already six weeks old, it will be admitted that no depressing influence is absent from the scene. This fact was keenly felt on a certain 12th of May, upwards of thirty years since,[1] by a lady who stood looking out of one of the windows of the best hotel in the ancient city of Boston. She had stood there for half an hour – stood there, that is, at intervals; for from time to time she turned back into the room and measured its length with a restless step. In the chimney-place was a red-hot fire which emitted a small blue flame; and in front of the fire, at a table, sat a young man who was busily plying a pencil. He had a number of sheets of paper cut into small equal squares, and he was apparently covering them with pictorial designs – strange-looking figures. He worked rapidly and attentively, sometimes threw back his head and held out his drawing at arm's-length, and kept up a soft, gay-sounding humming and whistling. The lady brushed past him in her walk; her much-trimmed skirts were voluminous. She never dropped her eyes upon his work; she only turned them, occasionally, as she passed, to a mirror suspended above the toilet-table on the other side of the room. Here she paused a moment, gave a pinch to her waist with her two hands, or raised these members

– they were very plump and pretty – to the multifold braids of her hair, with a movement half caressing, half corrective. An attentive observer might have fancied that during these periods of desultory self-inspection her face forgot its melancholy; but as soon as she neared the window again it began to proclaim that she was a very ill-pleased woman. And indeed, in what met her eyes there was little to be pleased with. The window-panes were battered by the sleet; the head-stones in the grave-yard beneath seemed to be holding themselves askance to keep it out of their faces. A tall iron railing protected them from the street, and on the other side of the railing an assemblage of Bostonians were trampling about in the liquid snow. Many of them were looking up and down; they appeared to be waiting for something. From time to time a strange vehicle drew near to the place where they stood, – such a vehicle as the lady at the window, in spite of a considerable acquaintance with human inventions, had never seen before: a huge, low omnibus, painted in brilliant colours, and decorated apparently with jangling bells, attached to a species of groove in the pavement, through which it was dragged, with a great deal of rumbling, bouncing and scratching, by a couple of remarkably small horses.[2] When it reached a certain point the people in front of the grave-yard, of whom much the greater number were women, carrying sat-chels and parcels, projected themselves upon it in a compact body – a movement suggesting the scramble for places in a life-boat at sea – and were engulfed in its large interior. Then the life-boat – or the life-car, as the lady at the window of the hotel vaguely designated it – went bumping and jingling away upon its invisible wheels, with the helmsman (the man at the wheel) guiding its course incongruously from the prow. This phenomenon was repeated every three minutes, and the supply of eagerly-moving women in cloaks, bearing reticules and bundles, renewed itself in the most liberal manner. On the other side of the grave-yard was a row of small red brick houses, showing a series of homely, domestic-looking backs; at the end opposite the hotel a tall wooden church-spire, painted white, rose high into the vagueness of the snow-flakes. The lady at the window looked at it for some time; for reasons of her own she thought it the ugliest thing she had ever seen. She hated it, she despised it; it threw her into a state of irritation that was quite out of proportion to any sensible motive. She had never known herself to care so much about church-spires.

She was not pretty; but even when it expressed perplexed irritation her face was most interesting and agreeable. Neither was she in her first youth; yet, though slender, with a great deal of extremely well-fashioned roundness of contour – a suggestion both of maturity and flexibility – she carried her three and thirty years as a light-wristed Hebe might have carried a brimming wine-cup.[3] Her complexion was fatigued, as the French say; her mouth was large, her lips too full, her teeth uneven, her chin rather commonly modelled; she had a thick nose, and when she smiled – she was constantly smiling – the lines beside it rose too high, toward her eyes. But these eyes were charming: grey in colour, brilliant, quickly glancing, gently resting, full of intelligence. Her forehead was very low – it was her only handsome feature; and she had a great abundance of crisp dark hair, finely frizzled, which was always braided in a manner that suggested some Southern or Eastern, some remotely foreign, woman. She had a large collection of earrings, and wore them in alternation; and they seemed to give a point to her Oriental or exotic aspect. A compliment had once been paid her, which, being repeated to her, gave her greater pleasure than anything she had ever heard. 'A pretty woman?' some one had said. 'Why, her features are very bad.' 'I don't know about her features,' a very discerning observer had answered; 'but she carries her head like a pretty woman.' You may imagine whether, after this, she carried her head less becomingly.

She turned away from the window at last, pressing her hands to her eyes. 'It's too horrible!' she exclaimed. 'I shall go back – I shall go back!' And she flung herself into a chair before the fire.

'Wait a little, dear child,' said the young man softly, sketching away at his little scraps of paper.

The lady put out her foot; it was very small, and there was an immense rosette on her slipper. She fixed her eyes for a while on this ornament, and then she looked at the glowing bed of anthracite coal in the grate. 'Did you ever see anything so hideous as that fire?' she demanded. 'Did you ever see anything so – so *affreux* as – as everything?' She spoke English with perfect purity; but she brought out this French epithet in a manner that indicated that she was accustomed to using French epithets.

'I think the fire is very pretty,' said the young man, glancing at it a moment. 'Those little blue tongues, dancing on top of the crimson embers, are extremely picturesque. They are like a fire in an alchemist's laboratory.'

'You are too good-natured, my dear,' his companion declared.

The young man held out one of his drawings, with his head on one side. His tongue was gently moving along his under-lip. 'Good-natured – yes. Too good-natured – no.'

'You are irritating,' said the lady, looking at her slipper.

He began to retouch his sketch. 'I think you mean simply that you are irritated.'

'Ah, for that, yes!' said his companion, with a little bitter laugh. 'It's the darkest day of my life – and you know what that means.'

'Wait till to-morrow,' rejoined the young man.

'Yes, we have made a great mistake. If there is any doubt about it to-day, there certainly will be none to-morrow. Ce sera clair, au moins!'

The young man was silent a few moments, driving his pencil. Then at last, 'There are no such things as mistakes,' he affirmed.

'Very true – for those who are not clever enough to perceive them. Not to recognize one's mistakes – that would be happiness in life,' the lady went on, still looking at her pretty foot.

'My dearest sister,' said the young man, always intent upon his drawing, 'it's the first time you have told me I am not clever.'

'Well, by your own theory I can't call it a mistake,' answered his sister, pertinently enough.

The young man gave a clear, fresh laugh. 'You, at least, are clever enough, dearest sister,' he said.

'I was not so when I proposed this.'

'Was it you who proposed it?' asked her brother.

She turned her head and gave him a little stare. 'Do you desire the credit of it?'

'If you like, I will take the blame,' he said, looking up with a smile.

'Yes,' she rejoined in a moment, 'you make no difference in these things. You have no sense of property.'

The young man gave his joyous laugh again. 'If that means I have no property, you are right!'

'Don't joke about your poverty,' said his sister. 'That is quite as vulgar as to boast about it.'

'My poverty! I have just finished a drawing that will bring me fifty francs!'

'Voyons,' said the lady, putting out her hand.

He added a touch or two, and then gave her his sketch. She looked at it, but she went on with her idea of a moment before. 'If a woman were to ask you to marry her you would say, "Certainly, my dear, with pleasure!" And you would marry her and be ridiculously happy. Then at the end of three months you would say to her, "You know that blissful day when I begged you to be mine!"'

The young man had risen from the table, stretching his arms a little; he walked to the window. 'That is a description of a charming nature,' he said.

'Oh, yes, you have a charming nature; I regard that as our capital. If I had not been convinced of that I should never have taken the risk of bringing you to this dreadful country.'

'This comical country, this delightful country!' exclaimed the young man, and he broke into the most animated laughter.

'Is it those women scrambling into the omnibus?' asked his companion. 'What do you suppose is the attraction?'

'I suppose there is a very good-looking man inside,' said the young man.

'In each of them? They come along in hundreds, and the men in this country don't seem at all handsome. As for the women – I have never seen so many at once since I left the convent.'

'The women are very pretty,' her brother declared, 'and the whole affair is very amusing. I must make a sketch of it.' And he came back to the table quickly, and picked up his utensils –

a small sketching-board, a sheet of paper, and three or four
crayons. He took his place at the window with these things,
and stood there glancing out, plying his pencil with an air of
easy skill. While he worked he wore a brilliant smile. Brilliant
is indeed the word at this moment for his strongly-lighted face.
He was eight and twenty years old; he had a short, slight,
well-made figure. Though he bore a noticeable resemblance to
his sister, he was a better favoured person: fair-haired, clear-
faced, witty-looking, with a delicate finish of feature and an
expression at once urbane and not at all serious, a warm blue
eye, an eyebrow finely drawn and excessively arched – an eyebrow which, if ladies wrote sonnets to those of their lovers,
might have been made the subject of such a piece of verse – and
a light moustache that flourished upwards as if blown that way
by the breath of a constant smile. There was something in his
physiognomy at once benevolent and picturesque. But, as I have
hinted, it was not at all serious. The young man's face was, in
this respect, singular; it was not at all serious, and yet it inspired
the liveliest confidence.

'Be sure you put in plenty of snow,' said his sister. 'Bonté
divine, what a climate!'

'I shall leave the sketch all white, and I shall put in the little
figures in black,' the young man answered, laughing. 'And I
shall call it – what is that line in Keats? – Mid-May's Eldest
Child!'[4]

'I don't remember,' said the lady, 'that mamma ever told me
it was like this.'

'Mamma never told you anything disagreeable. And it's not
like this – every day. You will see that to-morrow we shall have
a splendid day.'

'Qu'en savez-vous? To-morrow I shall go away.'

'Where shall you go?'

'Anywhere away from here. Back to Silberstadt. I shall write
to the Reigning Prince.'[5]

The young man turned a little and looked at her, with his
crayon poised. 'My dear Eugenia,' he murmured, 'were you so
happy at sea?'

Eugenia got up; she still held in her hand the drawing her

brother had given her. It was a bold, expressive sketch of a group of miserable people on the deck of a steamer, clinging together and clutching at each other, while the vessel lurched downward, at a terrific angle, into the hollow of a wave. It was extremely clever, and full of a sort of tragi-comical power. Eugenia dropped her eyes upon it and made a sad grimace. 'How can you draw such odious scenes?' she asked. 'I should like to throw it into the fire!' And she tossed the paper away. Her brother watched, quietly, to see where it went. It fluttered down to the floor, where he let it lie. She came toward the window, pinching in her waist. 'Why don't you reproach me – abuse me?' she asked. 'I think I should feel better then. Why don't you tell me that you hate me for bringing you here?'

'Because you would not believe it. I adore you, dear sister! I am delighted to be here, and I am charmed with the prospect.'

'I don't know what had taken possession of me. I had lost my head,' Eugenia went on.

The young man, on his side, went on plying his pencil. 'It is evidently a most curious and interesting country. Here we are, and I mean to enjoy it.'

His companion turned away with an impatient step, but presently came back. 'High spirits are doubtless an excellent thing,' she said; 'but you give one too much of them, and I can't see that they have done you any good.'

The young man stared, with lifted eyebrows, smiling; he tapped his handsome nose with his pencil. 'They have made me happy!'

'That was the least they could do; they have made you nothing else. You have gone through life thanking fortune for such very small favours that she has never put herself to any trouble for you.'

'She must have put herself to a little, I think, to present me with so admirable a sister.'

'Be serious, Felix. You forget that I am your elder.'

'With a sister, then, so elderly!' rejoined Felix, laughing. 'I hoped we had left seriousness in Europe.'

'I fancy you will find it here. Remember that you are nearly thirty years old, and that you are nothing but an obscure

Bohemian[6] – a penniless correspondent of an illustrated newspaper.'

'Obscure as much as you please, but not so much of a Bohemian as you think. And not at all penniless! I have a hundred pounds in my pocket. I have an engagement to make fifty sketches, and I mean to paint the portraits of all our cousins, and of all *their* cousins, at a hundred dollars a head.'

'You are not ambitious,' said Eugenia.

'You are, dear Baroness,' the young man replied.

The Baroness was silent a moment, looking out at the sleet-darkened grave-yard and the bumping horse-cars. 'Yes, I am ambitious,' she said at last. 'And my ambition has brought me to this dreadful place!' She glanced about her – the room had a certain vulgar nudity; the bed and the window were curtainless – and she gave a little passionate sigh. 'Poor old ambition!' she exclaimed. Then she flung herself down upon a sofa which stood near against the wall, and covered her face with her hands.

Her brother went on with his drawing, rapidly and skilfully; after some moments he sat down beside her and showed her his sketch. 'Now, don't you think that's pretty good for an obscure Bohemian?' he asked. 'I have knocked off another fifty francs.'

Eugenia glanced at the little picture as he laid it on her lap. 'Yes, it is very clever,' she said. And in a moment she added, 'Do you suppose our cousins do that?'

'Do what?'

'Get into those things, and look like that.'

Felix meditated awhile. 'I really can't say. It will be interesting to discover.'

'Oh, the rich people can't!' said the Baroness.

'Are you very sure they are rich?' asked Felix, lightly.

His sister slowly turned in her place, looking at him. 'Heavenly powers!' she murmured. 'You have a way of bringing out things!'

'It will certainly be much pleasanter if they are rich,' Felix declared.

'Do you suppose if I had not known they were rich I would ever have come?'

The young man met his sister's somewhat peremptory eye with his bright, contented glance. 'Yes, it certainly will be pleasanter,' he repeated.

'That is all I expect of them,' said the Baroness. 'I don't count upon their being clever or friendly – at first – or elegant or interesting. But I assure you I insist upon their being rich.'

Felix leaned his head upon the back of the sofa and looked awhile at the oblong patch of sky to which the window served as frame. The snow was ceasing; it seemed to him that the sky had begun to brighten. 'I count upon their being rich,' he said at last, 'and powerful, and clever, and friendly, and elegant, and interesting, and generally delightful! Tu vas voir.' And he bent forward and kissed his sister. 'Look there!' he went on. 'As a portent, even while I speak, the sky is turning the colour of gold; the day is going to be splendid.'

And indeed, within five minutes the weather had changed. The sun broke out through the snow-clouds and jumped into the Baroness's room. 'Bonté divine,' exclaimed this lady, 'what a climate!'

'We will go out and see the world,' said Felix.

And after a while they went out. The air had grown warm as well as brilliant; the sunshine had dried the pavements. They walked about the streets at hazard, looking at the people and the houses, the shops and the vehicles, the blazing blue sky and the muddy crossings, the hurrying men and the slow-strolling maidens, the fresh red bricks and the bright green trees, the extraordinary mixture of smartness and shabbiness. From one hour to another the day had grown vernal; even in the bustling streets there was an odour of earth and blossom. Felix was immensely entertained. He had called it a comical country, and he went about laughing at everything he saw. You would have said that American civilization expressed itself to his sense in a tissue of capital jokes. The jokes were certainly excellent, and the young man's merriment was joyous and genial. He possessed what is called the pictorial sense; and this first glimpse of democratic manners stirred the same sort of attention that he would have given to the movements of a lively young person with a bright complexion. Such attention would have been

demonstrative and complimentary; and in the present case Felix
might have passed for an undispirited young exile revisiting the
haunts of his childhood. He kept looking at the violent blue of
the sky, at the scintillating air, at the scattered and multiplied
patches of colour.

'Comme c'est bariolé, eh?' he said to his sister in that foreign
tongue which they both appeared to feel a mysterious prompting
occasionally to use.

'Yes, it is bariolé indeed,' the Baroness answered. 'I don't like
the colouring; it hurts my eyes.'

'It shows how extremes meet,' the young man rejoined. 'Instead of coming to the West we seem to have gone to the East.
The way the sky touches the house-tops is just like Cairo; and
the red and blue sign-boards patched over the face of everything
remind one of Mahometan[7] decorations.'

'The young women are not Mahometan,' said his companion.
'They can't be said to hide their faces. I never saw anything so
bold.'

'Thank Heaven they don't hide their faces!' cried Felix. 'Their
faces are uncommonly pretty.'

'Yes, their faces are often very pretty,' said the Baroness, who
was a very clever woman. She was too clever a woman not to
be capable of a great deal of just and fine observation. She clung
more closely than usual to her brother's arm; she was not exhilarated, as he was; she said very little, but she noted a great
many things and made her reflections. She was a little excited;
she felt that she had indeed come to a strange country, to make
her fortune. Superficially, she was conscious of a good deal of
irritation and displeasure; the Baroness was a very delicate and
fastidious person. Of old, more than once, she had gone, for
entertainment's sake and in brilliant company, to a fair in a
provincial town. It seemed to her now that she was at an
enormous fair – that the entertainment and the *désagréments*
were very much the same. She found herself alternately smiling
and shrinking; the show was very curious, but it was probable, from moment to moment, that one would be jostled. The
Baroness had never seen so many people walking about before;
she had never been so mixed up with people she did not know.

But little by little she felt that this fair was a more serious under-taking. She went with her brother into a large public garden, which seemed very pretty, but where she was surprised at seeing no carriages. The afternoon was drawing to a close; the coarse, vivid grass and the slender tree-boles were gilded by the level sunbeams – gilded as with gold that was fresh from the mine. It was the hour at which ladies should come out for an airing and roll past a hedge of pedestrians, holding their parasols askance. Here, however, Eugenia observed no indications of this custom, the absence of which was more anomalous as there was a charming avenue of remarkably graceful, arching elms in the most convenient contiguity to a large, cheerful street, in which, evidently, among the more prosperous members of the *bourgeoisie*, a great deal of pedestrianism went forward. Our friends passed out into this well-lighted promenade, and Felix noticed a great many more pretty girls and called his sister's attention to them. This latter measure, however, was superfluous; for the Baroness had inspected, narrowly, these charming young ladies.

'I feel an intimate conviction that our cousins are like that,' said Felix.

The Baroness hoped so, but this is not what she said. 'They are very pretty,' she said, 'but they are mere little girls. Where are the women – the women of thirty?'

'Of thirty-three, do you mean?' her brother was going to ask; for he understood often both what she said and what she did not say. But he only exclaimed upon the beauty of the sunset, while the Baroness, who had come to seek her fortune, reflected that it would certainly be well for her if the persons against whom she might need to measure herself should all be mere little girls. The sunset was superb; they stopped to look at it; Felix declared that he had never seen such a gorgeous mixture of colours. The Baroness also thought it splendid; and she was perhaps the more easily pleased from the fact that while she stood there she was conscious of much admiring observation on the part of various nice-looking people who passed that way, and to whom a distinguished, strikingly-dressed woman with a foreign air, exclaiming upon the beauties of nature on a

Boston street corner in the French tongue, could not be an object of indifference. Eugenia's spirits rose. She surrendered herself to a certain tranquil gaiety. If she had come to seek her fortune, it seemed to her that her fortune would be easy to find. There was a promise of it in the gorgeous purity of the western sky; there was an intimation in the mild, unimpertinent gaze of the passers of a certain natural facility in things.

'You will not go back to Silberstadt, eh?' asked Felix.

'Not to-morrow,' said the Baroness.

'Nor write to the Reigning Prince?'

'I shall write to him that they evidently know nothing about him over here.'

'He will not believe you,' said the young man. 'I advise you to let him alone.'

Felix himself continued to be in high good humour. Brought up among ancient customs and in picturesque cities, he yet found plenty of local colour in the little Puritan metropolis. That evening, after dinner, he told his sister that he should go forth early on the morrow to look up their cousins.

'You are very impatient,' said Eugenia.

'What can be more natural,' he asked, 'after seeing all those pretty girls today? If one's cousins are of that pattern, the sooner one knows them the better.'

'Perhaps they are not,' said Eugenia. 'We ought to have brought some letters – to some other people.'

'The other people would not be our kinsfolk.'

'Possibly they would be none the worse for that,' the Baroness replied.

Her brother looked at her with his eyebrows lifted. 'That was not what you said when you first proposed to me that we should come out here and fraternize with our relatives. You said that it was the prompting of natural affection; and when I suggested some reasons against it you declared that the *voix du sang* should go before everything.'

'You remember all that?' asked the Baroness.

'Vividly! I was greatly moved by it.'

She was walking up and down the room, as she had done in the morning; she stopped in her walk and looked at her brother.

She apparently was going to say something, but she checked herself and resumed her walk. Then, in a few moments, she said something different, which had the effect of an explanation of the suppression of her earlier thought. 'You will never be anything but a child, dear brother.'

'One would suppose that you, madam,' answered Felix, laughing, 'were a thousand years old.'

'I am – sometimes,' said the Baroness.

'I will go, then, and announce to our cousins the arrival of a personage so extraordinary. They will immediately come and pay you their respects.'

Eugenia paced the length of the room again, and then she stopped before her brother, laying her hand upon his arm. 'They are not to come and see me,' she said. 'You are not to allow that. That is not the way I shall meet them first.' And in answer to his interrogative glance she went on. 'You will go and examine, and report. You will come back and tell me who they are and what they are; their number, gender, their respective ages – all about them. Be sure you observe everything; be ready to describe to me the locality, the accessories – how shall I say it? – the mise en scène. Then, at my own time, at my own hour, under circumstances of my own choosing, I will go to them. I will present myself – I will appear before them!' said the Baroness, this time phrasing her idea with a certain frankness.

'And what message am I to take to them?' asked Felix, who had a lively faith in the justness of his sister's arrangements.

She looked at him a moment – at his expression of agreeable veracity; and, with that justness that he admired, she replied, 'Say what you please. Tell my story in the way that seems to you most – natural.' And she bent her forehead for him to kiss.

II

The next day was splendid, as Felix had prophesied; if the winter had suddenly leaped into spring, the spring had for the moment as quickly leaped into summer. This was an observation made by a young girl who came out of a large square house in the country, and strolled about in the spacious garden which separated it from a muddy road. The flowering shrubs and the neatly-disposed plants were basking in the abundant light and warmth; the transparent shade of the great elms – they were magnificent trees – seemed to thicken by the hour; and the intensely habitual stillness offered a submissive medium to the sound of a distant church-bell. The young girl listened to the church-bell; but she was not dressed for church. She was bare-headed; she wore a white muslin waist, with an embroidered border, and the skirt of her dress was of coloured muslin. She was a young lady of some two or three and twenty years of age, and though a young person of her sex walking bare-headed in a garden, of a Sunday morning in spring-time, can, in the nature of things, never be a displeasing object, you would not have pronounced this innocent Sabbath-breaker especially pretty. She was tall and pale, thin and a little awkward; her hair was fair and perfectly straight; her eyes were dark, and they had the singularity of seeming at once dull and restless – differing herein, as you see, fatally from the ideal 'fine eyes', which we always imagine to be both brilliant and tranquil. The doors and windows of the large square house were all wide open, to admit the purifying sunshine, which lay in generous patches upon the floor of a wide, high, covered piazza adjusted to two sides of the mansion – a piazza on which several straw-bottomed rocking-chairs and half a dozen of those small cylin-drical stools in green and blue porcelain, which suggest an affiliation between the residents and the Eastern trade, were symmetrically disposed. It was an ancient house – ancient in the sense of being eighty years old; it was built of wood, painted a clean, clear, faded grey, and adorned along the front, at inter-vals, with flat wooden pilasters, painted white. These pilasters appeared to support a kind of classic pediment, which was decor-ated in the middle by a large triple window in a boldly carved frame, and in each of its smaller angles by a glazed circular aperture. A large white door, furnished with a highly-polished brass knocker, presented itself to the rural-looking road, with which it was connected by a spacious pathway, paved with worn and cracked, but very clean, bricks. Behind it there were meadows and orchards, a barn and a pond; and facing it, a short distance along the road, on the opposite side, stood a smaller house, painted white, with external shutters painted green, a little garden on one hand and an orchard on the other. All this was shining in the morning air, through which the simple details of the picture addressed themselves to the eye as distinctly as the items of a 'sum' in addition.

A second young lady presently came out of the house, across the piazza, descended into the garden and approached the young girl of whom I have spoken. This second young lady was also thin and pale; but she was older than the other; she was shorter; she had dark, smooth hair. Her eyes, unlike the other's, were quick and bright; but they were not at all restless. She wore a straw bonnet with white ribbons, and a long, red, India scarf, which, on the front of her dress, reached to her feet. In her hand she carried a little key.

'Gertrude,' she said, 'are you very sure you had better not go to church?'

Gertrude looked at her a moment, plucked a small sprig from a lilac-bush, smelled it and threw it away. 'I am not very sure of anything!' she answered.

The other young lady looked straight past her, at the distant pond, which lay shining between the long banks of fir-trees. Then she said in a very soft voice, 'This is the key of the dining-room closet. I think you had better have it, if any one should want anything.'

'Who is there to want anything?' Gertrude demanded. 'I shall be all alone in the house.'

'Some one may come,' said her companion.

'Do you mean Mr. Brand?'

'Yes, Gertrude. He may like a piece of cake.'

'I don't like men that are always eating cake!' Gertrude declared, giving a pull at the lilac-bush.

Her companion glanced at her, and then looked down on the ground. 'I think father expected you would come to church,' she said. 'What shall I say to him?'

'Say I have a bad headache.'

'Would that be true?' asked the elder lady, looking straight at the pond again.

'No, Charlotte,' said the younger one simply.

Charlotte transferred her quiet eyes to her companion's face. 'I am afraid you are feeling restless.'

'I am feeling as I always feel,' Gertrude replied, in the same tone.

Charlotte turned away; but she stood there a moment. Presently she looked down at the front of her dress. 'Doesn't it seem to you, somehow, as if my scarf were too long?' she asked.

Gertrude walked half round her, looking at the scarf. 'I don't think you wear it right,' she said.

'How should I wear it, dear?'

'I don't know; differently from that. You should draw it differently over your shoulders, round your elbows; you should look differently behind.'

'How should I look?' Charlotte inquired.

'I don't think I can tell you,' said Gertrude, plucking out the scarf a little behind. 'I could do it myself, but I don't think I can explain it.'

Charlotte, by a movement of her elbows, corrected the laxity that had come from her companion's touch. 'Well, some day you must do it for me. It doesn't matter now. Indeed, I don't think it matters,' she added, 'how one looks behind.'

'I should say it mattered more,' said Gertrude. 'Then you

don't know who may be observing you. You are not on your guard. You can't try to look pretty.'

Charlotte received this declaration with extreme gravity. 'I don't think one should ever try to look pretty,' she rejoined, earnestly.

Her companion was silent. Then she said, 'Well, perhaps it's not of much use.'

Charlotte looked at her a little, and then kissed her. 'I hope you will be better when we come back.'

'My dear sister, I am very well!' said Gertrude.

Charlotte went down the large brick walk to the garden gate; her companion strolled slowly toward the house. At the gate Charlotte met a young man, who was coming in – a tall, fair young man, wearing a high hat and a pair of thread gloves. He was handsome, but rather too stout. He had a pleasant smile. 'Oh, Mr. Brand!' exclaimed the young lady.

'I came to see whether your sister was not going to church,' said the young man.

'She says she is not going; but I am very glad you have come. I think if you were to talk to her a little' ... And Charlotte lowered her voice. 'It seems as if she were restless.'

Mr. Brand smiled down on the young lady from his great height. 'I shall be very glad to talk to her. For that I should be willing to absent myself from almost any occasion of worship, however attractive.'

'Well, I suppose you know,' said Charlotte, softly, as if positive acceptance of this proposition might be dangerous. 'But I am afraid I shall be late.'

'I hope you will have a pleasant sermon,' said the young man.

'Oh, Mr. Gilman is always pleasant,' Charlotte answered. And she went on her way.

Mr. Brand went into the garden, where Gertrude, hearing the gate close behind him, turned and looked at him. For a moment she watched him coming; then she turned away. But almost immediately she corrected this movement, and stood still, facing him. He took off his hat and wiped his forehead as he approached. Then he put on his hat again and held out his hand. His hat being removed, you would have perceived that his forehead was very large and smooth, and his hair abundant but rather colourless. His nose was too large, and his mouth and eyes were too small; but for all this he was, as I have said, a young man of striking appearance. The expression of his little clean-coloured blue eyes was irresistibly gentle and serious; he looked, as the phrase is, as good as gold. The young girl, standing in the garden path, glanced, as he came up, at his thread gloves.

'I hoped you were going to church,' he said. 'I wanted to walk with you.'

'I am very much obliged to you,' Gertrude answered. 'I am not going to church.'

She had shaken hands with him; he held her hand a moment. 'Have you any special reason for not going?'

'Yes, Mr. Brand,' said the young girl.

'May I ask what it is?'

She looked at him smiling; and in her smile, as I have intimated, there was a certain dullness. But mingled with this dullness was something sweet and suggestive. 'Because the sky is so blue!' she said.

He looked at the sky, which was magnificent, and then said, smiling too, 'I have heard of young ladies staying at home for bad weather, but never for good. Your sister, whom I met at the gate, tells me you are depressed,' he added.

'Depressed? I am never depressed.'

'Oh, surely, sometimes,' replied Mr. Brand, as if he thought this a regrettable account of one's self.

'I am never depressed,' Gertrude repeated. 'But I am sometimes wicked. When I am wicked I am in high spirits. I was wicked just now to my sister.'

'What did you do to her?'

'I said things that puzzled her – on purpose.'

'Why did you do that, Miss Gertrude?' asked the young man.

She began to smile again. 'Because the sky is so blue!'

'You say things that puzzle *me*,' Mr. Brand declared.

'I always know when I do it,' proceeded Gertrude. 'But people puzzle me more, I think. And they don't seem to know!'

'This is very interesting,' Mr. Brand observed, smiling.

'You told me to tell you about my – my struggles,' the young girl went on.

'Let us talk about them. I have so many things to say.'

Gertrude turned away a moment; and then, turning back, 'You had better go to church,' she said.

'You know,' the young man urged, 'that I have always one thing to say.'

Gertrude looked at him a moment. 'Please don't say it now!'

'We are all alone,' he continued, taking off his hat; 'all alone in this beautiful Sunday stillness.'

Gertrude looked around her, at the breaking buds, the shining distance, the blue sky to which she had referred as a pretext for her irregularities. 'That's the reason,' she said, 'why I don't want you to speak. Do me a favour; go to church.'

'May I speak when I come back?' asked Mr. Brand.

'If you are still disposed,' she answered.

'I don't know whether you are wicked,' he said, 'but you are certainly puzzling.'

She had turned away; she raised her hands to her ears. He looked at her a moment, and then he slowly walked to church.

She wandered for a while about the garden, vaguely and without purpose. The church-bell had stopped ringing; the stillness was complete. This young lady relished highly, on occasions, the sense of being alone – the absence of the whole family and the emptiness of the house. To-day, apparently, the servants had also gone to church; there was never a figure at the open windows; behind the house there was no stout negress in a red turban, lowering the bucket into the great shingle-hooded well. And the front door of the big, unguarded home stood open, with the trustfulness of the golden age; or what is more to the purpose, with that of New England's silvery prime. Gertrude slowly passed through it, and went from one of the empty rooms to the other – large, clear-coloured rooms, with white wainscots, ornamented with thin-legged mahogany furniture, and, on the walls, with old-fashioned engravings, chiefly of scriptural subjects, hung very high. This agreeable sense of solitude, of having the house to herself, of which I have spoken, always excited Gertrude's imagination; she could not have told you why, and neither can her humble historian. It always seemed to her that she must do something particular – that she must honour the occasion; and while she roamed about, wondering what she could do, the occasion usually came to an end. To-day she wondered more than ever. At last she took down a book; there was no library in the house, but there were books in all the rooms. None of them were forbidden books, and Gertrude had not stopped at home for the sake of a chance to climb to the inaccessible shelves. She possessed herself of a very obvious volume – one of the series of the Arabian Nights – and she brought it out into the portico and sat down with it in her lap. There, for a quarter of an hour, she read the history of the loves of the Prince Camaralzaman and the Princess Badoura.[1] At last, looking up, she beheld, as it seemed to her, the Prince Camaralzaman standing before her. A beautiful young man was making her a very low bow – a magnificent bow, such as she had never seen before. He appeared to have dropped from the clouds; he was wonderfully handsome; he smiled – smiled as if he were smiling on purpose. Extreme surprise, for a moment, kept Gertrude sitting still; then she rose, without even keeping her finger in her book. The young man, with his hat in his hand, still looked at her, smiling and smiling. It was very strange.

'Will you kindly tell me,' said the mysterious visitor, at last, 'whether I have the honour of speaking to Miss Wentworth?'

'My name is Gertrude Wentworth,' murmured the young woman.

'Then – then – I have the honour – the pleasure – of being your cousin.'

The young man had so much the character of an apparition that this announcement seemed to complete his unreality. 'What cousin? Who are you?' said Gertrude.

He stepped back a few paces and looked up at the house; then glanced round him at the garden and the distant view. After this he burst out laughing. 'I see it must seem to you very strange,' he said. There was, after all, something substantial in his laughter. Gertrude looked at him from head to foot. Yes, he was remarkably handsome; but his smile was almost a grimace. 'It is very still,' he went on, coming nearer again. And as she only looked at him, for reply, he added, 'Are you all alone?'

'Every one has gone to church,' said Gertrude.

'I was afraid of that!' the young man exclaimed. 'But I hope you are not afraid of me.'

'You ought to tell me who you are,' Gertrude answered.

'I am afraid of you!' said the young man. 'I had a different plan. I expected the servant would take in my card, and that you would put your heads together, before admitting me, and make out my identity.'

Gertrude had been wondering with a quick intensity which brought its result; and the result seemed an answer – a wondrous, delightful answer – to her vague wish that something would befall her. 'I know – I know,' she said. 'You come from Europe.'

'We came two days ago. You have heard of us, then – you believe in us?'

'We have known, vaguely,' said Gertrude, 'that we had relations in France.'

'And have you ever wanted to see us?' asked the young man.

Gertrude was silent a moment. 'I have wanted to see you.'

'I am glad, then, it is you I have found. We wanted to see you, so we came.'

'On purpose?' asked Gertrude.

The young man looked round him, smiling still. 'Well, yes; on purpose. Does that sound as if we should bore you?' he added. 'I don't think we shall – I really don't think we shall. We are rather fond of wandering, too; and we were glad of a pretext.'

'And you have just arrived?'

'In Boston, two days ago. At the inn I asked for Mr. Wentworth. He must be your father. They found out for me where he lived; they seemed often to have heard of him. I determined to come, without ceremony. So, this lovely morning, they set my face in the right direction, and told me to walk straight before me, out of town. I came on foot because I wanted to see the country. I walked and walked, and here I am! It's a good many miles.'

'It is seven miles and a half,' said Gertrude, softly. Now that this handsome young man was proving himself a reality she found herself vaguely trembling; she was deeply excited. She had never in her life spoken to a foreigner, and she had often thought it would be delightful to do so. Here was one who had suddenly been engendered by the Sabbath stillness for her private use; and such a brilliant, polite, smiling one! She found time and means to compose herself, however: to remind herself that she must exercise a sort of official hospitality. 'We are very – very glad to see you,' she said. 'Won't you come into the house?' And she moved toward the open door.

'You are not afraid of me, then?' asked the young man again, with his light laugh.

She wondered a moment, and then, 'We are not afraid – here,' she said.

'Ah, comme vous devez avoir raison!' cried the young man, looking all round him, appreciatively. It was the first time that Gertrude had heard so many words of French spoken. They gave her something of a sensation. Her companion followed her, watching, with a certain excitement of his own, this tall, interesting-looking girl, dressed in her clear, crisp muslin. He paused in the hall, where there was a broad white staircase with a white balustrade. 'What a pleasant house!' he said. 'It's lighter inside than it is out.'

'It's pleasanter here,' said Gertrude, and she led the way into the parlour – a high, clean, rather empty-looking room. Here they stood looking at each other – the young man smiling more than ever; Gertrude, very serious, trying to smile.

'I don't believe you know my name,' he said. 'I am called Felix Young. Your father is my uncle. My mother was his half sister, and older than he.'

'Yes,' said Gertrude, 'and she turned Roman Catholic and married in Europe.'

'I see you know,' said the young man. 'She married and she died. Your father's family didn't like her husband. They called him a foreigner; but he was not. My poor father was born in Sicily, but his parents were American.'

'In Sicily?' Gertrude murmured.

'It is true,' said Felix Young, 'that they had spent their lives in Europe. But they were very patriotic. And so are we.'

'And you are Sicilian,' said Gertrude.

'Sicilian, no! Let's see. I was born at a little place – a dear little place – in France. My sister was born at Vienna.'

'So you are French,' said Gertrude.

'Heaven forbid!' cried the young man. Gertrude's eyes were fixed upon him almost insistently. He began to laugh again. 'I can easily be French, if that will please you.'

'You are a foreigner of some sort,' said Gertrude.

'Of some sort – yes; I suppose so. But who can say of what sort? I don't think we have ever had occasion to settle the question. You know there are people like that. About their country, their religion, their profession, they can't tell.'

Gertrude stood there gazing; she had not asked him to sit down. She had never heard of people like that; she wanted to hear. 'Where do you live?' she asked.

'They can't tell that, either!' said Felix. 'I am afraid you will think they are little better than vagabonds. I have lived any-where – everywhere. I really think I have lived in every city in Europe.' Gertrude gave a little long soft exhalation. It made the young man smile at her again; and his smile made her blush a little. To take refuge from blushing she asked him if, after his long walk, he was not hungry or thirsty. Her hand was in her pocket; she was fumbling with the little key that her sister had given her. 'Ah, my dear young lady,' he said, clasping his hands a little, 'if you could give me, in charity, a glass of wine!'

Gertrude gave a smile and a little nod, and went quickly out of the room. Presently she came back with a very large decanter in one hand and a plate in the other, on which was placed a big, round cake with a frosted top. Gertrude, in taking the cake from the closet, had had a moment of acute consciousness that it composed the refection[2] of which her sister had thought that Mr. Brand would like to partake. Her kinsman from across the seas was looking at the pale, high-hung engravings. When she came in he turned and smiled at her, as if they had been old friends meeting after a separation. 'You wait upon me yourself?' he asked. 'I am served like the gods!' She had waited upon a great many people, but none of them had ever told her that. The observation added a certain lightness to the step with which she went to a little table where there were some curious red glasses – glasses covered with little gold sprigs, which Charlotte used to dust every morning with her own hands. Gertrude thought the glasses very handsome, and it was a pleasure to her to know that the wine was good; it was her father's famous madeira. Felix Young thought it excellent; he wondered why he had been told that there was no wine in America. She cut him an immense triangle out of the cake, and again she thought of Mr. Brand. Felix sat there, with his glass in one hand and his huge morsel of cake in the other – eating, drinking, smiling, talking. 'I am very hungry,' he said. 'I am not at all tired; I am never tired. But I am very hungry.'

'You must stay to dinner,' said Gertrude. 'At two o'clock. They will all have come back from church; you will see the others.'

'Who are the others?' asked the young man. 'Describe them all.'

'You will see for yourself. It is you that must tell me; now, about your sister.'

'My sister is the Baroness Münster,' said Felix.

On hearing that his sister was a Baroness, Gertrude got up and walked about slowly, in front of him. She was silent a moment. She was thinking of it. 'Why didn't she come, too?' she asked.

'She did come; she is in Boston, at the hotel.'

'We will go and see her,' said Gertrude, looking at him.

'She begs you will not!' the young man replied. 'She sends you her love; she sent me to announce her. She will come and pay her respects to your father.'

Gertrude felt herself trembling again. A Baroness Münster, who sent a brilliant young man to 'announce' her; who was coming, as the Queen of Sheba came to Solomon,[3] to pay her 'respects' to quiet Mr. Wentworth – such a personage presented herself to Gertrude's vision with a most effective unexpectedness. For a moment she hardly knew what to say. 'When will she come?' she asked at last.

'As soon as you will allow her – to-morrow. She is very impatient,' answered Felix, who wished to be agreeable.

'To-morrow, yes,' said Gertrude. She wished to ask more about her; but she hardly knew what could be predicated of a Baroness Münster. 'Is she – is she – married?'

Felix had finished his cake and wine; he got up, fixing upon the young girl his bright, expressive eyes. 'She is married to a German prince – Prince Adolf, of Silberstadt-Schreckenstein.[4] He is not the reigning prince; he is a younger brother.'

Gertrude gazed at her informant; her lips were slightly parted. 'Is she a – a *Princess*?' she asked at last.

'Oh, no,' said the young man; 'her position is rather a singular one. It's a morganatic marriage.'

'Morganatic?' These were new names and new words to poor Gertrude.

'That's what they call a marriage, you know, contracted between a scion of a ruling house and – and a common mortal. They made Eugenia a Baroness, poor woman; but that was all they could do. Now they want to dissolve the marriage. Prince Adolf, between ourselves, is a ninny; but his brother, who is a clever man, has plans for him. Eugenia, naturally enough, makes difficulties; not, however, that I think she cares much – she's a very clever woman; I'm sure you'll like her – but she wants to bother them. Just now everything is *en l'air*.'

The cheerful off-hand tone in which her visitor related this darkly romantic tale seemed to Gertrude very strange; but it seemed also to convey a certain flattery to herself, a recognition of her wisdom and dignity. She felt a dozen impressions stirring within her, and presently the one that was uppermost found words. 'They want to dissolve her marriage?' she asked.

'So it appears.'

'And against her will?'

'Against her right.'

'She must be very unhappy!' said Gertrude.

Her visitor looked at her, smiling; he raised his hand to the back of his head and held it there a moment. 'So she says,' he answered. 'That's her story. She told me to tell it you.'

'Tell me more,' said Gertrude.

'No, I will leave that to her; she does it better.'

Gertrude gave her little excited sigh again. 'Well, if she is unhappy,' she said, 'I am glad she has come to us.'

She had been so interested that she failed to notice the sound of a footstep in the portico; and yet it was a footstep that she always recognized. She heard it in the hall, and then she looked out of the window. They were all coming back from church – her father, her sister and brother, and their cousins, who always came to dinner on Sunday. Mr. Brand had come in first; he was in advance of the others, because, apparently, he was still disposed to say what she had not wished him to say an hour before. He came into the parlour, looking for Gertrude. He had two little books in his hand. On seeing Gertrude's companion he slowly stopped, looking at him.

'Is this a cousin?' asked Felix.

Then Gertrude saw that she must introduce him; but her ears, and, by sympathy, her lips, were full of all that he had been telling her. 'This is the Prince,' she said, 'the Prince of Silberstadt-Schreckenstein!'

Felix burst out laughing, and Mr. Brand stood staring, while the others, who had passed into the house, appeared behind him in the open door-way.

III

That evening at dinner Felix Young gave his sister, the Baroness Münster, an account of his impressions. She saw that he had come back in the highest possible spirits; but this fact, to her own mind, was not a reason for rejoicing. She had but a limited confidence in her brother's judgement; his capacity for taking rose-coloured views was such as to vulgarize one of the prettiest of tints. Still, she supposed he could be trusted to give her the mere facts; and she invited him with some eagerness to communicate them. 'I suppose, at least, they didn't turn you out from the door,' she said. 'You have been away some ten hours.'

'Turn me from the door!' Felix exclaimed. 'They took me to their hearts; they killed the fatted calf.'[1]

'I know what you want to say: they are a collection of angels.'

'Exactly,' said Felix. 'They are a collection of angels – simply.'

'C'est bien vague,' remarked the Baroness. 'What are they like?'

'Like nothing you ever saw.'

'I am sure I am much obliged; but that is hardly more definite. Seriously, they were glad to see you?'

'Enchanted. It has been the proudest day of my life. Never, never have I been so lionized! I assure you, I was cock of the walk. My dear sister,' said the young man, 'nous n'avons qu'a nous tenir; we shall be great swells!'

Madame Münster looked at him, and her eye exhibited a slight responsive spark. She touched her lips to a glass of wine, and then she said, 'Describe them. Give me a picture.'

Felix drained his own glass. 'Well, it's in the country, among

the meadows and woods; a wild sort of place, and yet not far
from here. Only, such a road, my dear! Imagine one of the
Alpine glaciers reproduced in mud. But you will not spend
much time on it, for they want you to come and stay, once
for all.'

'Ah,' said the Baroness, 'they want me to come and stay, once
for all? Bon.'

'It's intensely rural, tremendously natural; and all overhung
with this strange white light, this far-away blue sky. There's a
big wooden house – a kind of three-storey bungalow; it looks
like a magnified Nüremberg toy.[2] There was a gentleman there
that made a speech to me about it and called it a "venerable
mansion"; but it looks as if it had been built last night.'

'Is it handsome – is it elegant?' asked the Baroness.

Felix looked at her a moment, smiling. 'It's very clean! No
splendours, no gilding, no troops of servants; rather straight-
backed chairs. But you might eat off the floors, and you can sit
down on the stairs.'

'That must be a privilege. And the inhabitants are straight-
backed too, of course.'

'My dear sister,' said Felix, 'the inhabitants are charming.'

'In what style?'

'In a style of their own. How shall I describe it? It's primitive;
it's patriarchal; it's the *ton* of the golden age.'

'And have they nothing golden but their ton? Are there no
symptoms of wealth?'

'I should say there was wealth without symptoms. A plain,
homely way of life: nothing for show, and very little for – what
shall I call it? – for the senses: but a great *aisance*, and a lot
of money, out of sight, that comes forward very quietly for
subscriptions to institutions, for repairing tenements, for paying
doctor's bills; perhaps even for portioning daughters.'

'And the daughters?' Madame Münster demanded. 'How
many are there?'

'There are two, Charlotte and Gertrude.'

'Are they pretty?'

'One of them,' said Felix.

'Which is that?'

The young man was silent, looking at his sister. 'Charlotte,' he said at last.

She looked at him in return. 'I see. You are in love with Gertrude. They must be Puritans to their finger-tips; anything but gay!'

'No, they are not gay,' Felix admitted. 'They are sober; they are even severe. They are of a pensive cast; they take things hard. I think there is something the matter with them; they have some melancholy memory or some depressing expectation. It's not the epicurean temperament. My uncle, Mr. Wentworth, is a tremendously high-toned old fellow; he looks as if he were undergoing martyrdom, not by fire, but by freezing. But we shall cheer them up; we shall do them good. They will take a good deal of stirring up; but they are wonderfully kind and gentle. And they are appreciative. They think one clever; they think one remarkable!'

'That is very fine, so far as it goes,' said the Baroness. 'But are we to be shut up to these three people. Mr. Wentworth and the two young women – what did you say their names were – Deborah and Hephzibah?'[3]

'Oh, no; there is another little girl, a cousin of theirs, a very pretty creature; a thorough little American. And then there is the son of the house.'

'Good!' said the Baroness. 'We are coming to the gentlemen. What of the son of the house?'

'I am afraid he gets tipsy.'

'He, then, has the epicurean temperament! How old is he?'

'He is a boy of twenty; a pretty young fellow, but I am afraid he has vulgar tastes. And then there is Mr. Brand – a very tall young man, a sort of lay-priest. They seem to think a good deal of him, but I don't exactly make him out.'

'And is there nothing,' asked the Baroness, 'between these extremes – this mysterious ecclesiastic and that intemperate youth?'

'Oh, yes, there is Mr. Acton. I think,' said the young man, with a nod at his sister, 'that you will like Mr. Acton.'

'Remember that I am very fastidious,' said the Baroness. 'Has he very good manners?'

'He will have them with you. He is a man of the world; he has been to China.'

Madame Münster gave a little laugh. 'A man of the Chinese world! He must be very interesting.'

'I have an idea that he brought home a fortune,' said Felix.

'That is always interesting. Is he young, good-looking, clever?'

'He is less than forty; he has a baldish head; he says witty things. I rather think,' added the young man, 'that he will admire the Baroness Münster.'

'It is very possible,' said this lady. Her brother never knew how she would take things; but shortly afterwards she declared that he had made a very pretty description and that on the morrow she would go and see for herself.

They mounted, accordingly, into a great barouche[4] – a vehicle as to which the Baroness found nothing to criticize but the price that was asked for it and the fact that the coachman wore a straw hat. (At Silberstadt Madame Münster had had liveries of yellow and crimson.) They drove into the country, and the Baroness, leaning far back and swaying her lace-fringed parasol, looked to right and to left and surveyed the way-side objects. After a while she pronounced them 'affreux'. Her brother remarked that it was apparently a country in which the foreground was inferior to the *plans reculés*: and the Baroness rejoined that the landscape seemed to be all foreground. Felix had fixed with his new friends the hour at which he should bring his sister; it was four o'clock in the afternoon. The large, clean-faced house wore, to his eyes, as the barouche drove up to it, a very friendly aspect; the high, slender elms made lengthening shadows in front of it. The Baroness descended; her American kinsfolk were stationed in the portico. Felix waved his hat to them, and a tall, lean gentleman, with a high forehead and a clean shaven face, came forward toward the garden gate. Charlotte Wentworth walked at his side. Gertrude came behind, more slowly. Both of these young ladies wore rustling silk dresses. Felix ushered his sister into the gate. 'Be very gracious,' he said to her. But he saw the admonition was superfluous. Eugenia was prepared to be gracious as only Eugenia could be. Felix knew no keener pleasure than to be able to admire his sister unrestrictedly; for if the opportunity was frequent, it was not inveterate. When she desired to please she was to him, as to every one else, the most charming woman in the world. Then he forgot that she was ever anything else; that she was sometimes hard and perverse; that he was occasionally afraid of her. Now, as she took his arm to pass into the garden, he felt that she desired, that she proposed, to please, and this situation made him very happy. Eugenia would please.

The tall gentleman came to meet her, looking very rigid and grave. But it was a rigidity that had no illiberal meaning. Mr. Wentworth's manner was pregnant, on the contrary, with a sense of grand responsibility, of the solemnity of the occasion, of its being difficult to show sufficient deference to a lady at once so distinguished and so unhappy. Felix had observed on the day before his characteristic pallor; and now he perceived that there was something almost cadaverous in his uncle's high-featured white face. But so clever were this young man's quick sympathies and perceptions that he already learned that in these semi-mortuary manifestations there was no cause for alarm. His light imagination had gained a glimpse of Mr. Wentworth's spiritual mechanism, and taught him that, the old man being infinitely conscientious, the special operation of conscience within him announced itself by several of the indications of physical faintness.

The Baroness took her uncle's hand, and stood looking at him with her ugly face and her beautiful smile. 'Have I done right to come?' she asked.

'Very right, very right,' said Mr. Wentworth, solemnly. He had arranged in his mind a little speech; but now it quite faded away. He felt almost frightened. He had never been looked at in just that way – with just that fixed, intense smile – by any woman; and it perplexed and weighed upon him, now, that the woman who was smiling so and who had instantly given him a vivid sense of her possessing other unprecedented attributes, was his own niece, the child of his own father's daughter. The idea that his niece should be a German Baroness, married 'morganatically' to a Prince, had already given him much to think about. Was it right, was it just, was it acceptable? He always slept badly, and the night before he had lain awake much more even than usual, asking himself these questions. The strange word 'morganatic' was constantly in his ears; it reminded him of a certain Mrs. Morgan whom he had once known and who had been a bold, unpleasant woman. He had a feeling that it was his duty, so long as the Baroness looked at him, smiling in that way, to meet her glance with his own scrupulously adjusted, consciously frigid organs of vision; but on this occasion he failed to perform his duty to the last. He looked away toward his daughters. 'We are very glad to see you,' he had said. 'Allow me to introduce my daughters – Miss Charlotte Wentworth, Miss Gertrude Wentworth.'

The Baroness thought she had never seen people less demonstrative. But Charlotte kissed her and took her hand, looking at her sweetly and solemnly. Gertrude seemed to her almost funereal, though Gertrude might have found a source of gaiety in the fact that Felix, with his magnificent smile, had been talking to her; he had greeted her as a very old friend. When she kissed the Baroness she had tears in her eyes. Madame Münster took each of these young women by the hand, and looked at them all over. Charlotte thought her very strange-looking and singularly dressed; she could not have said whether it was well or ill. She was glad, at any rate, that they had put on their silk gowns – especially Gertrude. 'My cousins are very pretty,' said the Baroness, turning her eyes from one to the other. 'Your daughters are very handsome, sir.'

Charlotte blushed quickly; she had never yet heard her personal appearance alluded to in a loud, expressive voice. Gertrude looked away – not at Felix; she was extremely pleased. It was not the compliment that pleased her; she did not believe it; she thought herself very plain. She could hardly have told you the source of her satisfaction; it came from something in the way the Baroness spoke, and it was not diminished – it was rather deepened, oddly enough – by the young girl's disbelief. Mr. Wentworth was silent; and then he asked, formally, 'Won't you come into the house?'

'These are not all; you have some other children,' said the Baroness.

'I have a son,' Mr. Wentworth answered.

'And why doesn't he come to meet me?' Eugenia cried. 'I am afraid he is not so charming as his sisters.'

'I don't know; I will see about it,' the old man declared.

'He is rather afraid of ladies,' Charlotte said, softly.

'He is very handsome,' said Gertrude, as loud as she could.

'We will go in and find him. We will draw him out of his *cachette*.' And the Baroness took Mr. Wentworth's arm, who was not aware that he had offered it to her, and who, as they walked toward the house, wondered whether he ought to have offered it and whether it was proper for her to take it if it had not been offered. 'I want to know you well,' said the Baroness, interrupting these meditations, 'and I want you to know me.'

'It seems natural that we should know each other,' Mr. Wentworth rejoined. 'We are near relatives.'

'Ah, there comes a moment in life when one reverts, irresistibly, to one's natural ties – to one's natural affections. You must have found that!' said Eugenia.

Mr. Wentworth had been told the day before by Felix that Eugenia was very clever, very brilliant, and the information had held him in some suspense. This was the cleverness, he supposed; the brilliancy was beginning. 'Yes, the natural affections are very strong,' he murmured.

'In some people,' the Baroness declared. 'Not in all.' Charlotte was walking beside her; she took hold of her hand again, smiling always. 'And you, *cousine*, where did you get that enchanting complexion?' she went on; 'such lilies and roses?' The roses in poor Charlotte's countenance began speedily to predominate over the lilies, and she quickened her step and reached the portico. 'This is the country of complexions,' the Baroness continued, addressing herself to Mr. Wentworth. 'I am convinced they are more delicate. There are very good ones in England – in Holland; but they are very apt to be coarse. There is too much red.'

'I think you will find,' said Mr. Wentworth, 'that this country is superior in many respects to those you mention. I have been to England and Holland.'

'Ah, you have been to Europe?' cried the Baroness. 'Why

didn't you come and see me? But it's better, after all, this way,'
she said. They were entering the house; she paused and looked
round her. 'I see you have arranged your house – your beautiful
house – in the – in the Dutch taste!'

'The house is very old,' remarked Mr. Wentworth. 'General
Washington once spent a week here.'

'Oh, I have heard of Washington,' cried the Baroness. 'My
father used to tell me of him.'

Mr. Wentworth was silent a moment, and then, 'I found he
was very well known in Europe,' he said.

Felix had lingered in the garden with Gertrude; he was standing before her and smiling, as he had done the day before. What
had happened the day before seemed to her a kind of dream.
He had been there and he had changed everything; the others
had seen him, they had talked with him; but that he should
come again, that he should be part of the future, part of her
small, familiar, much-meditating life – this needed, afresh, the
evidence of her senses. The evidence had come to her senses
now; and her senses seemed to rejoice in it. 'What do you think
of Eugenia?' Felix asked. 'Isn't she charming?'

'She is very brilliant,' said Gertrude. 'But I can't tell yet. She
seems to me like a singer singing an air. You can't tell till the
song is done.'

'Ah, the song will never be done!' exclaimed the young man,
laughing. 'Don't you think her handsome?'

Gertrude had been disappointed in the beauty of the Baroness
Münster; she had expected her, for mysterious reasons, to re-
semble a very pretty portrait of the Empress Josephine,[5] of which
there hung an engraving in one of the parlours, and which the
younger Miss Wentworth had always greatly admired. But the
Baroness was not at all like that – not at all. Though different,
however, she was very wonderful, and Gertrude felt herself most
suggestively corrected. It was strange, nevertheless, that Felix
should speak in that positive way about his sister's beauty. 'I
think I *shall* think her handsome,' Gertrude said. 'It must be
very interesting to know her. I don't feel as if I ever could.'

'Ah, you will know her well; you will become great friends,'
Felix declared, as if this were the easiest thing in the world.

'She is very graceful,' said Gertrude, looking after the Baroness, suspended to her father's arm. It was a pleasure to her to say that any one was graceful.

Felix had been looking about him. 'And your little cousin, of yesterday,' he said, 'who was so wonderfully pretty – what has become of her?'

'She is in the parlour,' Gertrude answered. 'Yes, she is very pretty.' She felt as if it were her duty to take him straight into the house, to where he might be near her cousin. But after hesitating a moment she lingered still. 'I didn't believe you would come back,' she said.

'Not come back!' cried Felix, laughing. 'You didn't know, then, the impression made upon this susceptible heart of mine.'

She wondered whether he meant the impression her cousin Lizzie had made. 'Well,' she said, 'I didn't think we should ever see you again.'

'And pray what did you think would become of me?'

'I don't know. I thought you would melt away.'

'That's a compliment to my solidity! I melt very often,' said Felix, 'but there is always something left of me.'

'I came and waited for you by the door, because the others did,' Gertrude went on. 'But if you had never appeared I should not have been surprised.'

'I hope,' declared Felix, looking at her, 'that you would have been disappointed.'

She looked at him a little, and shook her head. 'No – no!'

'Ah, *par exemple*!' cried the young man. 'You deserve that I should never leave you.'

Going into the parlour they found Mr. Wentworth performing introductions. A young man was standing before the Baroness, blushing a good deal, laughing a little, and shifting his weight from one foot to the other – a slim, mild-faced young man, with neatly-arranged features, like those of Mr. Wentworth. Two other gentlemen, behind him, had risen from their seats, and a little apart, near one of the windows, stood a remarkably pretty young girl. The young girl was knitting a stocking; but, while her fingers quickly moved, she looked with wide, brilliant eyes at the Baroness.

'And what is your son's name?' said Eugenia, smiling at the young man.

'My name is Clifford Wentworth, ma'am,' he said in a tremulous voice.

'Why didn't you come out to meet me, Mr. Clifford Wentworth?' the Baroness demanded, with her beautiful smile.

'I didn't think you would want me,' said the young man, slowly sidling about.

'One always wants a *beau cousin* – if one has one! But if you are very nice to me in future I won't remember it against you.' And Madame Münster transferred her smile to the other persons present. It rested first upon the candid countenance and long-skirted figure of Mr. Brand, whose eyes were intently fixed upon Mr. Wentworth, as if to beg him not to prolong an anomalous situation. Mr. Wentworth pronounced his name. Eugenia gave him a very charming glance, and then looked at the other gentleman.

This latter personage was a man of rather less than the usual stature and the usual weight, with a quick, observant, agreeable dark eye, a small quantity of thin dark hair, and a small moustache. He had been standing with his hands in his pockets; and when Eugenia looked at him he took them out. But he did not, like Mr. Brand, look evasively and urgently at their host. He met Eugenia's eyes; he appeared to appreciate the privilege of meeting them. Madame Münster instantly felt that he was, intrinsically, the most important person present. She was not unconscious that this impression was in some degree manifested in the little sympathetic nod with which she acknowledged Mr. Wentworth's announcement, 'My cousin, Mr. Acton!'

'Your cousin – not mine?' said the Baroness.

'It only depends upon you,' Mr. Acton declared, laughing.

The Baroness looked at him a moment, and noticed that he had very white teeth. 'Let it depend upon your behaviour,' she said. 'I think I had better wait. I have cousins enough. Unless I can also claim relationship,' she added, 'with that charming young lady,' and she pointed to the young girl at the window.

'That's my sister,' said Mr. Acton. And Gertrude Wentworth put her arm round the young girl and led her forward. It was not, apparently, that she needed much leading. She came toward the Baroness with a light, quick step, and with perfect self-possession, rolling her stocking round its needles. She had dark blue eyes and dark brown hair; she was wonderfully pretty.

Eugenia kissed her, as she had kissed the other young women, and then held her off a little, looking at her. 'Now this is quite another *type*,' she said; she pronounced the word in the French manner. 'This is a different outline, my uncle, a different character, from that of your own daughters. This, Felix,' she went on, 'is very much more what we have always thought of as the American type.'

The young girl, during this exposition, was smiling askance at every one in turn, and at Felix out of turn. 'I find only one type here!' cried Felix, laughing. 'The type adorable!'

This sally was received in perfect silence, but Felix, who learned all things quickly, had already learned that the silences frequently observed among his new acquaintances were not necessarily restrictive or resentful. It was, as one might say, the silence of expectation, of modesty. They were all standing round his sister, as if they were expecting her to acquit herself of the exhibition of some peculiar faculty, some brilliant talent. Their attitude seemed to imply that she was a kind of conversational mountebank, attired, intellectually, in gauze and spangles. This attitude gave a certain ironical force to Madame Münster's next words. 'Now this is your circle,' she said to her uncle. 'This is your *salon*. These are your regular habitués, eh? I am so glad to see you all together.'

'Oh,' said Mr. Wentworth, 'they are always dropping in and out. You must do the same.'

'Father,' interposed Charlotte Wentworth, 'they must do something more.' And she turned her sweet, serious face, that seemed at once timid and placid, upon their interesting visitor. 'What is your name?' she asked.

'Eugenia-Camilla-Dolores,' said the Baroness, smiling. 'But you needn't say all that.'

'I will say Eugenia, if you will let me. You must come and stay with us.'

The Baroness laid her hand upon Charlotte's arm very tenderly; but she reserved herself. She was wondering whether it would be possible to 'stay' with these people. 'It would be very charming – very charming,' she said; and her eyes wandered over the company, over the room. She wished to gain time before committing herself. Her glance fell upon young Mr. Brand, who stood there, with his arms folded and his hand on his chin, looking at her. 'The gentleman, I suppose, is a sort of ecclesiastic,' she said to Mr. Wentworth, lowering her voice a little.

'He is a minister,' answered Mr. Wentworth.

'A Protestant?' asked Eugenia.

'I am a Unitarian,[6] madam,' replied Mr. Brand, impressively.

'Ah, I see,' said Eugenia. 'Something new.' She had never heard of this form of worship.

Mr. Acton began to laugh, and Gertrude looked anxiously at Mr. Brand.

'You have come very far,' said Mr. Wentworth.

'Very far – very far,' the Baroness replied, with a graceful shake of her head – a shake that might have meant many different things.

'That's a reason why you ought to settle down with us,' said Mr. Wentworth, with that dryness of utterance which, as Eugenia was too intelligent not to feel, took nothing from the delicacy of his meaning.

She looked at him, and for an instant, in his cold, still face, she seemed to see a far-away likeness to the vaguely remembered image of her mother. Eugenia was a woman of sudden emotions, and now, unexpectedly, she felt one rising in her heart. She kept looking round the circle; she knew that there was admiration in all the eyes that were fixed upon her. She smiled at them all.

'I came to look – to try – to ask,' she said. 'It seems to me I have done well. I am very tired; I want to rest.' There were tears in her eyes. The luminous interior, the gentle, tranquil people, the simple, serious life – the sense of these things pressed upon her with an overmastering force, and she felt herself yielding to one of the most genuine emotions she had ever known. 'I should like to stay here,' she said. 'Pray take me in.'

Though she was smiling, there were tears in her voice as well as in her eyes. 'My dear niece,' said Mr. Wentworth, softly. And Charlotte put out her arms and drew the Baroness toward her; while Robert Acton turned away, with his hands stealing into his pockets.

IV

A few days after the Baroness Münster had presented herself
to her American kinsfolk she came, with her brother, and took
up her abode in that small white house adjacent to Mr. Wentworth's own dwelling of which mention has already been made.
It was on going with his daughters to return her visit that Mr.
Wentworth placed this comfortable cottage at her service; the
offer being the result of a domestic colloquy, diffused through
the ensuing twenty-four hours, in the course of which the two
foreign visitors were discussed and analysed with a great deal
of earnestness and subtlety. The discussion went forward, as I
say, in the family circle; but that circle on the evening following
Madame Münster's return to town, as on many other occasions,
included Robert Acton and his pretty sister. If you had been
present, it would probably not have seemed to you that the
advent of these brilliant strangers was treated as an exhilar-
ating occurrence, a pleasure the more in this tranquil household, a prospective source of entertainment. This was not
Mr. Wentworth's way of treating any human occurrence. The
sudden irruption into the well-ordered consciousness of the
Wentworths of an element not allowed for in its scheme of
usual obligations required a readjustment of that sense of responsibility which constituted its principal furniture. To consider an event, crudely and baldly, in the light of the pleasure
it might bring them was an intellectual exercise with which
Felix Young's American cousins were almost wholly un-
acquainted, and which they scarcely supposed to be largely
pursued in any section of human society. The arrival of Felix
and his sister was a satisfaction, but it was a singularly joyless

and inelastic satisfaction. It was an extension of duty, of the exercise of the more recondite virtues; but neither Mr. Wentworth, nor Charlotte, nor Mr. Brand, who, among these excellent people, was a great promoter of reflection and aspiration, frankly adverted to it as an extension of enjoyment. This function was ultimately assumed by Gertrude Wentworth, who was a peculiar girl, but the full compass of whose peculiarities had not been exhibited before they very ingeniously found their pretext in the presence of these possibly too agreeable foreigners. Gertrude, however, had to struggle with a great accumulation of obstructions, both of the subjective, as the metaphysicians say, and of the objective, order; and indeed it is no small part of the purpose of this little history to set forth her struggle. What seemed paramount in this abrupt enlargement of Mr. Wentworth's sympathies and those of his daughters was an extension of the field of possible mistakes; and the doctrine, as it may almost be called, of the oppressive gravity of mistakes was one of the most cherished traditions of the Wentworth family.

'I don't believe she wants to come and stay in this house,' said Gertrude; Madame Münster, from this time forward, receiving no other designation than the personal pronoun. Charlotte and Gertrude acquired considerable facility in addressing her, directly, as 'Eugenia'; but in speaking of her to each other they rarely called her anything but 'she'.

'Doesn't she think it good enough for her?' cried little Lizzie Acton, who was always asking unpractical questions that required, in strictness, no answer, and to which indeed she expected no other answer than such as she herself invariably furnished in a small, innocently-satirical laugh.

'She certainly expressed a willingness to come,' said Mr. Wentworth.

'That was only politeness,' Gertrude rejoined.

'Yes, she is very polite – very polite,' said Mr. Wentworth.

'She is too polite,' his son declared, in a softly growling tone which was habitual to him, but which was an indication of nothing worse than a vaguely humorous intention. 'It is very embarrassing.'

'That is more than can be said of you, sir,' said Lizzie Acton, with her little laugh.

'Well, I don't mean to encourage her,' Clifford went on.

'I'm sure I don't care if you do!' cried Lizzie.

'She will not think of you, Clifford,' said Gertrude, gravely.

'I hope not!' Clifford exclaimed.

'She will think of Robert,' Gertrude continued, in the same tone.

Robert Acton began to blush; but there was no occasion for it, for every one was looking at Gertrude – every one, at least, save Lizzie, who, with her pretty head on one side, contemplated her brother.

'Why do you attribute motives, Gertrude?' asked Mr. Wentworth.

'I don't attribute motives, father,' said Gertrude. 'I only say she will think of Robert; and she will!'

'Gertrude judges by herself!' Acton exclaimed, laughing. 'Don't you, Gertrude? Of course the Baroness will think of me. She will think of me from morning till night.'

'She will be very comfortable here,' said Charlotte, with something of a housewife's pride. 'She can have the large north-east room. And the French bedstead,' Charlotte added, with a constant sense of the lady's foreignness.

'She will not like it,' said Gertrude; 'not even if you pin little tidies all over the chairs.'

'Why not, dear?' asked Charlotte, perceiving a touch of irony here, but not resenting it.

Gertrude had left her chair; she was walking about the room; her stiff silk dress, which she had put on in honour of the Baroness, made a sound upon the carpet. 'I don't know,' she replied. 'She will want something more – more private.'

'If she wants to be private she can stay in her room,' Lizzie Acton remarked.

Gertrude paused in her walk, looking at her. 'That would not be pleasant,' she answered. 'She wants privacy and pleasure together.'

Robert Acton began to laugh again. 'My dear cousin, what a picture!'

Charlotte had fixed her serious eyes upon her sister; she wondered whence she had suddenly derived these strange notions. Mr. Wentworth also observed his younger daughter.

'I don't know what her manner of life may have been,' he said; 'but she certainly never can have enjoyed a more refined and salubrious home.'

Gertrude stood there looking at them all. 'She is the wife of a Prince,' she said.

'We are all princes here,' said Mr. Wentworth; 'and I don't know of any palace in this neighbourhood that is to let.'

'Cousin William,' Robert Acton interposed, 'do you want to do something handsome? Make them a present, for three months, of the little house over the way.'

'You are very generous with other people's things!' cried his sister.

'Robert is very generous with his own things,' Mr. Wentworth observed dispassionately, and looking, in cold meditation, at his kinsman.

'Gertrude,' Lizzie went on, 'I had an idea you were so fond of your new cousin.'

'Which new cousin?' asked Gertrude.

'I don't mean the Baroness!' the young girl rejoined, with her laugh. 'I thought you expected to see so much of him.'

'Of Felix? I hope to see a great deal of him,' said Gertrude, simply.

'Then why do you want to keep him out of the house?'

Gertrude looked at Lizzie Acton, and then looked away.

'Should you want me to live in the house with you, Lizzie?' asked Clifford.

'I hope you never will. I hate you!' Such was this young lady's reply.

'Father,' said Gertrude, stopping before Mr. Wentworth and smiling, with a smile the sweeter, as her smile always was, for its rarity; 'do let them live in the little house over the way. It will be lovely!'

Robert Acton had been watching her. 'Gertrude is right,' he said. 'Gertrude is the cleverest girl in the world. If I might take the liberty, I should strongly recommend their living there.'

'There is nothing there so pretty as the northeast room,' Charlotte urged.

'She will make it pretty. Leave her alone!' Acton exclaimed.

Gertrude, at his compliment, had blushed and looked at him: it was as if some one less familiar had complimented her. 'I am sure she will make it pretty. It will be very interesting. It will be a place to go to. It will be a foreign house.'

'Are we very sure that we need a foreign house?' Mr. Wentworth inquired. 'Do you think it desirable to establish a foreign house – in this quiet place?'

'You speak,' said Acton, laughing, 'as if it were a question of the poor Baroness opening a wine-shop or a gaming-table.'

'It would be too lovely!' Gertrude declared again, laying her hand on the back of her father's chair.

'That she should open a gaming-table?' Charlotte asked, with great gravity.

Gertrude looked at her a moment, and then, 'Yes, Charlotte,' she said, simply.

'Gertrude is growing pert,' Clifford Wentworth observed, with his humorous young growl. 'That comes of associating with foreigners.'

Mr. Wentworth looked up at his daughter, who was standing beside him; he drew her gently forward. 'You must be careful,' he said. 'You must keep watch. Indeed, we must all be careful. This is a great change; we are to be exposed to peculiar influences. I don't say they are bad. I don't judge them in advance. But they may perhaps make it necessary that we should exercise a great deal of wisdom and self-control. It will be a different tone.'

Gertrude was silent a moment, in deference to her father's speech; then she spoke in a manner that was not in the least an answer to it. 'I want to see how they will live. I am sure they will have different hours. She will do all kinds of little things differently. When we go over there it will be like going to Europe. She will have a boudoir. She will invite us to dinner – very late. She will breakfast in her room.'

Charlotte gazed at her sister again. Gertrude's imagination seemed to her to be fairly running riot. She had always known that Gertrude had a great deal of imagination – she had been very proud of it. But at the same time she had always felt that it was a dangerous and irresponsible faculty; and now, to her sense, for the moment, it seemed to threaten to make her sister a strange person who should come in suddenly, as from a journey, talking of the peculiar and possibly unpleasant things she had observed. Charlotte's imagination took no journeys whatever; she kept it, as it were, in her pocket, with the other furniture of this receptacle – a thimble, a little box of peppermint, and a morsel of court-plaster.[1] 'I don't believe she would have any dinner – or any breakfast,' said Miss Wentworth. 'I don't believe she knows how to do anything herself. I should have to get her ever so many servants, and she wouldn't like them.'

'She has a maid,' said Gertrude; 'a French maid. She mentioned her.'

'I wonder if the maid has a little fluted cap and red slippers,' said Lizzie Acton. 'There was a French maid in that play that Robert took me to see. She had pink stockings; she was very wicked.'

'She was a *soubrette*,'[2] Gertrude announced, who had never seen a play in her life. 'They call that a soubrette. It will be a great chance to learn French.' Charlotte gave a little soft, helpless groan. She had a vision of a wicked, theatrical person, clad in pink stockings and red shoes, and speaking, with confounding volubility, an incomprehensible tongue, flitting through the sacred penetralia of that large, clean house. 'That is one reason in favour of their coming here,' Gertrude went on. 'But we can make Eugenia speak French to us, and Felix. I mean to begin – the next time.'

Mr. Wentworth had kept her standing near him, and he gave her his earnest, thin, unresponsive glance again. 'I want you to make me a promise, Gertrude,' he said.

'What is it?' she asked, smiling.

'Not to get excited. Not to allow these – these occurrences to be an occasion for excitement.'

She looked down at him a moment, and then she shook her head. 'I don't think I can promise that, father. I am excited already.'

Mr. Wentworth was silent a while; they all were silent, as if in recognition of something audacious and portentous.

'I think they had better go to the other house,' said Charlotte, quietly.

'I shall keep them in the other house,' Mr. Wentworth subjoined, more pregnantly.

Gertrude turned away; then she looked across at Robert Acton. Her cousin Robert was a great friend of hers; she often looked at him this way instead of saying things. Her glance on this occasion, however, struck him as a substitute for a larger volume of diffident utterance than usual, inviting him to observe, among other things, the inefficiency of her father's design – if design it was – for diminishing, in the interest of quiet nerves, their occasions of contact with their foreign relatives. But Acton immediately complimented Mr. Wentworth upon his liberality. 'That's a very nice thing to do,' he said, 'giving them the little house. You will have treated them handsomely, and, whatever happens, you will be glad of it.' Mr. Wentworth was liberal, and he knew he was liberal. It gave him pleasure to know it, to feel it, to see it recorded; and this pleasure is the only palpable form of self-indulgence with which the narrator of these incidents will be able to charge him.

'A three days' visit at most, over there, is all I should have found possible,' Madame Münster remarked to her brother, after they had taken possession of the little white house. 'It would have been too *intime* – decidedly too intime. Breakfast, dinner, and tea *en famille* – it would have been the end of the world if I could have reached the third day.' And she made the same observation to her maid Augustine, an intelligent person, who enjoyed a liberal share of her confidence. Felix declared that he would willingly spend his life in the bosom of the Wentworth family; that they were the kindest, simplest, most amiable people in the world, and that he had taken a prodigious fancy to them all. The Baroness quite agreed with him that they were simple and kind; they were thoroughly nice people, and she liked them extremely. The girls were perfect ladies; it was impossible to be more of a lady than Charlotte Wentworth, in spite of her little village air. 'But as for thinking them the best company in the world,' said the Baroness, 'that is another thing; and as for wishing to live *porte à porte* with them, I should as soon think of wishing myself back in the convent again, to wear a bombazine[3] apron and sleep in a dormitory.' And yet the Baroness was in high good humour; she had been very much pleased. With her lively perception and her refined imagination, she was capable of enjoying anything that was characteristic, anything that was good of its kind. The Wentworth household seemed to her very perfect in its kind – wonderfully peaceful and unspotted; pervaded by a sort of dove-coloured freshness that had all the quietude and benevolence of what she deemed to be Quakerism,[4] and yet seemed to be founded upon a degree of material abundance for which, in certain matters of detail, one might have looked in vain at the frugal little court of Silberstadt-Schreckenstein. She perceived immediately that her American relatives thought and talked very little about money; and this of itself made an impression upon Eugenia's imagination. She perceived at the same time that if Charlotte or Gertrude should ask their father for a very considerable sum he would at once place it in their hands; and this made a still greater impression. The greatest impression of all, perhaps, was made by another rapid induction. The Baroness had an immediate conviction that Robert Acton would put his hand into his pocket every day in the week if that rattle-pated little sister of his should bid him. The men in this country, said the Baroness, are evidently very obliging. Her declaration that she was looking for rest and retirement had been by no means wholly untrue; nothing that the Baroness said was wholly untrue. It is but fair to add, perhaps, that nothing that she said was wholly true. She wrote to a friend in Germany that it was a return to nature; it was like drinking new milk, and she was very fond of new milk. She said to herself, of course, that it would be a little dull; but there can be no better proof of her good spirits than the fact that she thought she should not mind its being a little dull. It seemed to her, when from the piazza of her eleemosynary[5] cottage she looked out over the soundless fields, the stony pastures, the clear-faced ponds, the rugged little orchards, that she had never been in the midst of so peculiarly intense a stillness; it was almost a delicate sensual pleasure. It was all very good, very innocent and safe, and out of it something good must come. Augustine, indeed, who had an unbounded faith in her mistress's wisdom and far-sightedness, was a great deal perplexed and depressed. She was always ready to take her cue when she understood it; but she liked to understand it, and on this occasion comprehension failed. What, indeed, was the Baroness doing *dans cette galère*? what fish did she expect to land out of these very stagnant waters? The game was evidently a deep one. Augustine could trust her; but the sense of walking in the dark betrayed itself in the physiognomy of this spare, sober, sallow, middle-aged person, who had nothing in common with Gertrude Wentworth's conception of a soubrette, by the most ironical scowl that had ever rested upon the unpretending tokens of the peace and plenty of the Wentworths. Fortunately, Augustine could quench scepticism in action. She quite agreed with her mistress – or rather she quite out-stripped her mistress – in thinking that the little white house was pitifully bare. 'Il faudra,' said Augustine, 'lui faire un peu de toilette.' And she began to hang up *portières* in the doorways; to place wax candles, procured after some research, in unexpected situations; to dispose anomalous draperies over the arms of sofas and the backs of chairs. The Baroness had brought with her to the New World a copious provision of the element of costume; and the two Miss Wentworths, when they came over to see her, were somewhat bewildered by the obtrusive distribution of her wardrobe. There were India shawls suspended, curtain-wise, in the parlour door, and curious fabrics, corresponding to Gertrude's metaphysical vision of an opera-cloak, tumbled about in the sitting-places. There were pink silk blinds in the windows, by which the room was strangely bedimmed; and along the chimney-piece was disposed a remarkable band of velvet, covered with coarse, dirty-looking lace. 'I have been making myself a little comfortable,' said the Baroness, much to the confusion of Charlotte, who had been on the point of proposing to come and help her put her superfluous draperies away. But what Charlotte mistook for an almost culpably delayed subsidence Gertrude very

presently perceived to be the most ingenious, the most interesting, the most romantic intention. 'What is life, indeed, without
curtains?' she secretly asked herself; and she appeared to herself
to have been leading hitherto an existence singularly garish and
totally devoid of festoons.

Felix was not a young man who troubled himself greatly
about anything – least of all about the conditions of enjoyment.
His faculty of enjoyment was so large, so unconsciously eager,
that it may be said of it that it had a permanent advance upon
embarrassment and sorrow. His sentient faculty was intrinsically joyous, and novelty and change were in themselves a
delight to him. As they had come to him with a great deal of
frequency, his life had been more agreeable than appeared.
Never was a nature more perfectly fortunate. It was not a
restless, apprehensive, ambitious spirit, running a race with the
tyranny of fate, but a temper so unsuspicious as to put Adversity
off her guard, dodging and evading her with the easy, natural
motion of a wind-shifted flower. Felix extracted entertainment
from all things, and all his faculties – his imagination, his
intelligence, his affections, his senses – had a hand in the game.
It seemed to him that Eugenia and he had been very well treated;
there was something absolutely touching in that combination
of paternal liberality and social considerateness which marked
Mr. Wentworth's deportment. It was most uncommonly kind
of him, for instance, to have given them a house. Felix was
positively amused at having a house of his own; for the little
white cottage among the apple-trees – the chalet, as Madame
Münster always called it – was much more sensibly his own
than any domiciliary *quatrième*, looking upon a court, with
the rent overdue. Felix had spent a good deal of his life in looking into courts, with a perhaps slightly tattered pair of elbows
resting upon the ledge of a high-perched window, and the
thin smoke of a cigarette rising into an atmosphere in which
street-cries died away and the vibration of chimes from ancient
belfries became sensible. He had never known anything so
infinitely rural as these New England fields; and he took a great
fancy to all their pastoral roughnesses. He had never had a
greater sense of luxurious security; and at the risk of making

him seem a rather sordid adventurer I must declare that he
found an irresistible charm in the fact that he might dine every
day at his uncle's. The charm was irresistible, however, because
his fancy flung a rosy light over this homely privilege. He
appreciated highly the fare that was set before him. There was
a kind of fresh-looking abundance about it which made him
think that people must have lived so in the mythological era,
when they spread their tables upon the grass, replenished them
from cornucopias, and had no particular need of kitchen stoves.
But the great thing that Felix enjoyed was having found a family
– sitting in the midst of gentle, generous people whom he might
call by their first names. He had never known anything more
charming than the attention they paid to what he said. It was
like a large sheet of clean, fine-grained drawing-paper, all ready
to be washed over with effective splashes of water-colour. He
had never had any cousins, and he had never before found
himself in contact so unrestricted with young unmarried ladies.
He was extremely fond of the society of ladies, and it was new
to him that it might be enjoyed in just this manner. At first he
hardly knew what to make of his state of mind. It seemed to
him that he was in love, indiscriminately, with three girls at
once. He saw that Lizzie Acton was more brilliantly pretty than
Charlotte and Gertrude; but this was scarcely a superiority. His
pleasure came from something they had in common – a part of
which was, indeed, that physical delicacy which seemed to make
it proper that they should always dress in thin materials and
clear colours. But they were delicate in other ways, and it was
most agreeable to him to feel that these latter delicacies were
appreciable by contact, as it were. He had known, fortunately,
many virtuous gentlewomen, but it now appeared to him that
in his relations with them (especially when they were unmarried) he had been looking at pictures under glass. He perceived
at present what a nuisance the glass had been – how it perverted
and interfered, how it caught the reflection of other objects and
kept you walking from side to side. He had no need to ask
himself whether Charlotte and Gertrude, and Lizzie Acton,
were in the right light; they were always in the right light. He
liked everything about them: he was, for instance, not at all

above liking the fact that they had very slender feet and high insteps. He liked their pretty noses; he liked their surprised eyes and their hesitating, not at all positive way of speaking; he liked so much knowing that he was perfectly at liberty to be alone for hours, anywhere, with either of them; that preference for one to the other, as a companion of solitude, remained a minor affair. Charlotte Wentworth's sweetly severe features were as agreeable as Lizzie Acton's wonderfully expressive blue eyes; and Gertrude's air of being always ready to walk about and listen was as charming as anything else, especially as she walked very gracefully. After a while Felix began to distinguish; but even then he would often wish, suddenly, that they were not all so sad. Even Lizzie Acton, in spite of her fine little chatter and laughter, appeared sad. Even Clifford Wentworth, who had extreme youth in his favour, and kept a buggy with enormous wheels and a little sorrel mare with the prettiest legs in the world – even this fortunate lad was apt to have an averted, uncomfortable glance, and to edge away from you at times, in the manner of a person with a bad conscience. The only person in the circle with no sense of oppression of any kind was, to Felix's perception, Robert Acton.

It might perhaps have been feared that after the completion of those graceful domiciliary embellishments which have been mentioned Madame Münster would have found herself confronted with alarming possibilities of *ennui*. But as yet she had not taken the alarm. The Baroness was a restless soul, and she projected her restlessness, as it may be said, into any situation that lay before her. Up to a certain point her restlessness might be counted upon to entertain her. She was always expecting something to happen, and, until it was disappointed, expectancy itself was a delicate pleasure. What the Baroness expected just now it would take some ingenuity to set forth; it is enough that while she looked about her she found something to occupy her imagination. She assured herself that she was enchanted with her new relatives; she professed to herself that, like her brother, she felt it a sacred satisfaction to have found a family. It is certain that she enjoyed to the utmost the gentleness of her kinsfolk's deference. She had, first and last, received a great deal of admiration, and her experience of well-turned compliments was very considerable; but she knew that she had never been so real a power, never counted for so much, as now when, for the first time, the standard of comparison of her little circle was a prey to vagueness. The sense, indeed, that the good people about her had, as regards her remarkable self, no standard of comparison at all gave her a feeling of almost illimitable power. It was true, as she said to herself, that if for this reason they would be able to discover nothing against her, so they would perhaps neglect to perceive some of her superior points; but she always wound up her reflections by declaring that she would take care of that.

Charlotte and Gertrude were in some perplexity between their desire to show all proper attention to Madame Münster and their fear of being importunate. The little house in the orchard had hitherto been occupied during the summer months by intimate friends of the family, or by poor relations who found in Mr. Wentworth a landlord attentive to repairs and oblivious of quarter-day.[6] Under these circumstances the open door of the small house and that of the large one, facing each other across their homely gardens, levied no tax upon hourly visits. But the Misses Wentworth received an impression that Eugenia was no friend to the primitive custom of 'dropping in'; she evidently had no idea of living without a door-keeper. 'One goes into your house as into an inn – except that there are no servants rushing forward,' she said to Charlotte. And she added that that was very charming. Gertrude explained to her sister that she meant just the reverse; she didn't like it at all. Charlotte inquired why she should tell an untruth, and Gertrude answered that there was probably some very good reason for it which they should discover when they knew her better. 'There can surely be no good reason for telling an untruth,' said Charlotte. 'I hope she does not think so.'

They had of course desired, from the first, to do everything in the way of helping her to arrange herself. It had seemed to Charlotte that there would be a great many things to talk about; but the Baroness was apparently inclined to talk about nothing.

'Write her a note, asking her leave to come and see her. I think that is what she will like,' said Gertrude.

'Why should I give her the trouble of answering me?' Charlotte asked. 'She will have to write a note and send it over.'

'I don't think she will take any trouble,' said Gertrude, profoundly.

'What then will she do?'

'That is what I am curious to see,' said Gertrude, leaving her sister with an impression that her curiosity was morbid.

They went to see the Baroness without preliminary correspondence; and in the little salon which she had already created, with its becoming light and its festoons, they found Robert Acton.

Eugenia was intensely gracious, but she accused them of neglecting her cruelly. 'You see Mr. Acton has had to take pity upon me,' she said. 'My brother goes off sketching, for hours; I can never depend upon him. So I was to send Mr. Acton to beg you to come and give me the benefit of your wisdom.'

Gertrude looked at her sister. She wanted to say, '*That* is what she would have done.' Charlotte said that they hoped the Baroness would always come and dine with them; it would give them so much pleasure; and, in that case, she would spare herself the trouble of having a cook.

'Ah, but I must have a cook!' cried the Baroness. 'An old negress in a yellow turban. I have set my heart upon that. I want to look out of my window and see her sitting there on the grass, against the background of those crooked, dusky little apple-trees, pulling the husks off a lapful of Indian corn. That will be local colour, you know. There isn't much of it here – you don't mind my saying that, do you? – so one must make the most of what one can get. I shall be most happy to dine with you whenever you will let me; but I want to be able to ask you sometimes. And I want to be able to ask Mr. Acton,' added the Baroness.

'You must come and ask me at home,' said Acton. 'You must come and see me; you must dine with me first. I want to show you my place; I want to introduce you to my mother.' He called again upon Madame Münster, two days later. He was constantly at the other house; he used to walk across the fields from his own place, and he appeared to have fewer scruples than his cousins with regard to dropping in. On this occasion he found that Mr. Brand had come to pay his respects to the charming stranger; but after Acton's arrival the young theologian said nothing. He sat in his chair with his two hands clasped, fixing upon his hostess a grave, fascinated stare. The Baroness talked to Robert Acton, but, as she talked, she turned and smiled at Mr. Brand, who never took his eyes off her. The two men walked away together; they were going to Mr. Wentworth's. Mr. Brand still said nothing; but after they had passed into Mr. Wentworth's garden he stopped and looked back for some time at the little white house. Then, looking at his companion, with his head bent a little to one side and his eyes somewhat contracted, 'Now I suppose that's what is called conversation,' he said; 'real conversation.'

'It's what I call a very clever woman,' said Acton, laughing.

'It is most interesting,' Mr. Brand continued. 'I only wish she would speak French; it would seem more in keeping. It must be quite the style that we have heard about, that we have read about – the style of conversation of Madame de Staël, of Madame Récamier.'[7]

Acton also looked at Madame Münster's residence among its hollyhocks and apple-trees. 'What I should like to know,' he said, smiling, 'is just what has brought Madame Récamier to live in that place!'

V

Mr. Wentworth, with his cane and his gloves in his hand, went every afternoon to call upon his niece. A couple of hours later she came over to the great house to tea. She had let the proposal that she should regularly dine there fall to the ground; she was in the enjoyment of whatever satisfaction was to be derived from the spectacle of an old negress in a crimson turban shelling peas under the apple-trees. Charlotte, who had provided the ancient negress, thought it must be a strange household, Eugenia having told her that Augustine managed everything, the ancient negress included – Augustine who was naturally devoid of all acquaintance with the expurgatory English tongue. By far the most immoral sentiment which I shall have occasion to attribute to Charlotte Wentworth was a certain emotion of disappointment at finding that, in spite of these irregular conditions, the domestic arrangements at the small house were apparently not – from Eugenia's peculiar point of view – strikingly offensive. The Baroness found it amusing to go to tea; she dressed as if for dinner. The tea-table offered an anomalous and picturesque repast; and on leaving it they all sat and talked in the large piazza, or wandered about the garden in the starlight, with their ears full of those sounds of strange insects which, though they are supposed to be, all over the world, a part of the magic of summer nights, seemed to the Baroness to have beneath these western skies an incomparable resonance.

Mr. Wentworth, though, as I say, he went punctiliously to call upon her, was not able to feel that he was getting used to his niece. It taxed his imagination to believe that she was really his half-sister's child. His sister was a figure of his early years;

she had been only twenty when she went abroad, never to return, making in foreign parts a wilful and undesirable marriage. His aunt, Mrs. Whiteside, who had taken her to Europe for the benefit of the tour, gave, on her return, so lamentable an account of Mr. Adolphus Young, to whom the headstrong girl had united her destiny, that it operated as a chill upon family feeling – especially in the case of the half-brothers. Catherine had done nothing subsequently to propitiate her family; she had not even written to them in a way that indicated a lucid appreciation of their suspended sympathy; so that it had become a tradition in Boston circles that the highest charity, as regards this young lady, was to think it well to forget her, and to abstain from conjecture as to the extent to which her aberrations were reproduced in her descendants. Over these young people – a vague report of their existence had come to his ears – Mr. Wentworth had not, in the course of years, allowed his imagination to hover. It had plenty of occupation nearer home, and though he had many cares upon his conscience the idea that he had been an unnatural uncle was, very properly, never among the number. Now that his nephew and niece had come before him, he perceived that they were the fruit of influences and circumstances very different from those under which his own familiar progeny had reached a vaguely-qualified maturity. He felt no provocation to say that these influences had been exerted for evil; but he was sometimes afraid that he should not be able to like his distinguished, delicate, lady-like niece. He was paralysed and bewildered by her foreignness. She spoke, somehow, a different language. There was something strange in her words. He had a feeling that another man, in his place, would accommodate himself to her tone; would ask her questions and joke with her, reply to those pleasantries of her own which sometimes seemed startling as addressed to an uncle. But Mr. Wentworth could not do these things. He could not even bring himself to attempt to measure her position in the world. She was the wife of a foreign nobleman who desired to repudiate her. This had a singular sound, but the old man felt himself destitute of the materials for a judgement. It seemed to him that he ought to find them in his own experience, as a man of the world and an almost public character; but they were not there, and he was ashamed to confess to himself – much more to reveal to Eugenia by interrogations possibly too innocent – the unfurnished condition of this repository.

It appeared to him that he could get much nearer, as he would have said, to his nephew; though he was not sure that Felix was altogether safe. He was so bright and handsome and talkative that it was impossible not to think well of him; and yet it seemed as if there were something almost impudent, almost vicious – or as if there ought to be – in a young man being at once so joyous and so positive. It was to be observed that while Felix was not at all a serious young man there was somehow more of him – he had more weight and volume and resonance – than a number of young men who were distinctly serious. While Mr. Wentworth meditated upon this anomaly his nephew was admiring him unrestrictedly. He thought him a most delicate, generous, high-toned old gentleman, with a very handsome head, of the ascetic type, which he promised himself the profit of sketching. Felix was far from having made a secret of the fact that he wielded the paint-brush, and it was not his own fault if it failed to be generally understood that he was prepared to execute the most striking likenesses on the most reasonable terms. 'He is an artist – my cousin is an artist,' said Gertrude; and she offered this information to every one who would receive it. She offered it to herself, as it were, by way of admonition and reminder; she repeated to herself at odd moments, in lonely places, that Felix was invested with this sacred character. Gertrude had never seen an artist before; she had only read about such people. They seemed to her a romantic and mysterious class, whose life was made up of those agreeable accidents that never happened to other persons. And it merely quickened her meditations on this point that Felix should declare, as he repeatedly did, that he was really not an artist. 'I have never gone into the thing seriously,' he said. 'I have never studied; I have had no training. I do a little of everything, and nothing well. I am only an amateur.'

It pleased Gertrude even more to think that he was an amateur than to think that he was an artist; the former word, to her fancy, had an even subtler connotation. She knew, however, that it was a word to use more soberly. Mr. Wentworth used it freely; for though he had not been exactly familiar with it, he found it convenient as a help toward classifying Felix, who, as a young man extremely clever and active and apparently respectable and yet not engaged in any recognized business, was an importunate anomaly. Of course the Baroness and her brother – she was always spoken of first – were a welcome topic of conversation between Mr. Wentworth and his daughters and their occasional visitors.

'And the young man, your nephew, what is his profession?' asked an old gentleman – Mr. Broderip, of Salem – who had been Mr. Wentworth's classmate at Harvard College in the year 1809, and who came into his office in Devonshire Street. (Mr. Wentworth, in his later years, used to go but three times a week to his office, where he had a large amount of highly confidential trust-business to transact.)

'Well, he's an amateur,' said Felix's uncle, with folded hands, and with a certain satisfaction in being able to say it. And Mr. Broderip had gone back to Salem with a feeling that this was probably a 'European' expression for a broker or a grain exporter.

'I should like to do your head, sir,' said Felix to his uncle one evening, before them all – Mr. Brand and Robert Acton being also present. 'I think I should make a very fine thing of it. It's an interesting head; it's very mediaeval.'

Mr. Wentworth looked grave; he felt awkwardly, as if all the company had come in and found him standing before the looking-glass. 'The Lord made it,' he said. 'I don't think it is for man to make it over again.'

'Certainly the Lord made it,' replied Felix, laughing, 'and he made it very well. But life has been touching up the work. It is a very interesting type of head. It's delightfully wasted and emaciated. The complexion is wonderfully bleached.' And Felix looked round at the circle, as if to call their attention to these interesting points. Mr. Wentworth grew visibly paler. 'I should like to do you as an old prelate, an old cardinal, or the prior of an order.'

'A prelate, a cardinal?' murmured Mr. Wentworth. 'Do you refer to the Roman Catholic priesthood?'

'I mean an old ecclesiastic who should have led a very pure, abstinent life. Now I take it that has been the case with you, sir; one sees it in your face,' Felix proceeded. 'You have been very – a – very moderate. Don't you think one always sees that in a man's face?'

'You see more in a man's face than I should think of looking for,' said Mr. Wentworth coldly.

The Baroness rattled her fan, and gave her brilliant laugh. 'It is a risk to look so close!' she exclaimed. 'My uncle has some peccadilloes[1] on his conscience.' Mr. Wentworth looked at her, painfully at a loss; and in so far as the signs of a pure and abstinent life were visible in his face they were then probably peculiarly manifest. 'You are a *beau vieillard*, dear uncle,' said Madame Münster, smiling with her foreign eyes.

'I think you are paying me a compliment,' said the old man.

'Surely, I am not the first woman that ever did so!' cried the Baroness.

'I think you are,' said Mr. Wentworth gravely. And turning to Felix he added, in the same tone, 'Please don't take my likeness. My children have my daguerreotype.[2] That is quite satisfactory.'

'I won't promise,' said Felix, 'not to work your head into something!'

Mr. Wentworth looked at him and then at all the others; then he got up and slowly walked away.

'Felix,' said Gertrude, in the silence that followed, 'I wish you would paint my portrait.'

Charlotte wondered whether Gertrude was right in wishing this; and she looked at Mr. Brand as the most legitimate way of ascertaining. Whatever Gertrude did or said, Charlotte always looked at Mr. Brand. It was a standing pretext for looking at Mr. Brand – always, as Charlotte thought, in the interest of Gertrude's welfare. It is true that she felt a tremulous interest in Gertrude being right; for Charlotte, in her small, still way, was an heroic sister.

'We should be glad to have your portrait, Miss Gertrude,' said Mr. Brand.

'I should be delighted to paint so charming a model,' Felix declared.

'Do you think you are so lovely, my dear?' asked Lizzie Acton, with her little inoffensive pertness, biting off a knot in her knitting.

'It is not because I think I am beautiful,' said Gertrude, looking all round. 'I don't think I am beautiful, at all.' She spoke with a sort of conscious deliberateness; and it seemed very strange to Charlotte to hear her discussing this question so publicly. 'It is because I think it would be amusing to sit and be painted. I have always thought that.'

'I am sorry you have not had better things to think about, my daughter,' said Mr. Wentworth.

'You are very beautiful, cousin Gertrude,' Felix declared.

'That's a compliment,' said Gertrude. 'I put all the compliments I receive into a little money-jug that has a slit in the side. I shake them up and down, and they rattle. There are not many yet – only two or three.'

'No, it's not a compliment,' Felix rejoined. 'See; I am careful not to give it the form of a compliment. I didn't think you were beautiful at first. But you have come to seem so little by little.'

'Take care, now, your jug doesn't burst!' exclaimed Lizzie.

'I think sitting for one's portrait is only one of the various forms of idleness,' said Mr. Wentworth. 'Their name is legion.'[3]

'My dear sir,' cried Felix, 'you can't be said to be idle when you are making a man work so!'

'One might be painted while one is asleep,' suggested Mr. Brand, as a contribution to the discussion.

'Ah, do paint me while I am asleep,' said Gertrude to Felix, smiling. And she closed her eyes a little. It had by this time become a matter of almost exciting anxiety to Charlotte what Gertrude would say or would do next.

She began to sit for her portrait on the following day – in the open air, on the north side of the piazza. 'I wish you would tell me what you think of us – how we seem to you,' she said to Felix, as he sat before his easel.

'You seem to me the best people in the world,' said Felix.

'You say that,' Gertrude resumed, 'because it saves you the trouble of saying anything else.'

The young man glanced at her over the top of his canvas. 'What else should I say? It would certainly be a great deal of trouble to say anything different.'

'Well,' said Gertrude, 'you have seen people before that you have liked, have you not?'

'Indeed I have, thank Heaven!'

'And they have been very different from us,' Gertrude went on.

'That only proves,' said Felix, 'that there are a thousand different ways of being good company.'

'Do you think us good company?' asked Gertrude.

'Company for a king!'

Gertrude was silent a moment; and then, 'There must be a thousand different ways of being dreary,' she said; 'and sometimes I think we make use of them all.'

Felix stood up quickly, holding up his hand. 'If you could only keep that look on your face for half an hour – while I catch it!' he said. 'It is uncommonly handsome.'

'To look handsome for half an hour – that is a great deal to ask of me,' she answered.

'It would be the portrait of a young woman who has taken some vow, some pledge, that she repents of,' said Felix, 'and who is thinking it over at leisure.'

'I have taken no vow, no pledge,' said Gertrude, very gravely; 'I have nothing to repent of.'

'My dear cousin, that was only a figure of speech. I am very sure that no one in your excellent family has anything to repent of.'

'And yet we are always repenting!' Gertrude exclaimed. 'That is what I mean by our being dreary. You know it perfectly well; you only pretend that you don't.'

Felix gave a quick laugh. 'The half hour is going on, and yet you are handsomer than ever. One must be careful what one says, you see.'

'To me,' said Gertrude, 'you can say anything.'

Felix looked at her, as an artist might, and painted for some time in silence.

'Yes, you seem to me different from your father and sister – from most of the people you have lived with,' he observed.

'To say that one's self,' Gertrude went on, 'is like saying – by implication, at least – that one is better. I am not better; I am much worse. But they say themselves that I am different. It makes them unhappy.'

'Since you accuse me of concealing my real impressions, I may admit that I think the tendency – among you generally – is to be made unhappy too easily.'

'I wish you would tell that to my father,' said Gertrude.

'It might make him more unhappy!' Felix exclaimed, laughing.

'It certainly would. I don't believe you have seen people like that.'

'Ah, my dear cousin, how do you know what I have seen?' Felix demanded. 'How can I tell you?'

'You might tell me a great many things, if you only would. You have seen people like yourself – people who are bright and gay and fond of amusement. We are not fond of amusement.'

'Yes,' said Felix, 'I confess that rather strikes me. You don't seem to me to get all the pleasure out of life that you might. You don't seem to me to enjoy ... Do you mind my saying this?' he asked, pausing.

'Please go on,' said the girl, earnestly.

'You seem to me very well placed for enjoying. You have money and liberty and what is called in Europe a "position". But you take a painful view of life, as one may say.'

'One ought to think it bright and charming and delightful, eh?' asked Gertrude.

'I should say so – if one can. It is true it all depends upon that,' Felix added.

'You know there is a great deal of misery in the world,' said his model.

'I have seen a little of it,' the young man rejoined. 'But it was all over there – beyond the sea. I don't see any here. This is a paradise.'

Gertrude said nothing; she sat looking at the dahlias and the currant-bushes in the garden, while Felix went on with his work. 'To "enjoy",' she began at last, 'to take life – not painfully, must one do something wrong?'

Felix gave his long, light laugh again. 'Seriously, I think not. And for this reason, among others: you strike me as very capable of enjoying, if the chance were given you, and yet at the same time as incapable of wrong-doing.'

'I am sure,' said Gertrude, 'that you are very wrong in telling a person that she is incapable of that. We are never nearer to evil than when we believe that.'

'You are handsomer than ever,' observed Felix, irrelevantly.

Gertrude had got used to hearing him say this. There was not so much excitement in it as at first. 'What ought one to do?' she continued. 'To give parties, to go to the theatre, to read novels, to keep late hours?'

'I don't think it's what one does or one doesn't do that promotes enjoyment,' her companion answered. 'It is the general way of looking at life.'

'They look at it as a discipline – that's what they do here. I have often been told that.'

'Well, that's very good. But there is another way,' added Felix, smiling: 'to look at it as an opportunity.'

'An opportunity – yes,' said Gertrude. 'One would get more pleasure that way.'

'I don't attempt to say anything better for it than that it has been my own way – and that is not saying much!' Felix had laid down his palette and brushes; he was leaning back, with his arms folded, to judge the effect of his work. 'And you know,' he said, 'I am a very petty personage.'

'You have a great deal of talent,' said Gertrude.

'No – no,' the young man rejoined, in a tone of cheerful impartiality, 'I have not a great deal of talent. It is nothing at all remarkable. I assure you I should know if it were. I shall always be obscure. The world will never hear of me.' Gertrude looked at him with a strange feeling. She was thinking of the great world which he knew and which she did not, and how full of brilliant talents it must be, since it could afford to make light of his abilities. 'You needn't in general attach much importance to anything I tell you,' he pursued; 'but you may believe me when I say this – that I am little better than a good-natured feather-head.'

'A feather-head?' she repeated.

'I am a species of Bohemian.'

'A Bohemian?'[4] Gertrude had never heard this term before, save as a geographical denomination; and she quite failed to understand the figurative meaning which her companion appeared to attach to it. But it gave her pleasure.

Felix had pushed back his chair and risen to his feet; he slowly came toward her, smiling. 'I am a sort of adventurer,' he said, looking down at her.

She got up, meeting his smile. 'An adventurer?' she repeated. 'I should like to hear your adventures.'

For an instant she believed that he was going to take her hand; but he dropped his own hands suddenly into the pockets of his painting-jacket. 'There is no reason why you shouldn't,' he said. 'I have been an adventurer, but my adventures have been very innocent. They have all been happy ones; I don't think there are any I shouldn't tell. They were very pleasant and very pretty; I should like to go over them in memory. Sit down again, and I will begin,' he added in a moment, with his naturally persuasive smile.

Gertrude sat down again on that day, and she sat down on several other days. Felix, while he plied his brush, told her a great many stories, and she listened with charmed avidity. Her eyes rested upon his lips; she was very serious; sometimes, from her air of wondering gravity, he thought she was displeased. But Felix never believed for more than a single moment in any displeasure of his own producing. This would have been fatuity if the optimism it expressed had not been much more a hope than a prejudice. It is beside the matter to say that he had a good conscience; for the best conscience is a sort of self-reproach, and this young man's brilliantly healthy nature spent itself in objective good intentions which were ignorant of any test save exactness in hitting their mark. He told Gertrude how he had walked over France and Italy with a painter's knapsack on his back, paying his way often by knocking off a flattering portrait of his host or hostess. He told her how he had played the violin in a little band of musicians – not of high celebrity – who travelled through foreign lands giving provincial concerts. He told her also how he had been a momentary ornament of a troupe of strolling actors, engaged in the arduous task of interpreting Shakespeare to French and German, Polish and Hungarian audiences.

While this periodical recital was going on, Gertrude lived in a fantastic world; she seemed to herself to be reading a romance that came out in daily numbers. She had known nothing so delightful since the perusal of 'Nicholas Nickleby'.[5] One afternoon she went to see her cousin, Mrs. Acton, Robert's mother, who was a great invalid, never leaving the house. She came back alone, on foot, across the fields – this being a short way which they often used. Felix had gone to Boston with her father, who desired to take the young man to call upon some of his friends, old gentlemen who remembered his mother – remembered her, but said nothing about her – and several of whom, with the gentle ladies their wives, had driven out from town to pay their respects at the little house among the apple-trees, in vehicles which reminded the Baroness, who received her visitors with discriminating civility, of the large, light, rattling barouche in which she herself had made her journey to this neighbourhood. The afternoon was waning; in the western sky the great picture of a New England sunset, painted in crimson and silver, was suspended from the zenith; and the stony pastures, as Gertrude traversed them, thinking intently to herself, were covered with a light, clear glow. At the open gate of one of the fields she saw from the distance a man's figure; he stood there as if he were waiting for her, and as she came nearer she recognized Mr. Brand. She had a feeling as of not having seen him for some time; she could not have said for how long, for it yet seemed to her that he had been very lately at the house.

'May I walk back with you?' he asked. And when she had said that he might if he wanted, he observed that he had seen her and recognized her half a mile away.

'You must have very good eyes,' said Gertrude.

'Yes, I have very good eyes, Miss Gertrude,' said Mr. Brand. She perceived that he meant something; but for a long time past

Mr. Brand had constantly meant something, and she had almost got used to it. She felt, however, that what he meant had now a renewed power to disturb her, to perplex and agitate her. He walked beside her in silence for a moment, and then he added, 'I have had no trouble in seeing that you are beginning to avoid me. But perhaps,' he went on, 'one needn't have had very good eyes to see that.'

'I have not avoided you,' said Gertrude, without looking at him.

'I think you have been unconscious that you were avoiding me,' Mr. Brand replied. 'You have not even known that I was there.'

'Well, you are here now, Mr. Brand!' said Gertrude, with a little laugh. 'I know that very well.'

He made no rejoinder. He simply walked beside her slowly, as they were obliged to walk over the soft grass. Presently they came to another gate, which was closed. Mr. Brand laid his hand upon it, but he made no movement to open it; he stood and looked at his companion. 'You are very much interested – very much absorbed,' he said.

Gertrude glanced at him; she saw that he was pale and that he looked excited. She had never seen Mr. Brand excited before, and she felt that the spectacle, if fully carried out, would be impressive, almost painful. 'Absorbed in what?' she asked. Then she looked away at the illuminated sky. She felt guilty and uncomfortable, and yet she was vexed with herself for feeling so. But Mr. Brand, as he stood there looking at her with his small, kind, persistent eyes, represented an immense body of half-obliterated obligations, that were rising again into a certain distinctness.

'You have new interests, new occupations,' he went on. 'I don't know that I can say that you have new duties. We have always old ones, Gertrude,' he added.

'Please open the gate, Mr. Brand,' she said; and she felt as if, in saying so, she were cowardly and petulant. But he opened the gate, and allowed her to pass; then he closed it behind himself. Before she had time to turn away he put out his hand and held her an instant by the wrist.

'I want to say something to you,' he said.

'I know what you want to say,' she answered. And she was on the point of adding, 'And I know just how you will say it'; but these words she kept back.

'I love you, Gertrude,' he said. 'I love you very much; I love you more than ever.'

He said the words just as she had known he would; she had heard them before. They had no charm for her; she had said to herself before that it was very strange. It was supposed to be delightful for a woman to listen to such words; but these seemed to her flat and mechanical. 'I wish you would forget that,' she declared.

'How can I – why should I?' he asked.

'I have made you no promise – given you no pledge,' she said, looking at him, with her voice trembling a little.

'You have let me feel that I have an influence over you. You have opened your mind to me.'

'I never opened my mind to you, Mr. Brand!' Gertrude cried, with some vehemence.

'Then you were not so frank as I thought – as we all thought.'

'I don't see what any one else had to do with it!' cried the girl.

'I mean your father and your sister. You know it makes them happy to think you will listen to me.'

She gave a little laugh. 'It doesn't make them happy,' she said. 'Nothing makes them happy. No one is happy here.'

'I think your cousin is very happy – Mr. Young,' rejoined Mr. Brand, in a soft, almost timid tone.

'So much the better for him!' And Gertrude gave her little laugh again.

The young man looked at her a moment. 'You are very much changed,' he said.

'I am glad to hear it,' Gertrude declared.

'I am not. I have known you a long time, and I have loved you as you were.'

'I am much obliged to you,' said Gertrude. 'I must be going home.'

He on his side, gave a little laugh.

'You certainly do avoid me – you see!'

'Avoid me, then,' said the girl.

He looked at her again; and then, very gently, 'No I will not avoid you,' he replied; 'but I will leave you, for the present, to yourself. I think you will remember – after a while – some of the things you have forgotten. I think you will come back to me; I have great faith in that.'

This time his voice was very touching; there was a strong, reproachful force in what he said, and Gertrude could answer nothing. He turned away and stood there, leaning his elbows on the gate and looking at the beautiful sunset. Gertrude left him and took her way home again; but when she reached the middle of the next field she suddenly burst into tears. Her tears seemed to her to have been a long time gathering, and for some moments it was a kind of glee to shed them. But they presently passed away. There was something a little hard about Gertrude; and she never wept again.

VI

Going of an afternoon to call upon his niece, Mr. Wentworth more than once found Robert Acton sitting in her little drawing-room. This was in no degree, to Mr. Wentworth, a perturbing fact, for he had no sense of competing with his young kinsman for Eugenia's good graces. Madame Münster's uncle had the highest opinion of Robert Acton, who, indeed, in the family at large, was the object of a great deal of undemonstrative appreciation. They were all proud of him, in so far as the charge of being proud may be brought against people who were, habitually, distinctly guiltless of the misdemeanour known as 'taking credit'. They never boasted of Robert Acton, nor indulged in vainglorious reference to him; they never quoted the clever things he had said, nor mentioned the generous things he had done. But a sort of frigidly-tender faith in his unlimited goodness was a part of their personal sense of right; and there can, perhaps, be no better proof of the high esteem in which he was held than the fact that no explicit judgement was ever passed upon his actions. He was no more praised than he was blamed; but he was tacitly felt to be an ornament to his circle. He was the man of the world of the family. He had been to China and brought home a collection of curiosities; he had made a fortune – or rather he had quintupled a fortune already considerable; he was distinguished by that combination of celibacy, 'property', and good humour which appeals to even the most sub-dued imaginations; and it was taken for granted that he would presently place these advantages at the disposal of some well-regulated young woman of his own 'set'. Mr. Wentworth was not a man to admit to himself that – his paternal duties apart

– he liked any individual much better than all other individuals; but he thought Robert Acton extremely judicious; and this was perhaps as near an approach as he was capable of to the eagerness of preference, which his temperament repudiated as it would have disengaged itself from something slightly unchaste. Acton was, in fact, very judicious – and something more beside; and indeed it must be claimed for Mr. Wentworth that in the more illicit parts of his preference there hovered the vague adumbration of a belief that his cousin's final merit was a certain enviable capacity for whistling, rather gallantly, at the sanctions of mere judgement – for showing a larger courage, a finer quality of pluck, than common occasion demanded. Mr. Wentworth would never have risked the intimation that Acton was made, in the smallest degree, of the stuff of a hero; but this is small blame to him, for Robert would certainly never have risked it himself. Acton certainly exercised great discretion in all things – beginning with his estimate of himself. He knew that he was by no means so much of a man of the world as he was supposed to be in local circles; but it must be added that he knew also that his natural shrewdness had a reach of which he had never quite given local circles the measure. He was addicted to taking the humorous view of things, and he had discovered that even in the narrowest circles such a disposition may find frequent opportunities. Such opportunities had formed for some time – that is, since his return from China, a year and a half before – the most active element in this gentleman's life, which had just now a rather indolent air. He was perfectly willing to get married. He was very fond of books, and he had a handsome library; that is, his books were much more numerous than Mr. Wentworth's. He was also very fond of pictures; but it must be confessed, in the fierce light of contemporary criticism, that his walls were adorned with several rather abortive masterpieces. He had got his learning – and there was more of it than commonly appeared – at Harvard College; and he took a pleasure in old associations, which made it a part of his daily contentment to live so near this institution that he often passed it in driving to Boston. He was extremely interested in the Baroness Münster.

She was very frank with him; or at least she intended to be. 'I am sure you find it very strange that I should have settled down in this out-of-the-way part of the world!' she said to him three or four weeks after she had installed herself. 'I am certain you are wondering about my motives. They are very pure.' The Baroness by this time was an old inhabitant; the best society in Boston had called upon her, and Clifford Wentworth had taken her several times to drive in his buggy.

Robert Acton was seated near her, playing with a fan; there were always several fans lying about her drawing-room, with long ribbons of different colours attached to them, and Acton was always playing with one. 'No, I don't find it at all strange,' he said slowly, smiling. 'That a clever woman should turn up in Boston, or its suburbs – that does not require so much explanation. Boston is a very nice place.'

'If you wish to make me contradict you,' said the Baroness, '*vous vous y prenez mal*. In certain moods there is nothing I am not capable of agreeing to. Boston is a paradise, and we are in the suburbs of Paradise.'

'Just now I am not at all in the suburbs; I am in the place itself,' rejoined Acton, who was lounging a little in his chair. He was, however, not always lounging; and when he was he was not quite so relaxed as he pretended. To a certain extent, he sought refuge from shyness in this appearance of relaxation; and like many persons in the same circumstances he somewhat exaggerated the appearance. Beyond this, the air of being much at his ease was a cover for vigilant observation. He was more than interested in this clever woman, who, whatever he might say, was clever not at all after the Boston fashion; she plunged him into a kind of excitement, held him in vague suspense. He was obliged to admit to himself that he had never yet seen a woman just like this – not even in China. He was ashamed, for inscrutable reasons, of the vivacity of his emotion, and he carried it off, superficially, by taking, still superficially, the humorous view of Madame Münster. It was not at all true that he thought it very natural of her to have made this pious pilgrimage. It might have been said of him in advance that he was too good a Bostonian to regard in the light of an eccentricity the desire of even the remotest alien to visit the New England metropolis. This was an impulse for which, surely, no apology was needed; and Madame Münster was the fortunate possessor of several New England cousins. In fact, however, Madame Münster struck him as out of keeping with her little circle; she was at the best a very agreeable, a gracefully mystifying anomaly. He knew very well that it would not do to address these reflections too crudely to Mr. Wentworth; he would never have remarked to the old gentleman that he wondered what the Baroness was up to. And indeed he had no great desire to share his vague mistrust with any one. There was a personal pleasure in it; the greatest pleasure he had known at least since he had come from China. He would keep the Baroness, for better or worse, to himself; he had a feeling that he deserved to enjoy a monopoly of her, for he was certainly the person who had most adequately gauged her capacity for social intercourse. Before long it became apparent to him that the Baroness was disposed to lay no tax upon such a monopoly.

One day (he was sitting there again and playing with a fan) she asked him to apologize, should the occasion present itself, to certain people in Boston for her not having returned their calls. 'There are half a dozen places,' she said; 'a formidable list. Charlotte Wentworth has written it out for me, in a terrifically distinct hand. There is no ambiguity on the subject; I know perfectly where I must go. Mr. Wentworth informs me that the carriage is always at my disposal, and Charlotte offers to go with me, in a pair of tight gloves and a very stiff petticoat. And yet for three days I have been putting it off. They must think me horribly vicious.'

'You ask me to apologize,' said Acton, 'but you don't tell me what excuse I can offer.'

'That is more,' the Baroness declared, 'than I am held to. It would be like my asking you to buy me a bouquet and giving you the money. I have no reason except that – somehow – it's too violent an effort. It is not inspiring. Wouldn't that serve as an excuse, in Boston? I am told they are very sincere; they don't tell fibs. And then Felix ought to go with me, and he is never in readiness. I don't see him. He is always roaming about the fields and sketching old barns, or taking ten-mile walks, or painting some one's portrait, or rowing on the pond, or flirting with Gertrude Wentworth.'

'I should think it would amuse you to go and see a few people,' said Acton. 'You are having a very quiet time of it here. It's a dull life for you.'

'Ah, the quiet – the quiet!' the Baroness exclaimed. 'That's what I like. It's rest. That's what I came here for. Amusement? I have had amusement. And as for seeing people – I have already seen a great many in my life. If it didn't sound ungracious I should say that I wish very humbly your people here would leave me alone!'

Acton looked at her a moment, and she looked at him. She was a woman who took being looked at remarkably well. 'So you have come here for rest?' he asked.

'So I may say. I came for many of those reasons that are no reasons – don't you know? – and yet that are really the best: to come away, to change, to break with everything. When once one comes away one must arrive somewhere, and I asked myself why I shouldn't arrive here.'

'You certainly had time on the way!' said Acton, laughing.

Madame Münster looked at him again; and then, smiling: 'And I have certainly had time, since I got here, to ask myself why I came. However, I never ask myself idle questions. Here I am, and it seems to me you ought only to thank me.'

'When you go away you will see the difficulties I shall put in your path.'

'You mean to put difficulties in my path?' she asked, re-arranging the rosebud in her corsage.

'The greatest of all – that of having been so agreeable' –

'That I shall be unable to depart? Don't be too sure. I have left some very agreeable people over there.'

'Ah,' said Acton, 'but it was to come here, where I am!'

'I didn't know of your existence. Excuse me for saying anything so rude; but, honestly speaking, I did not. No,' the Baroness pursued, 'it was precisely not to see you – such people as you – that I came.'

'Such people as me?' cried Acton.

'I had a sort of longing to come into those natural relations which I knew I should find here. Over there I had only, as I may say, artificial relations. Don't you see the difference?'

'The difference tells against me,' said Acton. 'I suppose I am an artificial relation.'

'Conventional,' declared the Baroness; 'very conventional.'

'Well, there is one way in which the relation of a lady and a gentleman may always become natural,' said Acton.

'You mean by their becoming lovers? That may be natural or not. And at any rate,' rejoined Eugenia, '*nous n'en sommes pas là*!'

They were not, as yet; but a little later, when she began to go with him to drive, it might almost have seemed that they were. He came for her several times, alone, in his high 'wagon', drawn by a pair of charming light-limbed horses. It was different, her having gone with Clifford Wentworth, who was her cousin, and so much younger. It was not to be imagined that she should have a flirtation with Clifford, who was a mere shame-faced boy, and whom a large section of Boston society supposed to be 'engaged' to Lizzie Acton. Not, indeed, that it was to be conceived that the Baroness was a possible party to any flirtation whatever; for she was undoubtedly a married lady. It was generally known that her matrimonial condition was of the 'morganatic' order; but in its natural aversion to suppose that this meant anything less than absolute wedlock, the conscience of the community took refuge in the belief that it implied something even more.

Acton wished her to think highly of American scenery, and he drove her to great distances, picking out the prettiest roads and the largest points of view. If we are good when we are contented, Eugenia's virtues should now certainly have been uppermost; for she found a charm in the rapid movement through a wild country, and in a companion who from time to time made the vehicle dip, with a motion like a swallow's flight, over roads of primitive construction, and who, as she felt, would do a great many things that she might ask him. Sometimes, for a couple of hours together, there were almost no houses; there were nothing but woods and rivers and lakes and horizons adorned with bright-looking mountains. It seemed to the Baroness very wild, as I have said, and lovely; but the impression added something to that sense of the enlargement of opportunity which had been born of her arrival in the New World.

One day – it was late in the afternoon – Acton pulled up his horses on the crest of a hill which commanded a beautiful prospect. He let them stand a long time to rest, while he sat there and talked with Madame Münster. The prospect was beautiful in spite of there being nothing human within sight. There was a wilderness of woods, and the gleam of a distant river, and a glimpse of half the hill-tops in Massachusetts. The road had a wide, grassy margin, on the further side of which there flowed a deep, clear brook; there were wild flowers in the grass, and beside the brook lay the trunk of a fallen tree. Acton waited a while; at last a rustic wayfarer came trudging along the road. Acton asked him to hold the horses – a service he consented to render, as a friendly turn to a fellow-citizen. Then he invited the Baroness to descend, and the two wandered away, across the grass, and sat down on the log beside the brook.

'I imagine it doesn't remind you of Silberstadt,' said Acton. It was the first time that he had mentioned Silberstadt to her, for particular reasons. He knew she had a husband there, and this was disagreeable to him; and, furthermore, it had been repeated to him that this husband wished to put her away – a state of affairs to which even indirect reference was to be deprecated. It was true, nevertheless, that the Baroness herself had often alluded to Silberstadt; and Acton had often wondered why her husband wished to get rid of her. It was a curious position for a lady – this being known as a repudiated wife; and it is worthy of observation that the Baroness carried it off with exceeding grace and dignity. She had made it felt, from the first, that there were two sides to the question, and that her own side, when she should choose to present it, would be replete with touching interest.

'It does not remind me of the town, of course,' she said, 'of the sculptured gables and the Gothic churches, of the wonderful Schloss,[1] with its moat and its clustering towers. But it has a little look of some other parts of the principality. One might fancy one's self among those grand old German forests, those legendary mountains; the sort of country one sees from the windows at Shreckenstein.'

'What is Shreckenstein?' asked Acton.

'It is a great castle – the summer residence of the Reigning Prince.'

'Have you ever lived there?'

'I have stayed there,' said the Baroness. Acton was silent; he looked a while at the uncastled landscape before him. 'It is the first time you have ever asked me about Silberstadt,' she said. 'I should think you would want to know about my marriage; it must seem to you very strange.'

Acton looked at her a moment. 'Now you wouldn't like me to say that!'

'You Americans have such odd ways!' the Baroness declared. 'You never ask anything outright; there seem to be so many things you can't talk about.'

'We Americans are very polite,' said Acton, whose national consciousness had been complicated by a residence in foreign lands, and who yet disliked to hear Americans abused. 'We don't like to tread upon people's toes,' he said. 'But I should like very much to hear about your marriage. Now tell me how it came about.'

'The Prince fell in love with me,' replied the Baroness simply. 'He pressed his suit very hard. At first he didn't wish me to marry him; on the contrary. But on that basis I refused to listen to him. So he offered me marriage – in so far as he might. I was young, and I confess I was rather flattered. But if it were to be done again now, I certainly should not accept him.'

'How long ago was this?' asked Acton.

'Oh – several years,' said Eugenia. 'You should never ask a woman for dates.'

'Why, I should think that when a woman was relating history . . .' Acton answered. 'And now he wants to break it off?'

'They want him to make a political marriage. It is his brother's idea. His brother is very clever.'

'They must be a precious pair!' cried Robert Acton.

The Baroness gave a little philosophic shrug. 'Que voulez-vous? They are princes. They think they are treating me very well. Silberstadt is a perfectly despotic little state, and the Reigning Prince may annul the marriage by a stroke of his pen. But he has promised me, nevertheless, not to do so without my formal consent.'

'And this you have refused?'

'Hitherto. It is an indignity, and I have wished at least to make it difficult for them. But I have a little document in my writing-desk which I have only to sign and send back to the Prince.'

'Then it will be all over?'

The Baroness lifted her hand, and dropped it again. 'Of course I shall keep my title; at least, I shall be at liberty to keep it if I choose. And I suppose I shall keep it. One must have a name. And I shall keep my pension.[2] It is very small – it is wretchedly small; but it is what I live on.'

'And you have only to sign that paper?' Acton asked.

The Baroness looked at him a moment. 'Do you urge it?'

He got up slowly, and stood with his hands in his pockets. 'What do you gain by not doing it?'

'I am supposed to gain this advantage – that if I delay, or temporize, the Prince may come back to me, may make a stand against his brother. He is very fond of me, and his brother has pushed him only little by little.'

'If he were to come back to you,' said Acton, 'would you – would you take him back?'

The Baroness met his eyes; she coloured just a little. Then she rose. 'I should have the satisfaction of saying, "Now it is my turn. I break with your serene highness!"'

They began to walk toward the carriage. 'Well,' said Robert Acton, 'it's a curious story! How did you make his acquaintance?'

'I was staying with an old lady – an old Countess – in Dresden. She had been a friend of my father's. My father was dead; I was very much alone. My brother was wandering about the world in a theatrical troupe.'

'Your brother ought to have stayed with you,' Acton observed, 'and kept you from putting your trust in princes.'[3]

The Baroness was silent a moment, and then, 'He did what he could,' she said. 'He sent me money. The old Countess encouraged the Prince; she was even pressing. It seems to me,' Madame Münster added, gently, 'that – under the circumstances – I behaved very well.'

Acton glanced at her, and made the observation – he had made it before – that a woman looks the prettier for having unfolded her wrongs or her sufferings. 'Well,' he reflected, audibly, 'I should like to see you send his serene highness – somewhere!'

Madame Münster stooped and plucked a daisy from the grass. 'And not sign my renunciation?'

'Well, I don't know – I don't know,' said Acton.

'In one case I should have my revenge; in another case I should have my liberty.'

Acton gave a little laugh as he helped her into the carriage. 'At any rate,' he said, 'take good care of that paper.'

A couple of days afterward he asked her to come and see his house. The visit had already been proposed, but it had been put off in consequence of his mother's illness. She was a constant invalid, and she had passed these recent years, very patiently, in a great flowered arm-chair at her bedroom window. Lately, for some days, she had been unable to see any one; but now she was better, and she sent the Baroness a very civil message. Acton had wished their visitor to come to dinner; but Madame Münster preferred to begin with a simple call. She had reflected that if she should go to dinner Mr. Wentworth and his daughters would also be asked, and it had seemed to her that the peculiar character of the occasion would be best preserved in a *tête-à-tête* with her host. Why the occasion should have a peculiar character she explained to no one. As far as any one could see, it was simply very pleasant. Acton came for her and drove her to his door, an operation which was rapidly performed. His house the Baroness mentally pronounced a very good one; more articulately, she declared that it was enchanting. It was large and square and painted brown; it stood in a well-kept shrubbery, and was approached, from the gate, by a short drive. It was, moreover, a much more modern dwelling than Mr.

Wentworth's, and was more redundantly upholstered and expensively ornamented. The Baroness perceived that her entertainer had analysed material comfort to a sufficiently fine point. And then he possessed the most delightful *chinoiseries* – trophies of his sojourn in the Celestial Empire:[4] pagodas of ebony and cabinets of ivory; sculptured monsters, grinning and leering on chimney-pieces, in front of beautifully figured hand-screens; porcelain dinner-sets, gleaming behind the glass doors of mahogany buffets; large screens, in corners, covered with tense silk and embroidered with mandarins and dragons. These things were scattered all over the house, and they gave Eugenia a pretext for a complete domiciliary visit. She liked it, she enjoyed it; she thought it a very nice place. It had a mixture of the homely and the liberal, and though it was almost a museum, the large, little-used rooms were as fresh and clean as a well-kept dairy. Lizzie Acton told her that she dusted all the pagodas and other curiosities every day with her own hands; and the Baroness answered that she was evidently a household fairy. Lizzie had not at all the look of a young lady who dusted things; she wore such pretty dresses and had such delicate fingers that it was difficult to imagine her immersed in sordid cares. She came to meet Madame Münster on her arrival, but she said nothing, or almost nothing, and the Baroness again reflected – she had had occasion to do so before – that American girls had no manners. She disliked this little American girl, and she was quite prepared to learn that she had failed to commend herself to Miss Acton. Lizzie struck her as positive and explicit almost to pertness; and the idea of her combining the apparent incongruities of a taste for housework and the wearing of fresh, Parisian-looking dresses suggested the possession of a dangerous energy. It was a source of irritation to the Baroness that in this country it should seem to matter whether a little girl were a trifle less or a trifle more of a nonentity; for Eugenia had hitherto been conscious of no moral pressure as regards the appreciation of diminutive virgins. It was perhaps an indication of Lizzie's pertness that she very soon retired and left the Baroness on her brother's hands. Acton talked a great deal about his chinoiseries; he knew a good deal about porcelain and bric-a-brac. The Baroness, in her progress through the house, made, as it were, a great many stations. She sat down everywhere, confessed to being a little tired, and asked about the various objects with a curious mixture of alertness and inattention. If there had been any one to say it to she would have declared that she was positively in love with her host; but she could hardly make this declaration – even in the strictest confidence – to Acton himself. It gave her, nevertheless, a pleasure that had some of the charm of unwontedness to feel, with that admirable keenness with which she was capable of feeling things, that he had a disposition without any edges; that even his humorous irony always expanded toward the point. One's impression of his honesty was almost like carrying a bunch of flowers; the perfume was most agreeable, but they were occasionally an inconvenience. One could trust him, at any rate, round all the corners of the world; and, withal, he was not absolutely simple, which would have been excess; he was only relatively simple, which was quite enough for the Baroness.

Lizzie reappeared to say that her mother would now be happy to receive Madame Münster; and the Baroness followed her to Mrs. Acton's apartment. Eugenia reflected, as she went, that it was not the affectation of impertinence that made her dislike this young lady, for on that ground she could easily have beaten her. It was not an aspiration on the girl's part to rivalry, but a kind of laughing, childishly-mocking indifference to the results of comparison. Mrs. Acton was an emaciated, sweet-faced woman of five and fifty, sitting with pillows behind her, and looking out on a clump of hemlocks. She was very modest, very timid, and very ill; she made Eugenia feel grateful that she herself was not like that – neither so ill, nor, possibly, so modest. On a chair, beside her, lay a volume of Emerson's Essays.[5] It was a great occasion for poor Mrs. Acton, in her helpless condition, to be confronted with a clever foreign lady, who had more manner than any lady – any dozen ladies – that she had ever seen.

'I have heard a great deal about you,' she said, softly, to the Baroness.

'From your son, eh?' Eugenia asked. 'He has talked to me

immensely of you. Oh, he talks of you as you would like,' the Baroness declared; 'as such a son *must* talk of such a mother!'

Mrs. Acton sat gazing; this was part of Madame Münster's 'manner'. But Robert Acton was gazing too, in vivid consciousness that he had barely mentioned his mother to their brilliant guest. He never talked of this still maternal presence – a presence refined to such delicacy that it had almost resolved itself, with him, simply into the subjective emotion of gratitude. And Acton rarely talked of his emotions. The Baroness turned her smile toward him, and she instantly felt that she had been observed to be fibbing. She had struck a false note. But who were these people to whom such fibbing was not pleasing? If they were annoyed, the Baroness was equally so; and after the exchange of a few civil inquiries and low-voiced responses she took leave of Mrs. Acton. She begged Robert not to come home with her; she would get into the carriage alone; she preferred that. This was imperious, and she thought he looked disappointed. While she stood before the door with him – the carriage was turning in the gravel-walk – this thought restored her serenity.

When she had given him her hand in farewell she looked at him a moment. 'I have almost decided to dispatch that paper,' she said.

He knew that she alluded to the document that she had called her renunciation; and he assisted her into the carriage without saying anything. But just before the vehicle began to move he said, 'Well, when you have in fact dispatched it, I hope you will let me know!'

VII

Felix Young finished Gertrude's portrait, and he afterwards transferred to canvas the features of many members of that circle of which it may be said that he had become for the time the pivot and the centre. I am afraid it must be confessed that he was a decidedly flattering painter, and that he imparted to his models a romantic grace which seemed easily and cheaply acquired by the payment of a hundred dollars to a young man who made 'sitting' so entertaining. For Felix was paid for his pictures, making, as he did, no secret of the fact that in guiding his steps to the Western world affectionate curiosity had gone hand in hand with a desire to better his condition. He took his uncle's portrait quite as if Mr. Wentworth had never averted himself from the experiment; and as he compassed his end only by the exercise of gentle violence, it is but fair to add that he allowed the old man to give him nothing but his time. He passed his arm into Mr. Wentworth's one summer morning – very few arms indeed had ever passed into Mr. Wentworth's – and led him across the garden and along the road into the studio which he had extemporized in the little house among the apple-trees. The grave gentleman felt himself more and more fascinated by his clever nephew, whose fresh, demonstrative youth seemed a compendium of experiences so strangely numerous. It appeared to him that Felix must know a great deal; he would like to learn what he thought about some of those things as regards which his own conversation had always been formal, but his knowledge vague. Felix had a confident, gaily trenchant way of judging human actions which Mr. Wentworth grew little by little to envy; it seemed like criticism made easy. Forming an opinion

– say on a person's conduct – was, with Mr. Wentworth, a good deal like fumbling in a lock with a key chosen at hazard. He seemed to himself to go about the world with a big bunch of these ineffectual instruments at his girdle. His nephew, on the other hand, with a single turn of the wrist, opened any door as adroitly as a house-thief.[1] He felt obliged to keep up the convention that an uncle is always wiser than a nephew, even if he could keep it up no otherwise than by listening in serious silence to Felix's quick, light, constant discourse. But there came a day when he lapsed from consistency and almost asked his nephew's advice.

'Have you ever entertained the idea of settling in the United States?' he asked one morning, while Felix brilliantly plied his brush.

'My dear uncle,' said Felix, 'excuse me if your question makes me smile a little. To begin with, I have never entertained an idea. Ideas often entertain *me*; but I am afraid I have never seriously made a plan. I know what you are going to say; or rather, I know what you think, for I don't think you will say it – that this is very frivolous and loose-minded on my part. So it is; but I am made like that; I take things as they come, and somehow there is always some new thing to follow the last. In the second place, I should never propose to *settle*. I can't settle, my dear uncle; I'm not a settler. I know that is what strangers are supposed to do here; they always settle. But I haven't – to answer your question – entertained that idea.'

'You intend to return to Europe and resume your irregular manner of life?' Mr. Wentworth inquired.

'I can't say I intend. But it's very likely I shall go back to Europe. After all, I am a European. I feel that, you know. It will depend a good deal upon my sister. She's even more of a European than I; here, you know, she's a picture out of her setting. And as for "resuming", dear uncle, I really have never given up my irregular manner of life. What, for me, could be more irregular than this?'

'Than what?' asked Mr. Wentworth, with his pale gravity.

'Well, than everything! Living in the midst of you, this way; this charming, quiet, serious family life; fraternizing with

Charlotte and Gertrude; calling upon twenty young ladies and going out to walk with them; sitting with you in the evening on the piazza and listening to the crickets, and going to bed at ten o'clock.'

'Your description is very animated,' said Mr. Wentworth; 'but I see nothing improper in what you describe.'

'Neither do I, dear uncle. It is extremely delightful; I shouldn't like it if it were improper. I assure you I don't like improper things; though I dare say you think I do,' Felix went on, painting away.

'I have never accused you of that.'

'Pray don't,' said Felix, 'because, you see, at bottom I am a terrible Philistine.'

'A Philistine?'[2] repeated Mr. Wentworth.

'I mean, as one may say, a plain, God-fearing man.' Mr. Wentworth looked at him reservedly, like a mystified sage, and Felix continued, 'I trust I shall enjoy a venerable and venerated old age. I mean to live long. I can hardly call that a plan, perhaps; but it's a keen desire – a rosy vision. I shall be a lively, perhaps even a frivolous old man!'

'It is natural,' said his uncle, sententiously, 'that one should desire to prolong an agreeable life. We have perhaps a selfish indisposition to bring our pleasure to a close. But I presume,' he added, 'that you expect to marry.'

'That too, dear uncle, is a hope, a desire, a vision,' said Felix. It occurred to him for an instant that this was possibly a pre-face to the offer of the hand of one of Mr. Wentworth's admir-able daughters. But in the name of decent modesty and a proper sense of the hard realities of this world, Felix banished the thought. His uncle was the incarnation of benevolence, certainly; but from that to accepting – much more postulating – the idea of a union between a young lady with a dowry presumptively brilliant and a penniless artist with no prospect of fame, there was a very long way. Felix had lately become conscious of a luxurious preference for the society – if possible unshared with others – of Gertrude Wentworth; but he had relegated this young lady, for the moment, to the coldly brilliant category of unattainable possessions. She was not the first woman for whom he had entertained an unpractical admiration. He had been in love with duchesses and countesses, and he had made, once or twice, a perilously near approach to cynicism in declaring that the disinterestedness of women had been overrated. On the whole, he had tempered audacity with modesty; and it is but fair to him now to say explicitly that he would have been incapable of taking advantage of his present large allowance of familiarity to make love to the younger of his handsome cousins. Felix had grown up among traditions in the light of which such a proceeding looked like a grievous breach of hospitality. I have said that he was always happy, and it may be counted among the present sources of his happiness that he had as regards this matter of his relations with Gertrude a deliciously good conscience. His own deportment seemed to him suffused with the beauty of virtue – a form of beauty that he admired with the same vivacity with which he admired all other forms.

'I think that if you marry,' said Mr. Wentworth presently, 'it will conduce to your happiness.'

'*Sicurissimo!*'[3] Felix exclaimed; and then, arresting his brush, he looked at his uncle with a smile. 'There is something I feel tempted to say to you. May I risk it?'

Mr. Wentworth drew himself up a little. 'I am very safe; I don't repeat things.' But he hoped Felix would not risk too much.

Felix was laughing at his answer.

'It's odd to hear you telling me how to be happy. I don't think you know yourself, dear uncle. Now, does that sound brutal?'

The old man was silent a moment, and then, with a dry dignity that suddenly touched his nephew: 'We may sometimes point out a road we are unable to follow.'

'Ah, don't tell me you have had any sorrows,' Felix rejoined. 'I didn't suppose it, and I didn't mean to allude to them. I simply meant that you all don't amuse yourselves.'

'Amuse ourselves? We are not children.'

'Precisely not! You have reached the proper age. I was saying that the other day to Gertrude,' Felix added. 'I hope it was not indiscreet.'

'If it was,' said Mr. Wentworth, with a keener irony than Felix would have thought him capable of, 'it was but your way of amusing yourself. I am afraid you have never had a trouble.'

'Oh, yes, I have!' Felix declared, with some spirit; 'before I knew better. But you don't catch me at it again.'

Mr. Wentworth maintained for a while a silence more expressive than a deep-drawn sigh. 'You have no children,' he said at last.

'Don't tell me,' Felix exclaimed, 'that your charming young people are a source of grief to you!'

'I don't speak of Charlotte.' And then, after a pause, Mr. Wentworth continued, 'I don't speak of Gertrude. But I feel considerable anxiety about Clifford. I will tell you another time.'

The next time he gave Felix a sitting his nephew reminded him that he had taken him into his confidence. 'How is Clifford to-day?' Felix asked. 'He has always seemed to me a young man of remarkable discretion. Indeed, he is only too discreet; he seems on his guard against me – as if he thought me rather light company. The other day he told his sister – Gertrude repeated it to me – that I was always laughing at him. If I laugh it is simply from the impulse to try and inspire him with confidence. That is the only way I have.'

'Clifford's situation is no laughing matter,' said Mr. Wentworth. 'It is very peculiar, as I suppose you have guessed.'

'Ah, you mean his love affair with his cousin?'

Mr. Wentworth stared, blushing a little. 'I mean his absence from college. He has been suspended. We have decided not to speak of it unless we are asked.'

'Suspended?' Felix repeated.

'He has been requested by the Harvard authorities to absent himself for six months. Meanwhile he is studying with Mr. Brand. We think Mr. Brand will help him; at least we hope so.'

'What befell him at college?' Felix asked. 'He was too fond of pleasure? Mr. Brand certainly will not teach him any of those secrets!'

'He was too fond of something of which he should not have been fond. I suppose it is considered a pleasure.'

Felix gave his light laugh. 'My dear uncle, is there any doubt about its being a pleasure? *C'est de son âge*, as they say in France.'

'I should have said rather it was a vice of later life – of disappointed old age.'

Felix glanced at his uncle, with his lifted eyebrows, and then, 'Of what are you speaking?' he demanded, smiling.

'Of the situation in which Clifford was found.'

'Ah, he was found – he was caught?'

'Necessarily, he was caught. He couldn't walk; he staggered.'

'Oh,' said Felix, 'he drinks! I rather suspected that, from something I observed the first day I came here. I quite agree with you that it is a low taste. It's not a vice for a gentleman. He ought to give it up.'

'We hope for a good deal from Mr. Brand's influence,' Mr. Wentworth went on. 'He has talked to him from the first. And he never touches anything himself.'

'I will talk to him – I will talk to him!' Felix declared, gaily.

'What will you say to him?' asked his uncle, with some apprehension.

Felix for some moments answered nothing. 'Do you mean to marry him to his cousin?' he asked at last.

'Marry him?' echoed Mr. Wentworth. 'I shouldn't think his cousin would want to marry him.'

'You have no understanding, then, with Mrs. Acton?'

Mr. Wentworth stared, almost blankly. 'I have never discussed such subjects with her.'

'I should think it might be time,' said Felix. 'Lizzie Acton is admirably pretty, and if Clifford is dangerous . . .'

'They are not engaged,' said Mr. Wentworth. 'I have no reason to suppose they are engaged.'

'Par exemple!' cried Felix. 'A clandestine engagement? Trust me, Clifford, as I say, is a charming boy. He is incapable of that. Lizzie Acton, then, would not be jealous of another woman.'

'I certainly hope not,' said the old man, with a vague sense of jealousy being an even lower vice than a love of liquor.

'The best thing for Clifford, then,' Felix propounded, 'is to become interested in some clever, charming woman.' And he paused in his painting, and, with his elbows on his knees, looked with bright communicativeness at his uncle. 'You see, I believe greatly in the influence of women. Living with women helps to make a man a gentleman. It is very true Clifford has his sisters, who are so charming. But there should be a different sentiment in play from the fraternal, you know. He has Lizzie Acton; but she, perhaps, is rather immature.'

'I suspect Lizzie has talked to him, reasoned with him,' said Mr. Wentworth.

'On the impropriety of getting tipsy – on the beauty of temperance? That is dreary work for a pretty young girl. No,' Felix continued; 'Clifford ought to frequent some agreeable woman, who, without ever mentioning such unsavoury subjects, would give him a sense of its being very ridiculous to be fuddled. If he could fall in love with her a little, so much the better. The thing would operate as a cure.'

'Well, now, what lady should you suggest?' asked Mr. Wentworth.

'There is a clever woman under your hand. My sister.'

'Your sister – under my hand?' Mr. Wentworth repeated.

'Say a word to Clifford. Tell him to be bold. He is well disposed already; he has invited her two or three times to drive. But I don't think he comes to see her. Give him a hint to come – to come often. He will sit there of an afternoon, and they will talk. It will do him good.'

Mr. Wentworth meditated. 'You think she will exercise a helpful influence?'

'She will exercise a civilizing – I may call it a sobering – influence. A charming, clever, witty woman always does – especially if she is a little of a coquette. My dear uncle, the society of such women has been half my education. If Clifford is suspended, as you say, from college, let Eugenia be his preceptress.'

Mr. Wentworth continued thoughtful. 'You think Eugenia is a coquette?' he asked.

'What pretty woman is not?' Felix demanded in turn. But this, for Mr. Wentworth, could at the best have been no answer, for he did not think his niece pretty. 'With Clifford,' the young man pursued, 'Eugenia will simply be enough of a coquette to be a little ironical. That's what he needs. So you recommend him to be nice with her, you know. The suggestion will come best from you.'

'Do I understand,' asked the old man, 'that I am to suggest to my son to make a – a profession of – of affection to Madame Münster?'

'Yes, yes – a profession!' cried Felix sympathetically.

'But, as I understand it, Madame Münster is a married woman.'

'Ah,' said Felix, smiling, 'of course she can't marry him. But she will do what she can.'

Mr. Wentworth sat for some time with his eyes on the floor; at last he got up. 'I don't think,' he said, 'that I can undertake to recommend my son any such course.' And without meeting Felix's surprised glance he broke off his sitting, which was not resumed for a fortnight.

Felix was very fond of the little lake which occupied so many of Mr. Wentworth's numerous acres, and of a remarkable pine grove which lay upon the further side of it, planted upon a steep embankment and haunted by the summer breeze. The murmur of the air in the far off tree-tops had a strange distinctness; it was almost articulate. One afternoon the young man came out of his painting-room and passed the open door of Eugenia's little salon. Within, in the cool dimness, he saw his sister, dressed in white, buried in her arm-chair, and holding to her face an immense bouquet. Opposite to her sat Clifford Wentworth, twirling his hat. He had evidently just presented the bouquet to the Baroness, whose fine eyes, as she glanced at him over the big roses and geraniums, wore a conversational smile. Felix, standing on the threshold of the cottage, hesitated for a moment as to whether he should retrace his steps and enter the parlour. Then he went his way and passed into Mr. Wentworth's garden. That civilizing process to which he had suggested that Clifford should be subjected appeared to have come on of itself. Felix was very sure, at least, that Mr. Wentworth had not adopted his ingenious device for stimulating the young man's aesthetic consciousness. 'Doubtless he supposes,' he said to himself, after the conversation that has been narrated, 'that I desire, out of fraternal benevolence, to procure for Eugenia the amusement of a flirtation – or, as he probably calls it, an intrigue – with the too susceptible Clifford. It must be admitted – and I have noticed it before – that nothing exceeds the licence occasionally taken by the imagination of very rigid people.' Felix, on his own side, had of course said nothing to Clifford; but he had observed to Eugenia that Mr. Wentworth was much mortified at his son's low tastes. 'We ought to do something to help them, after all their kindness to us,' he had added. 'Encourage Clifford to come and see you, and inspire him with a taste for conversation. That will supplant the other, which only comes from his puerility, from his not taking his position in the world – that of a rich young man of ancient stock – seriously enough. Make him a little more serious. Even if he makes love to you it is no great matter.'

'I am to offer myself as a superior form of intoxication – a substitute for a brandy bottle, eh?' asked the Baroness. 'Truly, in this country one comes to strange uses.'

But she had not positively declined to undertake Clifford's higher education, and Felix, who had not thought of the matter again, being haunted with visions of more personal profit, now reflected that the work of redemption had fairly begun. The idea in prospect had seemed of the happiest, but in operation it made him a trifle uneasy. 'What if Eugenia – what if Eugenia' – he asked himself softly; the question dying away in his sense of Eugenia's undetermined capacity. But before Felix had time either to accept or to reject its admonition, even in this vague form, he saw Robert Acton turn out of Mr. Wentworth's enclosure, by a distant gate, and come toward the cottage in the orchard. Acton had evidently walked from his own house along a shady by-way and was intending to pay a visit to Madame Münster. Felix watched him a moment; then he turned away. Acton could be left to play the part of Providence and interrupt – if interruption were needed – Clifford's entanglement with Eugenia.

Felix passed through the garden toward the house and toward a postern gate which opened upon a path leading across the fields, beside a little wood, to the lake. He stopped and looked up at the house; his eyes rested more particularly upon a certain open window, on the shady side. Presently Gertrude appeared there, looking out into the summer light. He took off his hat to her and bade her good-day; he remarked that he was going to row across the pond, and begged that she would do him the honour to accompany him. She looked at him a moment; then, without saying anything, she turned away. But she soon reappeared below in one of those quaint and charming Leghorn hats,[4] tied with white satin bows, that were worn at that period; she also carried a green parasol. She went with him to the edge of the lake, where a couple of boats were always moored; they got into one of them, and Felix, with gentle strokes, propelled it to the opposite shore. The day was the perfection of summer weather; the little lake was the colour of sunshine; the plash of the oars was the only sound, and they found themselves listening to it. They disembarked, and, by a winding path, ascended the pine-crested mound which overlooked the water, whose white expanse glittered between the trees. The place was delightfully cool, and had the added charm that – in the softly sounding pine boughs – you seemed to hear the coolness as well as feel it. Felix and Gertrude sat down on the rust-coloured carpet of pine-needles and talked of many things. Felix spoke at last, in the course of talk, of his going away; it was the first time he had alluded to it.

'You are going away?' said Gertrude, looking at him.

'Some day – when the leaves begin to fall. You know I can't stay forever.'

Gertrude transferred her eyes to the outer prospect, and then, after a pause, she said, 'I shall never see you again.'

'Why not?' asked Felix. 'We shall probably both survive my departure.'

But Gertrude only repeated, 'I shall never see you again. I shall never hear of you,' she went on. 'I shall know nothing about you. I knew nothing about you before, and it will be the same again.'

'I knew nothing about you then, unfortunately,' said Felix. 'But now I shall write to you.'

'Don't write to me. I shall not answer you,' Gertrude declared.

'I should of course burn your letters,' said Felix.

Gertrude looked at him again. 'Burn my letters? You sometimes say strange things.'

'They are not strange in themselves,' the young man answered. 'They are only strange as said to you. You will come to Europe.'

'With whom shall I come?' She asked this question simply; she was very much in earnest. Felix was interested in her earnestness; for some moments he hesitated. 'You can't tell me that,' she pursued. 'You can't say that I shall go with my father and my sister; you don't believe that.'

'I shall keep your letters,' said Felix, presently, for all answer.

'I never write. I don't know how to write.' Gertrude, for some time, said nothing more; and her companion, as he looked at her, wished it had not been 'disloyal' to make love to the daughter of an old gentleman who had offered one hospitality. The afternoon waned; the shadows stretched themselves; and the light grew deeper in the western sky. Two persons appeared on the opposite side of the lake, coming from the house and crossing the meadow. 'It is Charlotte and Mr. Brand,' said Gertrude. 'They are coming over here.' But Charlotte and Mr. Brand only came down to the edge of the water, and stood there, looking across; they made no motion to enter the boat that Felix had left at the mooring-place. Felix waved his hat to them; it was too far to call. They made no visible response, and they presently turned away and walked along the shore.

'Mr. Brand is not demonstrative,' said Felix. 'He is never demonstrative to me. He sits silent, with his chin in his hand, looking at me. Sometimes he looks away. Your father tells me he is so eloquent; and I should like to hear him talk. He looks like such a noble young man. But with me he will never talk. And yet I am so fond of listening to brilliant imagery!'

'He is very eloquent,' said Gertrude; 'but he has no brilliant imagery. I have heard him talk a great deal. I knew that when they saw us they would not come over here.'

'Ah, he is making *la cour*, as they say, to your sister? They desire to be alone?'

'No,' said Gertrude, gravely, 'they have no such reason as that for being alone.'

'But why doesn't he make la cour to Charlotte?' Felix inquired. 'She is so pretty, so gentle, so good.'

Gertrude glanced at him, and then she looked at the distantly-seen couple they were discussing. Mr. Brand and Charlotte were walking side by side. They might have been a pair of lovers, and yet they might not. 'They think I should not be here,' said Gertrude.

'With me? I thought you didn't have those ideas.'

'You don't understand. There are a great many things you don't understand.'

'I understand my stupidity. But why, then, do not Charlotte and Mr. Brand, who, as an elder sister and a clergyman, are free to walk about together, come over and make me wiser by breaking up the unlawful interview into which I have lured you?'

'That is the last thing they would do,' said Gertrude.

Felix stared at her a moment, with his lifted eyebrows. 'Je n'y comprends rien!' he exclaimed; then his eyes followed for a while the retreating figures of this critical pair. 'You may say what you please,' he declared; 'it is evident to me that your sister is not indifferent to her clever companion. It is agreeable to her to be walking there with him. I can see that from here.' And in the excitement of observation Felix rose to his feet.

Gertrude rose also, but she made no attempt to emulate her companion's discovery; she looked rather in another direction. Felix's words had struck her; but a certain delicacy checked her. 'She is certainly not indifferent to Mr. Brand; she has the highest opinion of him.'

'One can see it – one can see it,' said Felix, in a tone of amused contemplation, with his head on one side. Gertrude turned her back to the opposite shore; it was disagreeable to her to look, but she hoped Felix would say something more. 'Ah, they have wandered away into the wood,' he added.

Gertrude turned round again. 'She is *not* in love with him,' she said; it seemed her duty to say that.

'Then he is in love with her; or if he is not, he ought to be.

She is such a perfect little woman of her kind. She reminds me of a pair of old-fashioned silver sugar-tongs; you know I am very fond of sugar. And she is very nice with Mr. Brand; I have noticed that; very gentle and gracious.'

Gertrude reflected a moment. Then she took a great resolution. 'She wants him to marry me,' she said. 'So of course she is nice.'

Felix's eyebrows rose higher than ever. 'To marry you! Ah, ah, this is interesting. And you think one must be very nice with a man to induce him to do that?'

Gertrude had turned a little pale, but she went on, 'Mr. Brand wants it himself.'

Felix folded his arms and stood looking at her. 'I see – I see,' he said quickly. 'Why did you never tell me this before?'

'It is disagreeable to me to speak of it even now. I wished simply to explain to you about Charlotte.'

'You don't wish to marry Mr. Brand, then?'

'No,' said Gertrude, gravely.

'And does your father wish it?'

'Very much.'

'And you don't like him – you have refused him?'

'I don't wish to marry him.'

'Your father and sister think you ought to, eh?'

'It is a long story,' said Gertrude. 'They think there are good reasons. I can't explain it. They think I have obligations, and that I have encouraged him.'

Felix smiled at her, as if she had been telling him an amusing story about some one else. 'I can't tell you how this interests me,' he said. 'Now you don't recognize these reasons – these obligations?'

'I am not sure; it is not easy.' And she picked up her parasol and turned away, as if to descend the slope.

'Tell me this,' Felix went on, going with her: 'are you likely to give in – to let them persuade you?'

Gertrude looked at him with the serious face that she had constantly worn, in opposition to his almost eager smile. 'I shall never marry Mr. Brand,' she said.

'I see!' Felix rejoined. And they slowly descended the hill

together, saying nothing till they reached the margin of the pond. 'It is your own affair,' he then resumed; 'but do you know, I am not altogether glad? If it were settled that you were to marry Mr. Brand I should take a certain comfort in the arrangement. I should feel more free. I have no right to make love to you myself, eh?' And he paused, lightly pressing his argument upon her.

'None whatever,' replied Gertrude quickly – too quickly.

'Your father would never hear of it; I haven't a penny. Mr. Brand, of course, has property of his own, eh?'

'I believe he has some property; but that has nothing to do with it.'

'With you, of course not; but with your father and sister it must have. So, as I say, if this were settled, I should feel more at liberty.'

'More at liberty?' Gertrude repeated. 'Please unfasten the boat.'

Felix untwisted the rope and stood holding it. 'I should be able to say things to you that I can't give myself the pleasure of saying now,' he went on. 'I could tell you how much I admire you, without seeming to pretend to that which I have no right to pretend to. I should make violent love to you,' he added, laughing, 'if I thought you were so placed as not to be offended by it.'

'You mean if I were engaged to another man? That is strange reasoning!' Gertrude exclaimed.

'In that case you would not take me seriously.'

'I take every one seriously,' said Gertrude. And without his help she stepped lightly into the boat.

Felix took up the oars and sent it forward. 'Ah, this is what you have been thinking about? It seemed to me you had something on your mind. I wish very much,' he added, 'that you would tell me some of these so-called reasons – these obligations.'

'They are not real reasons – good reasons,' said Gertrude, looking at the pink and yellow gleams in the water.

'I can understand that! Because a handsome girl has had a spark of coquetry, that is no reason.'

'If you mean me, it's not that. I have not done that.'

'It is something that troubles you, at any rate,' said Felix.

'Not so much as it used to,' Gertrude rejoined.

He looked at her, smiling always. 'That is not saying much, eh?' But she only rested her eyes, very gravely, on the lighted water. She seemed to him to be trying to hide the signs of the trouble of which she had just told him. Felix felt, at all times, much the same impulse to dissipate visible melancholy that a good housewife feels to brush away dust. There was something he wished to brush away now; suddenly he stopped rowing and poised his oars. 'Why should Mr. Brand have addressed himself to you, and not to your sister?' he asked. 'I am sure she would listen to him.'

Gertrude, in her family, was thought capable of a good deal of levity; but her levity had never gone so far as this. It moved her greatly, however, to hear Felix say that he was sure of something; so that, raising her eyes toward him, she tried intently, for some moments, to conjure up this wonderful image of a love-affair between her own sister and her own suitor. We know that Gertrude had an imaginative mind; so that it is not impossible that this effort should have been partially successful. But she only murmured, 'Ah, Felix! ah, Felix!'

'Why shouldn't they marry? Try and make them marry!' cried Felix.

'Try and make them?'

'Turn the tables on them. Then they will leave you alone. I will help you as far as I can.'

Gertrude's heart began to beat; she was greatly excited; she had never had anything so interesting proposed to her before. Felix had begun to row again, and he now sent the boat home with long strokes. 'I believe she does care for him!' said Gertrude, after they had disembarked.

'Of course she does, and we will marry them off. It will make them happy; it will make every one happy. We shall have a wedding and I will write an epithalamium.'[5]

'It seems as if it would make me happy,' said Gertrude.

'To get rid of Mr. Brand, eh? To recover your liberty?'

Gertrude walked on. 'To see my sister married to so good a man.'

Felix gave his light laugh. 'You always put things on those grounds; you will never say anything for yourself. You are all so afraid, here, of being selfish. I don't think you know how,' he went on. 'Let me show you! It will make me happy for myself, and for just the reverse of what I told you a while ago. After that, when I make love to you, you will have to think I mean it.'

'I shall never think you mean anything,' said Gertrude. 'You are too fantastic.'

'Ah,' cried Felix, 'that's a licence to say everything! Gertrude, I adore you!'

VIII

Charlotte and Mr. Brand had not returned when they reached the house; but the Baroness had come to tea, and Robert Acton also, who now regularly asked for a place at this generous repast or made his appearance later in the evening. Clifford Wentworth, with his juvenile growl, remarked upon it.

'You are always coming to tea nowadays, Robert,' he said. 'I should think you had drunk enough tea in China.'

'Since when is Mr. Acton more frequent?' asked the Baroness.

'Since you came,' said Clifford. 'It seems as if you were a kind of attraction.'

'I suppose I am a curiosity,' said the Baroness. 'Give me time and I will make you a salon.'

'It would fall to pieces after you go!' exclaimed Acton.

'Don't talk about her going, in that familiar way,' Clifford said. 'It makes me feel gloomy.'

Mr. Wentworth glanced at his son, and taking note of these words, wondered if Felix had been teaching him, according to the programme he had sketched out, to make love to the wife of a German prince.

Charlotte came in late with Mr. Brand; but Gertrude, to whom, at least, Felix had taught something, looked in vain, in her face, for the traces of a guilty passion. Mr. Brand sat down by Gertrude, and she presently asked him why they had not crossed the pond to join Felix and herself.

'It is cruel of you to ask me that,' he answered, very softly. He had a large morsel of cake before him; but he fingered it without eating it. 'I sometimes think you are growing cruel,' he added.

Gertrude said nothing; she was afraid to speak. There was a kind of rage in her heart; she felt as if she could easily persuade herself that she was persecuted. She said to herself that it was quite right that she should not allow him to make her believe she was wrong. She thought of what Felix had said to her; she wished indeed Mr. Brand would marry Charlotte. She looked away from him and spoke no more. Mr. Brand ended by eating his cake, while Felix sat opposite, describing to Mr. Wentworth the students' duels at Heidelberg. After tea they all dispersed themselves, as usual, upon the piazza and in the garden; and Mr. Brand drew near to Gertrude again.

'I didn't come to you this afternoon because you were not alone,' he began; 'because you were with a newer friend.'

'Felix? He is an old friend by this time.'

Mr. Brand looked at the ground for some moments. 'I thought I was prepared to hear you speak in that way,' he resumed. 'But I find it very painful.'

'I don't see what else I can say,' said Gertrude.

Mr. Brand walked beside her for a while in silence; Gertrude wished he would go away. 'He is certainly very accomplished. But I think I ought to advise you.'

'To advise me?'

'I think I know your nature.'

'I think you don't,' said Gertrude, with a soft laugh.

'You make yourself out worse than you are – to please him,' Mr. Brand said, gently.

'Worse – to please him? What do you mean?' asked Gertrude, stopping.

Mr. Brand stopped also, and with the same soft straightforwardness, 'He doesn't care for the things you care for – the great questions of life.'

Gertrude, with her eyes on his, shook her head. 'I don't care for the great questions of life. They are much beyond me.'

'There was a time when you didn't say that,' said Mr. Brand.

'Oh,' rejoined Gertrude, 'I think you made me talk a great deal of nonsense. And it depends,' she added, 'upon what you call the great questions of life. There are some things I care for.'

'Are they the things you talk about with your cousin?'

'You should not say things to me against my cousin, Mr. Brand,' said Gertrude. 'That is dishonourable.'

He listened to this respectfully; then he answered, with a little vibration of the voice, 'I should be very sorry to do anything dishonourable. But I don't see why it is dishonourable to say that your cousin is frivolous.'

'Go and say it to himself!'

'I think he would admit it,' said Mr. Brand. 'That is the tone he would take. He would not be ashamed of it.'

'Then I am not ashamed of it!' Gertrude declared. 'That is probably what I like him for. I am frivolous myself.'

'You are trying, as I said just now, to lower yourself.'

'I am trying for once to be natural!' cried Gertrude passionately. 'I have been pretending, all my life; I have been dishonest; it is you that have made me so!' Mr. Brand stood gazing at her, and she went on, 'Why shouldn't I be frivolous, if I want? One has a right to be frivolous, if it's one's nature. No, I don't care for the great questions. I care for pleasure – for amusement. Perhaps I am fond of wicked things; it is very possible!'

Mr. Brand remained staring; he was even a little pale, as if he had been frightened. 'I don't think you know what you are saying!' he exclaimed.

'Perhaps not. Perhaps I am talking nonsense. But it is only with you that I talk nonsense. I never do so with my cousin.'

'I will speak to you again, when you are less excited,' said Mr. Brand.

'I am always excited when you speak to me. I must tell you that – even if it prevents you altogether, in future. Your speaking to me irritates me. With my cousin it is very different. That seems quiet and natural.'

He looked at her, and then he looked away, with a kind of helpless distress, at the dusky garden and the faint summer stars. After which, suddenly turning back, 'Gertrude, Gertrude!' he softly groaned. 'Am I really losing you?'

She was touched – she was pained; but it had already occurred to her that she might do something better than say so. It would not have alleviated her companion's distress to perceive, just then, whence she had sympathetically borrowed this ingenuity.

'I am not sorry for you,' Gertrude said; 'for in paying so much attention to me you are following a shadow – you are wasting something precious. There is something else you might have that you don't look at – something better than I am. That is a reality!' And then, with intention, she looked at him and tried to smile a little. He thought this smile of hers very strange; but she turned away and left him.

She wandered about alone in the garden wondering what Mr. Brand would make of her words, which it had been a singular pleasure for her to utter. Shortly after, passing in front of the house, she saw at a distance two persons standing near the garden gate. It was Mr. Brand going away and bidding good-night to Charlotte, who had walked down with him from the house. Gertrude saw that the parting was prolonged. Then she turned her back upon it. She had not gone very far, however, when she heard her sister slowly following her. She neither turned round nor waited for her; she knew what Charlotte was going to say. Charlotte, who at last overtook her, in fact presently began; she had passed her arm into Gertrude's.

'Will you listen to me, dear, if I say something very particular?'

'I know what you are going to say,' said Gertrude. 'Mr. Brand feels very badly.'

'Oh, Gertrude, how can you treat him so?' Charlotte demanded. And as her sister made no answer she added, 'After all he has done for you!'

'What has he done for me?'

'I wonder you can ask, Gertrude. He has helped you so. You told me so yourself, a great many times. You told me that he helped you to struggle with your – your peculiarities. You told me that he had taught you how to govern your temper.'

For a moment Gertrude said nothing. Then, 'Was my temper very bad?' she asked.

'I am not accusing you, Gertrude,' said Charlotte.

'What are you doing, then?' her sister demanded, with a short laugh.

'I am pleading for Mr. Brand – reminding you of all you owe him.'

'I have given it all back,' said Gertrude, still with her little laugh. 'He can take back the virtue he imparted! I want to be wicked again.'

Her sister made her stop in the path, and fixed upon her, in the darkness, a sweet, reproachful gaze. 'If you talk this way I shall almost believe it. Think of all we owe Mr. Brand. Think of how he has always expected something of you. Think how much he has been to us. Think of his beautiful influence upon Clifford.'

'He is very good,' said Gertrude, looking at her sister. 'I know he is very good. But he shouldn't speak against Felix.'

'Felix is good,' Charlotte answered, softly but promptly. 'Felix is very wonderful. Only he is so different. Mr. Brand is much nearer to us. I should never think of going to Felix with a trouble – with a question. Mr. Brand is much more to us, Gertrude.'

'He is very – very good,' Gertrude repeated. 'He is more to you; yes, much more. Charlotte,' she added suddenly, 'you are in love with him!'

'Oh, Gertrude!' cried poor Charlotte; and her sister saw her blushing in the darkness.

Gertrude put her arm round her. 'I wish he would marry you!' she went on.

Charlotte shook herself free. 'You must not say such things!' she exclaimed, beneath her breath.

'You like him more than you say, and he likes you more than he knows.'

'This is very cruel of you!' Charlotte Wentworth murmured.

But if it was cruel Gertrude continued pitiless. 'Not if it's true,' she answered. 'I wish he would marry you.'

'Please don't say that.'

'I mean to tell him so!' said Gertrude.

'Oh, Gertrude, Gertrude!' her sister almost moaned.

'Yes, if he speaks to me again about myself. I will say, "Why don't you marry Charlotte? She's a thousand times better than I."'

'You *are* wicked; you *are* changed!' cried her sister.

'If you don't like it you can prevent it,' said Gertrude. 'You can prevent it by keeping him from speaking to me!' And with this she walked away, very conscious of what she had done; measuring it and finding a certain joy and a quickened sense of freedom in it.

Mr. Wentworth was rather wide of the mark in suspecting that Clifford had begun to pay unscrupulous compliments to his brilliant cousin; for the young man had really more scruples than he received credit for in his family. He had a certain transparent shamefacedness which was in itself a proof that he was not at his ease in dissipation. His collegiate peccadilloes had aroused a domestic murmur as disagreeable to the young man as the creaking of his boots would have been to a house-breaker. Only, as the house-breaker would have simplified matters by removing his *chaussures*, it had seemed to Clifford that the shortest cut to comfortable relations with people – relations which should make him cease to think that when they spoke to him they meant something improving – was to renounce all ambition toward a nefarious development. And, in fact, Clifford's ambition took the most commendable form. He thought of himself in the future as the well-known and much-liked Mr. Wentworth, of Boston, who should, in the natural course of prosperity, have married his pretty cousin, Lizzie Acton; should live in a wide-fronted house, in view of the Common;[1] and should drive, behind a light wagon, over the damp autumn roads, a pair of beautifully matched sorrel horses. Clifford's vision of the coming years was very simple; its most definite features were this element of familiar matrimony and the duplication of his resources for trotting. He had not yet asked his cousin to marry him; but he meant to do so as soon as he had taken his degree. Lizzie was serenely conscious of his intention, and she had made up her mind that he would improve. Her brother, who was very fond of this light, quick, competent little Lizzie, saw on his side no reason to interpose. It seemed to him a graceful social law that Clifford and his sister should become engaged; he himself was not engaged, but every one else, fortunately, was not such a fool as he. He was fond of Clifford, as well, and had his own way – of which it must be confessed he was a little ashamed – of looking at those

aberrations which had led to the young man's compulsory
retirement from the neighbouring seat of learning. Acton had
seen the world, as he said to himself; he had been to China and
had knocked about among men. He had learned the essential
difference between a nice young fellow and a mean young
fellow, and was satisfied that there was no harm in Clifford.
He believed – although it must be added that he had not quite
the courage to declare it – in the doctrine of wild oats, and
thought it a useful preventive of superfluous fears. If Mr. Wentworth and Charlotte and Mr. Brand would only apply it in
Clifford's case, they would be happier; and Acton thought it a
pity they should not be happier. They took the boy's misde-
meanours too much to heart; they talked to him too solemnly;
they frightened and bewildered him. Of course there was the
great standard of morality, which forbade that a man should
get tipsy, play at billiards for money, or cultivate his sensual
consciousness; but what fear was there that poor Clifford was
going to run a tilt at any great standard? It had, however, never
occurred to Acton to dedicate the Baroness Münster to the
redemption of a refractory collegian. The instrument, here,
would have seemed to him quite too complex for the operation. Felix, on the other hand, had spoken in obedience to the
belief that the more charming a woman is the more numerous,
literally, are her definite social uses.

Eugenia herself, as we know, had plenty of leisure to enumerate her uses. As I have had the honour of intimating, she had
come four thousand miles to seek her fortune; and it is not to
be supposed that after this great effort she could neglect any
apparent aid to advancement. It is my misfortune that in
attempting to describe in a short compass the deportment of
this remarkable woman I am obliged to express things rather
brutally. I feel this to be the case, for instance, when I say that
she had primarily detected such an aid to advancement in the
person of Robert Acton, but that she had afterwards remembered that a prudent archer has always a second bowstring.
Eugenia was a woman of finely-mingled motive, and her intentions were never sensibly gross. She had a sort of aesthetic
ideal for Clifford which seemed to her a disinterested reason for

taking him in hand. It was very well for a fresh-coloured young gentleman to be ingenuous; but Clifford, really, was crude. With such a pretty face he ought to have prettier manners. She would teach him that, with a beautiful name, the expectation of a large property, and, as they said in Europe, a social position, an only son should know how to carry himself.

Once Clifford had begun to come and see her by himself and for himself, he came very often. He hardly knew why he should come; he saw her almost every evening at his father's house; he had nothing particular to say to her. She was not a young girl, and fellows of his age called only upon young girls. He exaggerated her age; she seemed to him an old woman; it was happy that the Baroness, with all her intelligence, was incapable of guessing this. But gradually it struck Clifford that visiting old women might be, if not a natural, at least, as they say of some articles of diet, an acquired taste. The Baroness was certainly a very amusing old woman; she talked to him as no lady – and indeed no gentleman – had ever talked to him before.

'You should go to Europe and make the tour,' she said to him one afternoon. 'Of course, on leaving college you will go.'

'I don't want to go,' Clifford declared. 'I know some fellows who have been to Europe. They say you can have better fun here.'

'That depends. It depends upon your idea of fun. Your friends probably were not introduced.'

'Introduced?' Clifford demanded.

'They had no opportunity of going into society; they formed no *relations*.' This was one of a certain number of words that the Baroness often pronounced in the French manner.

'They went to a ball, in Paris; I know that,' said Clifford.

'Ah, there are balls and balls; especially in Paris. No, you must go, you know; it is not a thing from which you can dispense yourself. You need it.'

'Oh, I'm very well,' said Clifford. 'I'm not sick.'

'I don't mean for your health, my poor child. I mean for your manners.'

'I haven't got any manners!' growled Clifford.

'Precisely. You don't mind my assenting to that, eh?' asked the Baroness with a smile. 'You must go to Europe and get a few. You can get them better there. It is a pity you might not have come while I was living in – in Germany. I would have introduced you; I had a charming little circle. You would perhaps have been rather young; but the younger one begins, I think, the better. Now, at any rate, you have no time to lose, and when I return you must immediately come to me.'

All this, to Clifford's apprehension, was a great mixture – his beginning young, Eugenia's return to Europe, his being introduced to her charming little circle. What was he to begin, and what was her little circle? His ideas about her marriage had a good deal of vagueness; but they were in so far definite as that he felt it to be a matter not to be freely mentioned. He sat and looked all round the room; he supposed she was alluding in some way to her marriage.

'Oh, I don't want to go to Germany,' he said; it seemed to him the most convenient thing to say.

She looked at him a while, smiling with her lips, but not with her eyes.

'You have scruples?' she asked.

'Scruples?' said Clifford.

'You young people, here, are very singular; one doesn't know where to expect you. When you are not extremely improper you are so terribly proper. I dare say you think that, owing to my irregular marriage, I live with loose people. You were never more mistaken. I have been all the more particular.'

'Oh, no,' said Clifford, honestly distressed. 'I never thought such a thing as that.'

'Are you very sure? I am convinced that your father does, and your sisters. They say to each other that here I am on my good behaviour, but that over there – married by the left hand – I associate with light women.'

'Oh, no,' cried Clifford, energetically, 'they don't say such things as that to each other!'

'If they think them they had better say them,' the Baroness rejoined. 'Then they can be contradicted. Please contradict that whenever you hear it, and don't be afraid of coming to see me

on account of the company I keep. I have the honour of knowing more distinguished men, my poor child, than you are likely
to see in a lifetime. I see very few women; but those are women
of rank. So, my dear young Puritan, you needn't be afraid. I
am not in the least one of those who think that the society of
women who have lost their place in the *vrai monde* is necessary
to form a young man. I have never taken that tone. I have kept
my place myself, and I think we are a much better school than
the others. Trust me, Clifford, and I will prove that to you,' the
Baroness continued, while she made the agreeable reflection
that she could not, at least, be accused of perverting her young
kinsman. 'So if you ever fall among thieves don't go about
saying I sent you to them.'

Clifford thought it so comical that he should know – in spite
of her figurative language – what she meant, and that she should
mean what he knew, that he could hardly help laughing a little,
although he tried hard. 'Oh, no! oh, no!' he murmured.

'Laugh out, laugh out, if I amuse you!' cried the Baroness. 'I
am here for that!' And Clifford thought her a very amusing
person indeed. 'But remember,' she said on this occasion, 'that
you are coming – next year – to pay me a visit over there.'

About a week afterwards she said to him, point-blank, 'Are
you seriously making love to your little cousin?'

'Seriously making love' – these words, on Madame Münster's
lips, had to Clifford's sense a portentous and embarrassing
sound; he hesitated about assenting, lest he should commit
himself to more than he understood. 'Well, I shouldn't say it if
I was!' he exclaimed.

'Why wouldn't you say it?' the Baroness demanded. 'Those
things ought to be known.'

'I don't care whether it is known or not,' Clifford rejoined.
'But I don't want people looking at me.'

'A young man of your importance ought to learn to bear
observation – to carry himself as if he were quite indifferent to
it. I won't say, exactly, unconscious,' the Baroness explained.
'No, he must seem to know he is observed, and to think it
natural he should be; but he must appear perfectly used to it.
Now you haven't that, Clifford; you haven't that at all. You

must have that, you know. Don't tell me you are not a young man of importance,' Eugenia added. 'Don't say anything so flat as that.'

'Oh, no, you don't catch me saying that!' cried Clifford.

'Yes, you must come to Germany,' Madame Münster continued. 'I will show you how people can be talked about, and yet not seem to know it. You will be talked about, of course, with me; it will be said you are my lover. I will show you how little one may mind that – how little I shall mind it.'

Clifford sat staring, blushing and laughing. 'I shall mind it a good deal!' he declared.

'Ah, not too much, you know; that would be uncivil. But I give you leave to mind it a little; especially if you have a passion for Miss Acton. Voyons; as regards that, you either have or you have not. It is very simple to say it.'

'I don't see why you want to know,' said Clifford.

'You ought to want me to know. If one is arranging a marriage, one tells one's friends.'

'Oh, I'm not arranging anything,' said Clifford.

'You don't intend to marry your cousin?'

'Well, I expect I shall do as I choose!'

The Baroness leaned her head upon the back of her chair and closed her eyes, as if she were tired. Then opening them again, 'Your cousin is very charming!' she said.

'She is the prettiest girl in this place,' Clifford rejoined.

'"In this place" is saying little; she would be charming anywhere. I am afraid you are entangled.'

'Oh, no, I'm not entangled.'

'Are you engaged? At your age that is the same thing.'

Clifford looked at the Baroness with some audacity. 'Will you tell no one?'

'If it's as sacred as that – no.'

'Well, then – we are not!' said Clifford.

'That's the great secret – that you are not, eh?' asked the Baroness, with a quick laugh. 'I am very glad to hear it. You are altogether too young. A young man in your position must choose and compare; he must see the world first. Depend upon it,' she added, 'you should not settle that matter before you have come abroad and paid me that visit. There are several things I should like to call your attention to first.'

'Well, I am rather afraid of that visit,' said Clifford. 'It seems to me it will be rather like going to school again.'

The Baroness looked at him a moment.

'My dear child,' she said, 'there is no agreeable man who has not, at some moment, been to school to a clever woman – probably a little older than himself. And you must be thankful when you get your instructions gratis. With me you would get it gratis.'

The next day Clifford told Lizzie Acton that the Baroness thought her the most charming girl she had ever seen.

Lizzie shook her head. 'No, she doesn't!' she said.

'Do you think everything she says,' asked Clifford, 'is to be taken the opposite way?'

'I think that is!' said Lizzie.

Clifford was going to remark that in this case the Baroness must desire greatly to bring about a marriage between Mr. Clifford Wentworth and Miss Elizabeth Acton; but he resolved, on the whole, to suppress this observation.

IX

It seemed to Robert Acton, after Eugenia had come to his house, that something had passed between them which made them a good deal more intimate. It was hard to say exactly what, except her telling him that she had taken her resolution with regard to the Prince Adolf; for Madame Münster's visit had made no difference in their relations. He came to see her very often; but he had come to see her very often before. It was agreeable to him to find himself in her little drawing-room; but this was not a new discovery. There was a change, however, in this sense: that if the Baroness had been a great deal in Acton's thoughts before, she was now never out of them. From the first she had been personally fascinating; but the fascination now had become intellectual as well. He was constantly pondering her words and motions; they were as interesting as the factors in an algebraic problem. This is saying a good deal; for Acton was extremely fond of mathematics. He asked himself whether it could be that he was in love with her, and then hoped he was not; hoped it not so much for his own sake as for that of the amatory passion itself. If this was love, love had been overrated. Love was a poetic impulse, and his own state of feeling with regard to the Baroness was largely characterized by that eminently prosaic sentiment – curiosity. It was true, as Acton with his quietly cogitative habit observed to himself, that curiosity, pushed to a given point, might become a romantic passion; and he certainly thought enough about this charming woman to make him restless and even a little melancholy. It puzzled and vexed him at times to feel that he was not more ardent. He was not in the least bent upon remaining a bachelor. In his younger years he had been – or he had tried to be – of the opinion that it would be a good deal 'jollier' not to marry, and he had flattered himself that his single condition was something of a citadel. It was a citadel, at all events, of which he had long since levelled the outworks. He had removed the guns from the ramparts; he had lowered the draw-bridge across the moat. The draw-bridge had swayed lightly under Madame Münster's step; why should be not cause it to be raised again, so that she might be kept prisoner? He had an idea that she would become – in time at least, and on learning the conveniences of the place for making a lady comfortable – a tolerably patient captive. But the draw-bridge was never raised, and Acton's brilliant visitor was as free to depart as she had been to come. It was part of his curiosity to know why the deuce so susceptible a man was *not* in love with so charming a woman. If her various graces were, as I have said, the factors in an algebraic problem, the answer to this question was the indispensable unknown quantity. The pursuit of the unknown quantity was extremely absorbing; for the present it taxed all Acton's faculties.

Toward the middle of August he was obliged to leave home for some days; an old friend, with whom he had been associated in China, had begged him to come to Newport,[1] where he lay extremely ill. His friend got better, and at the end of a week Acton was released. I use the word 'released' advisedly; for in spite of his attachment to his Chinese comrade he had been but a half-hearted visitor. He felt as if he had been called away from the theatre during the progress of a remarkably interesting drama. The curtain was up all this time, and he was losing the fourth act; that fourth act which would have been so essential to a just appreciation of the fifth. In other words, he was thinking about the Baroness, who, seen at this distance, seemed a truly brilliant figure. He saw at Newport a great many pretty women, who certainly were figures as brilliant as beautiful light dresses could make them; but though they talked a great deal – and the Baroness's strong point was perhaps also her conversation – Madame Münster appeared to lose nothing by the comparison. He wished she had come to Newport too. Would it not be possible to make up, as they said, a party for visiting the famous watering-place and invite Eugenia to join it? It was true that the complete satisfaction would be to spend a fortnight at Newport with Eugenia alone. It would be a great pleasure to see her, in society, carry everything before her, as he was sure she would do. When Acton caught himself thinking these thoughts he began to walk up and down, with his hands in his pockets, frowning a little and looking at the floor. What did it prove – for it certainly proved something – this lively disposition to be 'off' somewhere with Madame Münster, away from all the rest of them? Such a vision, certainly, seemed a refined implication of matrimony, after the Baroness should have formally got rid of her informal husband. At any rate, Acton, with his characteristic discretion, forbore to give expression to whatever else it might imply, and the narrator of these incidents is not obliged to be more definite.

He returned home rapidly, and, arriving in the afternoon, lost as little time as possible in joining the familiar circle at Mr. Wentworth's. On reaching the house, however, he found the piazzas empty. The doors and windows were open, and their emptiness was made clear by the shafts of lamp-light from the parlours. Entering the house, he found Mr. Wentworth sitting alone in one of these apartments, engaged in the perusal of the 'North American Review'.[2] After they had exchanged greetings and his cousin had made discreet inquiry about his journey, Acton asked what had become of Mr. Wentworth's companions.

'They are scattered about, amusing themselves as usual,' said the old man. 'I saw Charlotte, a short time since, seated, with Mr. Brand, upon the piazza. They were conversing with their customary animation. I suppose they have joined her sister, who, for the hundredth time, was doing the honours of the garden to her foreign cousin.'

'I suppose you mean Felix,' said Acton. And on Mr. Wentworth's assenting, he said, 'And the others?'

'Your sister has not come this evening. You must have seen her at home,' said Mr. Wentworth.

'Yes. I proposed to her to come. She declined.'

'Lizzie, I suppose, was expecting a visitor,' said the old man, with a kind of solemn slyness.

'If she was expecting Clifford, he had not turned up.'

Mr. Wentworth, at this intelligence, closed the 'North American Review' and remarked that he had understood Clifford to say that he was going to see his cousin. Privately, he reflected that if Lizzie Acton had had no news of his son, Clifford must have gone to Boston for the evening: an unnatural course of a summer night, especially when accompanied with disingenuous representations.

'You must remember that he has two cousins,' said Acton, laughing. And then, coming to the point, 'If Lizzie is not here,' he added, 'neither apparently is the Baroness.'

Mr. Wentworth stared a moment, and remembered that queer proposition of Felix's. For a moment he did not know whether it was not to be wished that Clifford, after all, might have gone to Boston. 'The Baroness has not honoured us tonight,' he said. 'She has not come over for three days.'

'Is she ill?' Acton asked.

'No; I have been to see her.'

'What is the matter with her?'

'Well,' said Mr. Wentworth, 'I infer she has tired of us.'

Acton pretended to sit down, but he was restless; he found it impossible to talk with Mr. Wentworth. At the end of ten minutes he took up his hat and said that he thought he would 'go off'. It was very late; it was ten o'clock.

His quiet-faced kinsman looked at him a moment. 'Are you going home?' he asked.

Acton hesitated, and then answered that he had proposed to go over and take a look at the Baroness.

'Well, *you* are honest, at least,' said Mr. Wentworth, sadly.

'So are you, if you come to that!' cried Acton, laughing. 'Why shouldn't I be honest?'

The old man opened the 'North American' again, and read a few lines. 'If we have ever had any virtue among us, we had better keep hold of it now,' he said. He was not quoting.

'We have a Baroness among us,' said Acton. 'That's what we must keep hold of!' He was too impatient to see Madame Münster again to wonder what Mr. Wentworth was talking about. Nevertheless, after he had passed out of the house and traversed the garden and the little piece of road that separated him from Eugenia's provisional residence, he stopped a moment outside. He stood in her little garden; the long window of her parlour was open, and he could see the white curtains, with the lamp-light shining through them, swaying softly to and fro in the warm night wind. There was a sort of excitement in the idea of seeing Madame Münster again; he became aware that his heart was beating rather faster than usual. It was this that made him stop, with a half-amused surprise. But in a moment he went along the piazza, and, approaching the open window, tapped upon its lintel with his stick. He could see the Baroness within; she was standing in the middle of the room. She came to the window and pulled aside the curtain; then she stood looking at him a moment. She was not smiling; she seemed serious.

'Mais entrez donc!' she said at last. Acton passed in across the window-sill; he wondered, for an instant, what was the matter with her. But the next moment she had begun to smile and had put out her hand. 'Better late than never,' she said. 'It is very kind of you to come at this hour.'

'I have just returned from my journey,' said Acton.

'Ah, very kind, very kind,' she repeated, looking about her where to sit.

'I went first to the other house,' Acton continued. 'I expected to find you there.'

She had sunk into her usual chair; but she got up again, and began to move about the room. Acton had laid down his hat and stick; he was looking at her, conscious that there was in fact a great charm in seeing her again. 'I don't know whether I ought to tell you to sit down,' she said. 'It is too late to begin a visit.'

'It's too early to end one,' Acton declared; 'and we needn't mind the beginning.'

She looked at him again, and, after a moment, dropped once more into her low chair, while he took a place near her. 'We are in the middle, then?' she asked. 'Was that where we were when you went away? No, I haven't been to the other house.'

'Not yesterday, nor the day before, eh?'

'I don't know how many days it is.'

'You are tired of it,' said Acton.

She leaned back in her chair; her arms were folded. 'That is a terrible accusation, but I have not the courage to defend myself.'

'I am not attacking you,' said Acton. 'I expected something of this kind.'

'It's a proof of extreme intelligence. I hope you enjoyed your journey.'

'Not at all,' Acton declared. 'I would much rather have been here with you.'

'Now you *are* attacking me,' said the Baroness. 'You are contrasting my inconstancy with your own fidelity.'

'I confess I never get tired of people I like.'

'Ah, you are not a poor wicked foreign woman, with irritable nerves and a sophisticated mind!'

'Something has happened to you since I went away,' said Acton, changing his place.

'Your going away – that is what has happened to me.'

'Do you mean to say that you have missed me?' he asked.

'If I had meant to say it, it would not be worth your making a note of. I am very dishonest and my compliments are worthless.'

Acton was silent for some moments. 'You have broken down,' he said at last.

Madame Münster left her chair, and began to move about.

'Only for a moment. I shall pull myself together again.'

'You had better not take it too hard. If you are bored, you needn't be afraid to say so – to me at least.'

'You shouldn't say such things as that,' the Baroness answered. 'You should encourage me.'

'I admire your patience; that is encouraging.'

'You shouldn't even say that. When you talk of my patience you are disloyal to your own people. Patience implies suffering; and what have I had to suffer?'

'Oh, not hunger, not unkindness, certainly,' said Acton, laughing. 'Nevertheless, we all admire your patience.'

'You all detest me!' cried the Baroness, with a sudden vehemence, turning her back toward him.

'You make it hard,' said Acton, getting up, 'for a man to say something tender to you.' This evening there was something particularly striking and touching about her; an unwonted softness and a look of suppressed emotion. He felt himself suddenly appreciating the fact that she had behaved very well. She had come to this quiet corner of the world under the weight of a cruel indignity, and she had been so gracefully, modestly thankful for the rest she found there. She had joined that simple circle over the way; she had mingled in its plain, provincial talk; she had shared its meagre and savourless pleasures. She had set herself a task, and she had rigidly performed it. She had conformed to the angular conditions of New England life, and she had had the tact and pluck to carry it off as if she liked them. Acton felt a more downright need than he had ever felt before to tell her that he admired her and that she struck him as a very superior woman. All along, hitherto, he had been on his guard with her; he had been cautious, observant, suspicious. But now a certain light tumult in his blood seemed to tell him that a finer degree of confidence in this charming woman would be its own reward. 'We don't detest you,' he went on. 'I don't know what you mean. At any rate, I speak for myself; I don't know anything about the others. Very likely, you detest them for the dull life they make you lead. Really, it would give me a sort of pleasure to hear you say so.'

Eugenia had been looking at the door on the other side of the room; now she slowly turned her eyes toward Robert Acton. 'What can be the motive,' she asked, 'of a man like you – an honest man, a *galant homme* – in saying so base a thing as that?'

'Does it sound very base?' asked Acton, candidly. 'I suppose it does, and I thank you for telling me so. Of course, I don't mean it literally.'

The Baroness stood looking at him. 'How do you mean it?' she asked.

This question was difficult to answer, and Acton, feeling the least bit foolish, walked to the open window and looked out. He stood there, thinking a moment, and then he turned back. 'You know that document that you were to send to Germany,' he said. 'You called it your "renunciation". Did you ever send it?'

Madame Münster's eyes expanded; she looked very grave. 'What a singular answer to my question!'

'Oh, it isn't an answer,' said Acton. 'I have wished to ask you, many times. I thought it probable you would tell me yourself. The question, on my part, seems abrupt now; but it would be abrupt at any time.'

The Baroness was silent a moment; and then, 'I think I have told you too much!' she said.

This declaration appeared to Acton to have a certain force; he had indeed a sense of asking more of her than he offered her. He returned to the window, and watched, for a moment, a little star that twinkled through the lattice of the piazza. There were at any rate offers enough he could make; perhaps he had hitherto not been sufficiently explicit in doing so. 'I wish you would ask something of me,' he presently said. 'Is there nothing I can do for you? If you can't stand this dull life any more, let me amuse you!'

The Baroness had sunk once more into a chair, and she had taken up a fan which she held, with both hands, to her mouth. Over the top of the fan her eyes were fixed on him. 'You are very strange to-night,' she said, with a little laugh.

'I will do anything in the world,' he rejoined, standing in front of her. 'Shouldn't you like to travel about and see something of the country? Won't you go to Niagara? You ought to see Niagara, you know.'

'With you, do you mean?'

'I should be delighted to take you.'

'You alone?'

Acton looked at her, smiling, and yet with a serious air. 'Well, yes; we might go alone,' he said.

'If you were not what you are,' she answered, 'I should feel insulted.'

'How do you mean – what I am?'

'If you were one of the gentlemen I have been used to all my life. If you were not a queer Bostonian.'

'If the gentlemen you have been used to have taught you to expect insults,' said Acton, 'I am glad I am what I am. You had much better come to Niagara.'

'If you wish to "amuse" me,' the Baroness declared, 'you need go to no further expense. You amuse me very effectually.'

He sat down opposite to her; she still held her fan up to her face, with her eyes only showing above it. There was a moment's silence, and then he said, returning to his former question, 'Have you sent that document to Germany?'

Again there was a moment's silence. The expressive eyes of Madame Münster seemed, however, half to break it.

'I will tell you – at Niagara!' she said.

She had hardly spoken when the door at the further end of the room opened – the door upon which, some minutes previous, Eugenia had fixed her gaze. Clifford Wentworth stood there, blushing and looking rather awkward. The Baroness rose, quickly, and Acton, more slowly, did the same. Clifford gave him no greeting; he was looking at Eugenia.

'Ah, you were here?' exclaimed Acton.

'He was in Felix's studio,' said Madame Münster. 'He wanted to see his sketches.'

Clifford looked at Robert Acton, but said nothing; he only fanned himself with his hat. 'You chose a bad moment,' said Acton; 'you hadn't much light.'

'I hadn't any!' said Clifford, laughing.

'Your candle went out?' Eugenia asked. 'You should have come back here and lighted it again.'

Clifford looked at her a moment. 'So I have – come back. But I have left the candle!'

Eugenia turned away. 'You are very stupid, my poor boy. You had better go home.'

'Well,' said Clifford, 'good night!'

'Haven't you a word to throw to a man when he has safely returned from a dangerous journey?' Acton asked.

'How do you do?' said Clifford. 'I thought – I thought you were –' and he paused, looking at the Baroness again.

'You thought I was at Newport, eh? So I was – this morning.'

'Good night, clever child!' said Madame Münster, over her shoulder.

Clifford stared at her – not at all like a clever child; and then, with one of his little facetious growls, took his departure.

'What is the matter with him?' asked Acton, when he was gone. 'He seemed rather in a muddle.'

Eugenia, who was near the window, glanced out, listening a moment. 'The matter – the matter' – she answered. 'But you don't say such things here.'

'If you mean that he had been drinking a little, you can say that.'

'He doesn't drink any more. I have cured him. And in return – he's in love with me.'

It was Acton's turn to stare. He instantly thought of his sister; but he said nothing about her. He began to laugh. 'I don't wonder at his passion! But I wonder at his forsaking your society for that of your brother's paint-brushes.'

Eugenia was silent a little. 'He had not been in the studio. I invented that at the moment.'

'Invented it? For what purpose?'

'He has an idea of being romantic. He has adopted the habit of coming to see me at midnight – passing only through the orchard and through Felix's painting-room, which has a door opening that way. It seems to amuse him,' added Eugenia, with a little laugh.

Acton felt more surprise than he confessed to, for this was a new view of Clifford, whose irregularities had hitherto been quite without the romantic element. He tried to laugh again, but he felt rather too serious, and after a moment's hesitation his seriousness explained itself. 'I hope you don't encourage him,' he said. 'He must not be inconstant to poor Lizzie.'

'To your sister?'

'You know they are decidedly intimate,' said Acton.

'Ah,' cried Eugenia, smiling, 'has she – has she –'

'I don't know,' Acton interrupted, 'what she has. But I always supposed that Clifford had a desire to make himself agreeable to her.'

'Ah, par exemple!' the Baroness went on. 'The little monster! The next time he becomes sentimental I will him tell that he ought to be ashamed of himself.'

Acton was silent a moment. 'You had better say nothing about it.'

'I had told him as much already, on general grounds,' said the Baroness. 'But in this country, you know, the relations of young people are so extraordinary that one is quite at sea. They are not engaged when you would quite say they ought to be. Take Charlotte Wentworth, for instance, and that young ecclesiastic. If I were her father I should insist upon his marrying her; but it appears to be thought there is no urgency. On the other hand, you suddenly learn that a boy of twenty and a little girl who is still with her governess – your sister has no governess? Well, then, who is never away from her mamma – a young couple, in short, between whom you have noticed nothing beyond an exchange of the childish pleasantries characteristic of their age, are on the point of setting up as man and wife.' The Baroness spoke with a certain exaggerated volubility which was in contrast with the languid grace that had characterized her manner before Clifford made his appearance. It seemed to Acton that there was a spark of irritation in her eye – a note of irony (as when she spoke of Lizzie being never away from her mother) in her voice. If Madame Münster was irritated, Robert Acton was vaguely mystified; she began to move about the room again, and he looked at her without saying anything. Presently she took out her watch, and, glancing at it, declared that it was three o'clock in the morning and that he must go.

'I have not been here an hour,' he said, 'and they are still sitting up at the other house. You can see the lights. Your brother has not come in.'

'Oh, at the other house,' cried Eugenia, 'they are terrible people! I don't know what they may do over there. I am a quiet little humdrum woman; I have rigid rules and I keep them. One of them is not to have visitors in the small hours – especially clever men like you. So good night!'

Decidedly, the Baroness was incisive; and though Acton bade her good night and departed, he was still a good deal mystified.

The next day Clifford Wentworth came to see Lizzie, and Acton, who was at home and saw him pass through the garden, took note of the circumstance. He had a natural desire to make it tally with Madame Münster's account of Clifford's disaffection; but his ingenuity, finding itself unequal to the task, resolved at last to ask help of the young man's candour. He waited till he saw him going away, and then he went out and overtook him in the grounds.

'I wish very much you would answer me a question,' Acton said. 'What were you doing, last night, at Madame Münster's?'

Clifford began to laugh and to blush, by no means like a young man with a romantic secret. 'What did she tell you?' he asked.

'That is exactly what I don't want to say.'

'Well, I want to tell you the same,' said Clifford; 'and unless I know it perhaps I can't.'

They had stopped in a garden path; Acton looked hard at his rosy young kinsman. 'She said she couldn't fancy what had got into you; you appeared to have taken a violent dislike to her.'

Clifford stared, looking a little alarmed. 'Oh, come,' he growled, 'you don't mean that!'

'And that when – for common civility's sake – you came occasionally to the house you left her alone and spent your time in Felix's studio, under pretext of looking at his sketches.'

'Oh, come!' growled Clifford, again.

'Did you ever know me to tell an untruth?'

'Yes, lots of them!' said Clifford, seeing an opening, out of the discussion, for his sarcastic powers. 'Well,' he presently added, 'I thought you were my father.'

'You knew some one was there?'

'We heard you coming in.'

Acton meditated. 'You had been with the Baroness, then?'

'I was in the parlour. We heard your step outside. I thought it was my father.'

'And on that,' asked Acton, 'you ran away?'

'She told me to go – to go out by the studio.'

Acton meditated more intensely; if there had been a chair at hand he would have sat down. 'Why should she wish you not to meet your father?'

'Well,' said Clifford, 'father doesn't like to see me there.'

Acton looked askance at his companion and forbore to make

any comment upon this assertion. 'Has he said so,' he asked, 'to the Baroness?'

'Well, I hope not,' said Clifford. 'He hasn't said so – in so many words – to me. But I know it worries him; and I want to stop worrying him. The Baroness knows it, and she wants me to stop, too.'

'To stop coming to see her?'

'I don't know about that; but to stop worrying father. Eugenia knows everything,' Clifford added, with an air of knowingness of his own.

'Ah,' said Acton, interrogatively, 'Eugenia knows everything?'

'She knew it was not father coming in.'

'Then why did you go?'

Clifford blushed and laughed afresh. 'Well, I was afraid it was. And besides, she told me to go, at any rate.'

'Did she think it was I?' Acton asked.

'She didn't say so.'

Again Robert Acton reflected. 'But you didn't go,' he presently said; 'you came back.'

'I couldn't get out of the studio,' Clifford rejoined. 'The door was locked, and Felix has nailed some planks across the lower half of the confounded windows to make the light come in from above. So they were no use. I waited there a good while, and then, suddenly, I felt ashamed. I didn't want to be hiding away from my own father. I couldn't stand it any longer. I bolted out, and when I found it was you I was a little flurried. But Eugenia carried it off, didn't she?' Clifford added, in the tone of a young humorist whose perception had not been permanently clouded by the sense of his own discomfort.

'Beautifully!' said Acton. 'Especially,' he continued, 'when one remembers that you were very imprudent and that she must have been a good deal annoyed.'

'Oh,' cried Clifford, with the indifference of a young man who feels that however he may have failed of felicity in behaviour he is extremely just in his impressions, 'Eugenia doesn't care for anything!'

Acton hesitated a moment. 'Thank you for telling me this,'

he said at last. And then, laying his hand on Clifford's shoulder, he added, 'Tell me one thing more: are you by chance a little in love with the Baroness?'

'No, sir!' said Clifford, almost shaking off his hand.

X

The first Sunday that followed Robert Acton's return from Newport witnessed a change in the brilliant weather that had long prevailed. The rain began to fall and the day was cold and dreary. Mr. Wentworth and his daughters put on overshoes and went to church, and Felix Young, without overshoes, went also, holding an umbrella over Gertrude. It is to be feared that, in the whole observance, this was the privilege he most highly valued. The Baroness remained at home; she was in neither a cheerful nor a devotional mood. She had, however, never been, during her residence in the United States, what is called a regular attendant at divine service; and on this particular Sunday morning of which I began with speaking she stood at the window of her little drawing-room, watching the long arm of a rose-tree that was attached to her piazza, but a portion of which had disengaged itself, sway to and fro, shake and gesticulate, against the dusky drizzle of the sky. Every now and then, in a gust of wind, the rose-tree scattered a shower of water-drops against the window-pane; it appeared to have a kind of human movement – a menacing, warning intention. The room was very cold; Madame Münster put on a shawl and walked about. Then she determined to have some fire; and summoning her ancient negress, the contrast of whose polished ebony and whose crimson turban had been at first a source of satisfaction to her, she made arrangements for the production of a crackling flame. This old woman's name was Azarina. The Baroness had begun by thinking that there would be a savoury wildness in her talk, and, for amusement, she had encouraged her to chatter. But Azarina was dry and prim; her conversation was anything but

African; she reminded Eugenia of the tiresome old ladies she met in society. She knew, however, how to make a fire; so that after she had laid the logs, Eugenia, who was terribly bored, found a quarter of an hour's entertainment in sitting and watching them blaze and sputter. She had thought it very likely Robert Acton would come and see her; she had not met him since that infelicitous evening. But the morning waned without his coming; several times she thought she heard his step on the piazza; but it was only a window-shutter shaking in a rain-gust. The Baroness, since the beginning of that episode in her career of which a slight sketch has been attempted in these pages, had had many moments of irritation. But to-day her irritation had a peculiar keenness; it appeared to feed upon itself. It urged her to do something; but it suggested no particularly profitable line of action. If she could have done something at the moment, on the spot, she would have stepped upon a European steamer and turned her back, with a kind of rapture, upon that profoundly mortifying failure, her visit to her American relations. It is not exactly apparent why she should have termed this enterprise a failure, inasmuch as she had been treated with the highest distinction for which allowance had been made in American institutions. Her irritation came, at bottom, from the sense, which, always present, had suddenly grown acute, that the social soil on this big, vague continent was somehow not adapted for growing those plants whose fragrance she especially inclined to inhale and by which she liked to see herself surrounded – a species of vegetation for which she carried a collection of seedlings, as we may say, in her pocket. She found her chief happiness in the sense of exerting a certain power and making a certain impression; and now she felt the annoyance of a rather wearied swimmer who, on nearing shore, to land, finds a smooth straight wall of rock when he had counted upon a clean firm beach. Her power, in the American air, seemed to have lost its prehensile attributes; the smooth wall of rock was insurmountable. 'Surely je n'en suis pas là,' she said to herself, 'that I let it make me uncomfortable that a Mr. Robert Acton shouldn't honour me with a visit!' Yet she was vexed that he had not come; and she was vexed at her vexation.

Her brother, at least, came in, stamping in the hall and shaking the wet from his coat. In a moment he entered the room, with a glow in his cheek and half-a-dozen rain-drops glistening on his moustache. 'Ah, you have a fire,' he said.

'Les beaux jours sont passés,' replied the Baroness.

'Never, never! They have only begun,' Felix declared, planting himself before the hearth. He turned his back to the fire, placed his hands behind him, extended his legs and looked away through the window with an expression of face which seemed to denote the perception of rose-colour even in the tints of a wet Sunday.

His sister, from her chair, looked up at him, watching him; and what she saw in his face was not grateful to her present mood. She was puzzled by many things, but her brother's disposition was a frequent source of wonder to her. I say frequent and not constant, for there were long periods during which she gave her attention to other problems. Sometimes she had said to herself that his happy temper, his eternal gaiety, was an affectation, a *pose*; but she was vaguely conscious that during the present summer he had been a highly successful comedian. They had never yet had an explanation; she had not known the need of one. Felix was presumably following the bent of his disinterested genius, and she felt that she had no advice to give him that he would understand. With this, there was always a certain element of comfort about Felix – the assurance that he would not interfere. He was very delicate, this pure-minded Felix; in effect, he was her brother, and Madame Münster felt that there was a great propriety, every way, in that. It is true that Felix was delicate; he was not fond of explanations with his sister; this was one of the very few things in the world about which he was uncomfortable. But now he was not thinking of anything uncomfortable.

'Dear brother,' said Eugenia at last, 'do stop making *les yeux doux* at the rain.'

'With pleasure. I will make them at you!' answered Felix.

'How much longer,' asked Eugenia, in a moment, 'do you propose to remain in this lovely spot?'

Felix stared. 'Do you want to go away – already?'

'"Already" is delicious. I am not so happy as you.'

Felix dropped into a chair, looking at the fire. 'The fact is I *am* happy,' he said in his light, clear tone.

'And do you propose to spend your life in making love to Gertrude Wentworth?'

'Yes!' said Felix, smiling sidewise at his sister.

The Baroness returned his glance, much more gravely; and then, 'Do you like her?' she asked.

'Don't you?' Felix demanded.

The Baroness was silent a moment. 'I will answer you in the words of the gentleman who was asked if he liked music: "Je ne la crains pas!"'

'She admires you immensely,' said Felix.

'I don't care for that. Other women should not admire one.'

'They should dislike you?'

Again Madame Münster hesitated. 'They should hate me! It's a measure of the time I have been losing here that they don't.'

'No time is lost in which one has been happy!' said Felix, with a bright sententiousness which may well have been a little irritating.

'And in which,' rejoined his sister, with a harsher laugh, 'one has secured the affections of a young lady with a fortune!'

Felix explained, very candidly and seriously. 'I have secured Gertrude's affection, but I am by no means sure that I have secured her fortune. That may come – or it may not.'

'Ah, well, it *may*! That's the great point.'

'It depends upon her father. He doesn't smile upon our union. You know he wants her to marry Mr. Brand.'

'I know nothing about it!' cried the Baroness. 'Please to put on a log.' Felix complied with her request and sat watching the quickening of the flame. Presently his sister added, 'And you propose to elope with mademoiselle?'

'By no means. I don't wish to do anything that's disagreeable to Mr. Wentworth. He has been far too kind to us.'

'But you must choose between pleasing yourself and pleasing him.'

'I want to please every one!' exclaimed Felix, joyously. 'I have a good conscience. I made up my mind at the outset that it was not my place to make love to Gertrude.'

'So, to simplify matters, she made love to you!'

Felix looked at his sister with sudden gravity. 'You say you are not afraid of her,' he said. 'But perhaps you ought to be – a little. She's a very clever person.'

'I begin to see it!' cried the Baroness. Her brother, making no rejoinder, leaned back in his chair, and there was a long silence. At last, with an altered accent, Madame Münster put another question. 'You expect, at any rate, to marry?'

'I shall be greatly disappointed if we don't.'

'A disappointment or two will do you good!' the Baroness declared. 'And, afterwards, do you mean to turn American?'

'It seems to me I am a very good American already. But we shall go to Europe. Gertrude wants extremely to see the world.'

'Ah, like me, when I came here!' said the Baroness, with a little laugh.

'No, not like you,' Felix rejoined, looking at his sister with a certain gentle seriousness. While he looked at her she rose from her chair, and he also got up. 'Gertrude is not at all like you,' he went on; 'but in her own way she is almost as clever.' He paused a moment; his soul was full of an agreeable feeling and of a lively disposition to express it. His sister, to his spiritual vision, was always like the lunar disc when only a part of it is lighted. The shadow on this bright surface seemed to him to expand and to contract; but whatever its proportions, he always appreciated the moonlight. He looked at the Baroness, and then he kissed her. 'I am very much in love with Gertrude,' he said. Eugenia turned away and walked about the room, and Felix continued. 'She is very interesting, and very different from what she seems. She has never had a chance. She is very brilliant. We will go to Europe and amuse ourselves.'

The Baroness had gone to the window, where she stood looking out. The day was drearier than ever; the rain was doggedly falling. 'Yes, to amuse yourselves,' she said at last, 'you had decidedly better go to Europe!' Then she turned round, looking at her brother. A chair stood near her; she leaned her hands upon the back of it. 'Don't you think it is very good of me,' she asked, 'to come all this way with you simply to see you properly married – if properly it is?'

'Oh, it will be properly!' cried Felix, with light eagerness.

The Baroness gave a little laugh. 'You are thinking only of yourself, and you don't answer my question. While you are amusing yourself – with the brilliant Gertrude – what shall I be doing?'

'Vous serez de la partie!' cried Felix.

'Thank you: I should spoil it.' The Baroness dropped her eyes for some moments. 'Do you propose, however, to leave me here?' she inquired.

Felix smiled at her. 'My dearest sister, where you are concerned I never propose. I execute your commands.'

'I believe,' said Eugenia, slowly, 'that you are the most heartless person living. Don't you see that I am in trouble?'

'I saw that you were not cheerful, and I gave you some good news.'

'Well, let me give you some news,' said the Baroness. 'You probably will not have discovered it for yourself. Robert Acton wants to marry me.'

'No, I had not discovered that. But I quite understand it. Why does it make you unhappy?'

'Because I can't decide.'

'Accept him, accept him!' cried Felix, joyously. 'He is the best fellow in the world.'

'He is immensely in love with me,' said the Baroness.

'And he has a large fortune. Permit me in turn to remind you of that.'

'Oh, I am perfectly aware of it,' said Eugenia. 'That's a great item in his favour. I am terribly candid.' And she left her place and came nearer her brother, looking at him hard. He was turning over several things; she was wondering in what manner he really understood her.

There were several ways of understanding her: there was what she said, and there was what she meant, and there was something, between the two, that was neither. It is probable that, in the last analysis, what she meant was that Felix should spare her the necessity of stating the case more exactly and should hold himself commissioned to assist her by all honourable means to marry the best fellow in the world. But in all this it was never discovered what Felix understood.

'Once you have your liberty, what are your objections?' he asked.

'Well, I don't particularly like him.'

'Oh, try a little.'

'I am trying now,' said Eugenia. 'I should succeed better if he didn't live here. I could never live here.'

'Make him go to Europe,' Felix suggested.

'Ah, there you speak of happiness based upon violent effort,' the Baroness rejoined. 'That is not what I am looking for. He would never live in Europe.'

'He would live anywhere, with you!' said Felix, gallantly.

His sister looked at him still, with a ray of penetration in her charming eyes; then she turned away again. 'You see, at all events,' she presently went on, 'that if it had been said of me that I had come over here to seek my fortune it would have to be added that I have found it!'

'Don't leave it lying!' urged Felix, with smiling solemnity.

'I am much obliged to you for your interest,' his sister declared, after a moment. 'But promise me one thing: *pas de zèle*! If Mr. Acton should ask you to plead his cause, excuse yourself.'

'I shall certainly have the excuse,' said Felix, 'that I have a cause of my own to plead.'

'If he should talk of me – favourably,' Eugenia continued, 'warn him against dangerous illusions. I detest importunities; I want to decide at my leisure, with my eyes open.'

'I shall be discreet,' said Felix, 'except to you. To you I will say, Accept him outright.'

She had advanced to the open door-way, and she stood looking at him. 'I will go and dress and think of it,' she said; and he heard her moving slowly to her apartments.

Late in the afternoon the rain stopped, and just afterwards there was a great flaming, flickering, trickling sunset. Felix sat in his painting-room and did some work; but at last, as the light, which had not been brilliant, began to fade, he laid down his brushes and came out to the little piazza of the cottage. Here he walked up and down for some time, looking at the splendid blaze of the western sky and saying, as he had often said before, that this was certainly the country of sunsets. There was something in these glorious deeps of fire that quickened his imagination; he always found images and promises in the western sky. He thought of a good many things – of roaming about the world with Gertrude Wentworth; he seemed to see their possible adventures, in a glowing frieze, between the cloud-bars; then of what Eugenia had just been telling him. He wished very much that Madame Münster would make a comfortable and honourable marriage. Presently, as the sunset expanded and deepened, the fancy took him of making a note of so magnificent a piece of colouring. He returned to his studio and fetched out a small panel, with his palette and brushes, and, placing the panel against a window-sill, he began to daub with great gusto. While he was so occupied he saw Mr. Brand, in the distance, slowly come down from Mr. Wentworth's house, nursing a large folded umbrella. He walked with a joyless, meditative tread, and his eyes were bent upon the ground. Felix poised his brush for a moment, watching him; then, by a sudden impulse, as he drew nearer, advanced to the garden-gate and signalled to him – the palette and bunch of brushes contributing to this effect.

Mr. Brand stopped and started; then he appeared to decide to accept Felix's invitation. He came out of Mr. Wentworth's gate and passed along the road; after which he entered the little garden of the cottage. Felix had gone back to his sunset; but he made his visitor welcome while he rapidly brushed it in.

'I wanted so much to speak to you that I thought I would call you,' he said, in the friendliest tone. 'All the more that you have been to see me so little. You have come to see my sister; I know that. But you haven't come to see me – the celebrated artist. Artists are very sensitive, you know; they notice those things.' And Felix turned round, smiling, with a brush in his mouth.

Mr. Brand stood there with a certain blank, candid majesty, pulling together the large flaps of his umbrella. 'Why should I come to see you?' he asked. 'I know nothing of Art.'

'It would sound very conceited, I suppose,' said Felix, 'if I were to say that it would be a good little chance for you to learn something. You would ask me why you should learn; and I should have no answer to that. I suppose a minister has no need for Art, eh?'

'He has need for good temper, sir,' said Mr. Brand, with decision.

Felix jumped up, with his palette on his thumb and a movement of the liveliest deprecation. 'That's because I keep you standing there while I splash my red paint! I beg a thousand pardons! You see what bad manners Art gives a man; and how right you are to let it alone. I didn't mean you should stand, either. The piazza, as you see, is ornamented with rustic chairs; though indeed I ought to warn you that they have nails in the wrong places. I was just making a note of that sunset. I never saw such a blaze of different reds. It looks as if the Celestial City were in flames, eh? If that were really the case I suppose it would be the business of you theologians to put out the fire. Fancy me – an ungodly artist – quietly sitting down to paint it!'

Mr. Brand had always credited Felix Young with a certain impudence, but it appeared to him that on this occasion his impudence was so great as to make a special explanation – or even an apology – necessary. And the impression, it must be added, was sufficiently natural. Felix had at all times a brilliant assurance of manner which was simply the vehicle of his good spirits and his good will; but at present he had a special design, and as he would have admitted that the design was audacious, so he was conscious of having summoned all the arts of conversation to his aid. But he was so far from desiring to offend his visitor that he was rapidly asking himself what personal compliment he could pay the young clergyman that would gratify him most. If he could think of it, he was prepared to pay it down. 'Have you been preaching one of your beautiful sermons to-day?' he suddenly asked, laying down his palette. This was not what Felix had been trying to think of, but it was a tolerable stop-gap.

Mr. Brand frowned – as much as a man can frown who has very fair, soft eyebrows, and, beneath them, very gentle, tranquil eyes. 'No, I have not preached any sermon to-day. Did you bring me over here for the purpose of making that inquiry?'

Felix saw that he was irritated, and he regretted it immensely; but he had no fear of not being, in the end, agreeable to Mr. Brand. He looked at him, smiling and laying his hand on his arm. 'No, no, not for that – not for that. I wanted to ask you something; I wanted to tell you something. I am sure it will interest you very much. Only – as it is something rather private – we had better come into my little studio. I have a western window; we can still see the sunset. *Andiamo*!'[1] And he gave a little pat to his companion's arm.

He led the way in; Mr. Brand stiffly and softly followed. The twilight had thickened in the little studio; but the wall opposite the western window was covered with a deep pink flush. There were a great many sketches and half-finished canvasses suspended in this rosy glow, and the corners of the room were vague and dusky. Felix begged Mr. Brand to sit down; then glancing round him, 'By Jove, how pretty it looks!' he cried. But Mr. Brand would not sit down; he went and leaned against the window; he wondered what Felix wanted of him. In the shadow, on the darker parts of the wall, he saw the gleam of three or four pictures that looked fantastic and surprising. They seemed to represent naked figures. Felix stood there, with his head a little bent and his eyes fixed upon his visitor, smiling intensely, pulling his moustache. Mr. Brand felt vaguely uneasy. 'It is very delicate – what I want to say,' Felix began. 'But I have been thinking of it for some time.'

'Please to say it as quickly as possible,' said Mr. Brand.

'It's because you are a clergyman, you know,' Felix went on. 'I don't think I should venture to say it to a common man.'

Mr. Brand was silent a moment. 'If it is a question of yielding to a weakness, of resenting an injury, I am afraid I am a very common man.'

'My dearest friend,' cried Felix, 'this is not an injury; it's a benefit – a great service! You will like it extremely. Only it's so delicate!' And, in the dim light, he continued to smile intensely. 'You know I take a great interest in my cousins – in Charlotte and Gertrude Wentworth. That's very evident from my having travelled some five thousand miles to see them.' Mr. Brand said nothing and Felix proceeded. 'Coming into their society as a perfect stranger I received of course a great many new impressions, and my impressions had a great freshness, a great keenness. Do you know what I mean?'

'I am not sure that I do; but I should like you to continue.'

'I think my impressions have always a good deal of freshness,' said Mr. Brand's entertainer; 'but on this occasion it was perhaps particularly natural that – coming in, as I say, from outside – I should be struck with things that passed unnoticed among yourselves. And then I had my sister to help me; and she is simply the most observant woman in the world.'

'I am not surprised,' said Mr. Brand, 'that in our little circle two intelligent persons should have found food for observation. I am sure that, of late, I have found it myself!'

'Ah, but I shall surprise you yet!' cried Felix, laughing. 'Both my sister and I took a great fancy to my cousin Charlotte.'

'Your cousin Charlotte?' repeated Mr. Brand.

'We fell in love with her from the first!'

'You fell in love with Charlotte?' Mr. Brand murmured.

'*Dame!*' exclaimed Felix, 'she's a very charming person; and Eugenia was especially smitten.' Mr. Brand stood staring, and he pursued, 'Affection, you know, opens one's eyes, and we noticed something. Charlotte is not happy! Charlotte is in love.' And Felix, drawing nearer, laid his hand again upon his companion's arm.

There was something akin to an acknowledgment of fascination in the way Mr. Brand looked at him; but the young clergyman retained as yet quite enough self-possession to be able to say, with a good deal of solemnity, 'She is not in love with you.'

Felix gave a light laugh, and rejoined with the alacrity of a maritime adventurer who feels a puff of wind in his sail. 'Ah, no; if she were in love with me I should know it! I am not so blind as you.'

'As I?'

'My dear sir, you are stone blind. Poor Charlotte is dead in love with *you*!'

Mr. Brand said nothing for a moment; he breathed a little heavily. 'Is that what you wanted to say to me?' he asked.

'I have wanted to say it these three weeks. Because of late she has been worse. I told you,' added Felix, 'it was very delicate.'

'Well, sir –' Mr. Brand began; 'well, sir –'

'I was sure you didn't know it,' Felix continued. 'But don't you see – as soon as I mention it – how everything is explained?' Mr. Brand answered nothing; he looked for a chair and softly sat down. Felix could see that he was blushing; he had looked straight at his host hitherto, but now he looked away. The foremost effect of what he had heard had been a sort of irritation of his modesty. 'Of course,' said Felix, 'I suggest nothing; it would be very presumptuous in me to advise you. But I think there is no doubt about the fact.'

Mr. Brand looked hard at the floor for some moments; he was oppressed with a mixture of sensations. Felix, standing there, was very sure that one of them was profound surprise. The innocent young man had been completely unsuspicious of poor Charlotte's hidden flame. This gave Felix great hope; he was sure that Mr. Brand would be flattered. Felix thought him very transparent, and indeed he was so; he could neither simulate nor dissimulate. 'I scarcely know what to make of this,' he said at last, without looking up; and Felix was struck with the fact that he offered no protest or contradiction. Evidently Felix had kindled a train of memories – a retrospective illumination. It was making, to Mr. Brand's astonished eyes, a very pretty blaze; his second emotion had been a gratification of vanity.

'Thank me for telling you,' Felix rejoined. 'It's a good thing to know.'

'I am not sure of that,' said Mr. Brand.

'Ah, don't let her languish!' Felix murmured, lightly and softly.

'You *do* advise me, then?' And Mr. Brand looked up.

'I congratulate you!' said Felix, smiling. He had thought at first his visitor was simply appealing; but he saw he was a little ironical.

'It is in your interest; you have interfered with me,' the young clergyman went on.

Felix still stood and smiled. The little room had grown darker, and the crimson glow had faded; but Mr. Brand could see the brilliant expression of his face. 'I won't pretend not to know what you mean,' said Felix at last. 'But I have not really interfered with you. Of what you had to lose – with another person – you have lost nothing. And think what you have gained!'

'It seems to me I am the proper judge, on each side,' Mr. Brand declared. He got up, holding the brim of his hat against his mouth and staring at Felix through the dusk.

'You have lost an illusion!' said Felix.

'What do you call an illusion?'

'The belief that you really know – that you have ever really known – Gertrude Wentworth. Depend upon that,' pursued Felix. 'I don't know her yet; but I have no illusions; I don't pretend to.'

Mr. Brand kept gazing, over his hat. 'She has always been a lucid, limpid nature,' he said, solemnly.

'She has always been a dormant nature. She was waiting for a touchstone. But now she is beginning to awaken.'

'Don't praise her to me!' said Mr. Brand, with a little quaver in his voice. 'If you have the advantage of me that is not generous.'

'My dear sir, I am melting with generosity!' exclaimed Felix. 'And I am not praising my cousin. I am simply attempting a scientific definition of her. She doesn't care for abstractions. Now I think the contrary is what you have always fancied – is the basis on which you have been building. She is extremely preoccupied with the concrete. I care for the concrete, too. But Gertrude is stronger than I; she whirls me along!'

Mr. Brand looked for a moment into the crown of his hat. 'It's a most interesting nature.'

'So it is,' said Felix. 'But it pulls – it pulls – like a runaway horse. Now I like the feeling of a runaway horse; and if I am thrown out of the vehicle it is no great matter. But if *you* should be thrown, Mr. Brand' – and Felix paused a moment – 'another person also would suffer from the accident.'

'What other person?'

'Charlotte Wentworth!'

Mr. Brand looked at Felix for a moment sidewise, mistrustfully; then his eyes slowly wandered over the ceiling. Felix was sure he was secretly struck with the romance of the situation. 'I think this is none of our business,' the young minister murmured.

'None of mine, perhaps; but surely yours!'

Mr. Brand lingered still, looking at the ceiling; there was evidently something he wanted to say. 'What do you mean by Miss Gertrude being strong?' he asked abruptly.

'Well,' said Felix meditatively, 'I mean that she has had a great deal of self-possession. She was waiting – for years; even when she seemed, perhaps, to be living in the present. She knew how to wait; she had a purpose. That's what I mean by her being strong.'

'But what do you mean by her purpose?'

'Well – the purpose to see the world!'

Mr. Brand eyed his strange informant askance again; but he said nothing. At last he turned away, as if to take leave. He seemed bewildered, however; for instead of going to the door he moved toward the opposite corner of the room. Felix stood and watched him for a moment – almost groping about in the dusk; then he led him to the door, with a tender, almost fraternal movement. 'Is that all you have to say?' asked Mr. Brand.

'Yes, it's all – but it will bear a good deal of thinking of.'

Felix went with him to the garden-gate, and watched him slowly walk away into the thickening twilight with a relaxed rigidity that tried to rectify itself. 'He is offended, excited, bewildered, perplexed – and enchanted!' Felix said to himself. 'That's a capital mixture.'

XI

Since that visit paid by the Baroness Münster to Mrs. Acton, of which some account was given at an earlier stage of this narrative, the intercourse between these two ladies had been neither frequent nor intimate. It was not that Mrs. Acton had failed to appreciate Madame Münster's charms; on the contrary, her perception of the graces of manner and conversation of her brilliant visitor had been only too acute. Mrs. Acton was, as they said in Boston, very 'intense', and her impressions were apt to be too many for her. The state of her health required the restriction of emotion; and this is why, receiving, as she sat in her eternal arm-chair, very few visitors, even of the soberest local type, she had been obliged to limit the number of her interviews with a lady whose costume and manner recalled to her imagination – Mrs. Acton's imagination was a marvel – all that she had ever read of the most stirring historical periods. But she had sent the Baroness a great many quaintly-worded messages and a great many nosegays from her garden and baskets of beautiful fruit. Felix had eaten the fruit, and the Baroness had arranged the flowers and returned the baskets and the messages. On the day that followed that rainy Sunday of which mention has been made, Eugenia determined to go and pay the beneficent invalid a *'visite d'adieux'*; so it was that, to herself, she qualified her enterprise. It may be noted that neither on the Sunday evening nor on the Monday morning had she received that expected visit from Robert Acton. To his own consciousness, evidently he was 'keeping away'; and as the Baroness, on her side, was keeping away from her uncle's, whither, for several days, Felix had been the unembarrassed bearer of apologies and regrets for absence, chance had not taken the cards from the hands of design. Mr. Wentworth and his daughters had respected Eugenia's seclusion; certain intervals of mysterious retirement appeared to them, vaguely, a natural part of the graceful, rhythmic movement of so remarkable a life. Gertrude especially held these periods in honour; she wondered what Madame Münster did at such times, but she would not have permitted herself to inquire too curiously.

The long rain had freshened the air, and twelve hours' brilliant sunshine had dried the roads; so that the Baroness, in the late afternoon, proposing to walk to Mrs. Acton's, exposed herself to no great discomfort. As with her charming undulating step she moved along the clean, grassy margin of the road, beneath the thickly-hanging boughs of the orchards, through the quiet of the hour and place and the rich maturity of the summer, she was even conscious of a sort of luxurious melancholy. The Baroness had the amiable weakness of attaching herself to places – even when she had begun with a little aversion; and now, with the prospect of departure, she felt tenderly toward this well-wooded corner of the Western world, where the sunsets were so beautiful and one's ambitions were so pure. Mrs. Acton was able to receive her; but on entering this lady's large, freshly-scented room the Baroness saw that she was looking very ill. She was wonderfully white and transparent, and, in her flowered arm-chair, she made no attempt to move. But she flushed a little – like a young girl, the Baroness thought – and she rested her clear, smiling eyes upon those of her visitor. Her voice was low and monotonous, like a voice that had never expressed any human passions.

'I have come to bid you good-bye,' said Eugenia. 'I shall soon be going away.'

'When are you going away?'

'Very soon – any day.'

'I am very sorry,' said Mrs. Acton. 'I hoped you would stay – always.'

'Always?' Eugenia demanded.

'Well, I mean a long time,' said Mrs. Acton, in her sweet,

feeble tone. 'They tell me you are so comfortable – that you
have got such a beautiful little house.'

Eugenia stared – that is, she smiled; she thought of her poor
little *chalet* and she wondered whether her hostess were jesting. 'Yes, my house is exquisite,' she said; 'though not to be
compared to yours.'

'And my son is so fond of going to see you,' Mrs. Acton
added. 'I am afraid my son will miss you.'

'Ah, dear madame,' said Eugenia, with a little laugh, 'I can't
stay in America for your son!'

'Don't you like America?'

The Baroness looked at the front of her dress. 'If I liked it –
that would not be staying for your son!'

Mrs. Acton gazed at her with her grave, tender eyes, as if she
had not quite understood. The Baroness at last found something
irritating in the sweet, soft stare of her hostess; and if one were
not bound to be merciful to great invalids she would almost
have taken the liberty of pronouncing her, mentally, a fool. 'I
am afraid, then, I shall never see you again,' said Mrs. Acton.
'You know I am dying.'

'Ah, dear madame,' murmured Eugenia.

'I want to leave my children cheerful and happy. My daughter
will probably marry her cousin.'

'Two such interesting young people,' said the Baroness,
vaguely. She was not thinking of Clifford Wentworth.

'I feel so tranquil about my end,' Mrs. Acton went on. 'It is
coming so easily, so surely.' And she paused, with her mild gaze
always on Eugenia's.

The Baroness hated to be reminded of death; but even in its
imminence, so far as Mrs. Acton was concerned, she preserved
her good manners. 'Ah, madame, you are too charming an
invalid,' she rejoined.

But the delicacy of this rejoinder was apparently lost upon
her hostess, who went on in her low, reasonable voice. 'I want
to leave my children bright and comfortable. You seem to me
all so happy here – just as you are. So I wish you could stay. It
would be so pleasant for Robert.'

Eugenia wondered what she meant by its being pleasant for

Robert; but she felt that she would never know what such a woman as that meant. She got up; she was afraid Mrs. Acton would tell her again that she was dying. 'Good-bye, dear madame,' she said. 'I must remember that your strength is precious.'

Mrs. Acton took her hand and held it a moment. 'Well, you *have* been happy here, haven't you? And you like us all, don't you? I wish you would stay,' she added, 'in your beautiful little house.'

She had told Eugenia that her waiting-woman would be in the hall, to show her down-stairs; but the large landing outside her door was empty, and Eugenia stood there looking about. She felt irritated; the dying lady had not '*la main heureuse*'. She passed slowly down-stairs, still looking about. The broad staircase made a great bend, and in the angle was a high window, looking westward, with a deep bench, covered with a row of flowering plants in curious old pots of blue china-ware. The yellow afternoon light came in through the flowers and flickered a little on the white wainscots. Eugenia paused a moment; the house was perfectly still, save for the ticking, somewhere, of a great clock. The lower hall stretched away at the foot of the stairs, half covered over with a large Oriental rug. Eugenia lingered a little, noticing a great many things. 'Comme c'est bien!' she said to herself; such a large, solid, irreproachable basis of existence the place seemed to her to indicate. And then she reflected that Mrs. Acton was soon to withdraw from it. The reflection accompanied her the rest of the way down-stairs, where she paused again, making more observations. The hall was extremely broad, and on either side of the front door was a wide, deeply-set window, which threw the shadows of everything back into the house. There were high-backed chairs along the wall and big Eastern vases upon tables, and, on either side, a large cabinet with a glass front and little curiosities within, dimly gleaming. The doors were open – into the darkened parlour, the library, the dining-room. All these rooms seemed empty. Eugenia passed along, and stopped a moment on the threshold of each. 'Comme c'est bien!' she murmured again; she had thought of just such a house as this when she decided to come to America. She opened the front door for herself – her light tread had summoned none of the servants – and on the threshold she gave a last look. Outside, she was still in the humour for curious contemplation; so instead of going directly down the little drive, to the gate, she wandered away towards the garden, which lay to the right of the house. She had not gone many yards over the grass before she paused quickly; she perceived a gentleman stretched upon the level verdure, beneath a tree. He had not heard her coming, and he lay motionless, flat on his back, with his hands clasped under his head, staring up at the sky; so that the Baroness was able to reflect, at her leisure, upon the question of his identity. It was that of a person who had lately been much in her thoughts; but her first impulse, nevertheless, was to turn away; the last thing she desired was to have the air of coming in quest of Robert Acton. The gentleman on the grass, however, gave her no time to decide; he could not long remain unconscious of so agreeable a presence. He rolled back his eyes, stared, gave an exclamation, and then jumped up. He stood an instant, looking at her.

'Excuse my ridiculous position,' he said.

'I have just now no sense of the ridiculous. But, in case you have, don't imagine I came to see you.'

'Take care,' rejoined Acton, 'how you put it into my head! I was thinking of you.'

'The occupation of extreme leisure!' said the Baroness. 'To think of a woman when you are in that position is no compliment.'

'I didn't say I was thinking well!' Acton affirmed, smiling.

She looked at him, and then she turned away.

'Though I didn't come to see you,' she said, 'remember at least that I am within your gates.'

'I am delighted – I am honoured! Won't you come into the house?'

'I have just come out of it. I have been calling upon your mother. I have been bidding her farewell.'

'Farewell?' Acton demanded.

'I am going away,' said the Baroness. And she turned away again, as if to illustrate her meaning.

'When are you going?' asked Acton, standing a moment in his place. But the Baroness made no answer, and he followed her.

'I came this way to look at your garden,' she said, walking back to the gate, over the grass. 'But I must go.'

'Let me at least go with you.' He went with her, and they said nothing till they reached the gate. It was open, and they looked down the road which was darkened over with long bosky shadows. 'Must you go straight home?' Acton asked.

But she made no answer. She said, after a moment, 'Why have you not been to see me?' He said nothing, and then she went on, 'Why don't you answer me?'

'I am trying to invent an answer,' Acton confessed.

'Have you none ready?'

'None that I can tell you,' he said. 'But let me walk with you now.'

'You may do as you like.'

She moved slowly along the road, and Acton went with her. Presently he said, 'If I had done as I liked I would have come to see you several times.'

'Is that invented?' asked Eugenia.

'No, that is natural. I stayed away because –'

'Ah, here comes the reason, then!'

'Because I wanted to think about you.'

'Because you wanted to lie down!' said the Baroness. 'I have seen you lie down – almost – in my drawing-room.'

Acton stopped in the road, with a movement which seemed to beg her to linger a little. She paused, and he looked at her awhile; he thought her very charming. 'You are jesting,' he said; 'but if you are really going away it is very serious.'

'If I stay,' and she gave a little laugh, 'it is more serious still!'

'When shall you go?'

'As soon as possible.'

'And why?'

'Why should I stay?'

'Because we all admire you so.'

'That is not a reason. I am admired also in Europe.' And she began to walk homeward again.

'What could I say to keep you?' asked Acton. He wanted to keep her, and it was a fact that he had been thinking of her for a week. He was in love with her now; he was conscious of that, or he thought he was; and the only question with him was whether he could trust her.

'What you can say to keep me?' she repeated. 'As I want very much to go it is not in my interest to tell you. Besides, I can't imagine.'

He went on with her in silence; he was much more affected by what she had told him than appeared. Ever since that evening of his return from Newport her image had had a terrible power to trouble him. What Clifford Wentworth had told him – that had affected him, too, in an adverse sense; but it had not liberated him from the discomfort of a charm of which his intelligence was impatient. 'She is not honest, she is not honest,' he kept murmuring to himself. That is what he had been saying to the summer sky, ten minutes before. Unfortunately, he was unable to say it finally, definitively; and now that he was near her it seemed to matter wonderfully little. 'She is a woman who will lie,' he had said to himself. Now, as he went along, he reminded himself of this observation; but it failed to frighten him as it had done before. He almost wished he could make her lie and then convict her of it, so that he might see how he should like that. He kept thinking of this as he walked by her side, while she moved forward with her light, graceful dignity. He had sat with her before; he had driven with her; but he had never walked with her.

'By Jove, how *comme il faut* she is!' he said, as he observed her sidewise. When they reached the cottage in the orchard she passed into the gate without asking him to follow; but she turned round, as he stood there, to bid him good-night.

'I asked you a question the other night which you never answered,' he said. 'Have you sent off that document – liberating yourself?'

She hesitated for a single moment – very naturally. Then, 'Yes,' she said, simply.

He turned away; he wondered whether that would do for his lie. But he saw her again that evening, for the Baroness reappeared at her uncle's. He had little talk with her, however; two gentlemen had driven out from Boston, in a buggy, to call upon Mr. Wentworth and his daughters, and Madame Münster was an object of absorbing interest to both of the visitors. One of them, indeed, said nothing to her; he only sat and watched with intense gravity, and leaned forward solemnly, presenting his ear (a very large one), as if he were deaf, whenever she dropped an observation. He had evidently been impressed with the idea of her misfortunes and reverses: he never smiled. His companion adopted a lighter, easier style; sat as near as possible to Madame Münster; attempted to draw her out, and proposed every few moments a new topic of conversation. Eugenia was less vividly responsive than usual and had less to say than, from her brilliant reputation, her interlocutor expected, upon the relative merits of European and American institutions; but she was inaccessible to Robert Acton, who roamed about the piazza with his hands in his pockets, listening for the grating sound of the buggy from Boston, as it should be brought round to the side-door. But he listened in vain, and at last he lost patience. His sister came to him and begged him to take her home, and he presently went off with her. Eugenia observed him leaving the house with Lizzie; in her present mood the fact seemed a contribution to her irritated conviction that he had several precious qualities. 'Even that *mal-élevée* little girl,' she reflected, 'makes him do what she wishes.'

She had been sitting just within one of the long windows that opened upon the piazza; but very soon after Acton had gone away she got up abruptly, just when the talkative gentleman from Boston was asking her what she thought of the 'moral tone' of that city. On the piazza she encountered Clifford Wentworth, coming round from the other side of the house. She stopped him; she told him she wished to speak to him.

'Why didn't you go home with your cousin?' she asked.

Clifford stared. 'Why, Robert has taken her,' he said.

'Exactly so. But you don't usually leave that to him.'

'Oh,' said Clifford, 'I want to see those fellows start off. They don't know how to drive.'

'It is not, then, that you have quarrelled with your cousin?'

Clifford reflected a moment, and then with a simplicity which had, for the Baroness, a singularly baffling quality, 'Oh, no; we have made up!' he said.

She looked at him for some moments; but Clifford had begun to be afraid of the Baroness's looks, and he endeavoured, now, to shift himself out of their range. 'Why do you never come to see me any more?' she asked. 'Have I displeased you?'

'Displeased me? Well, I guess not!' said Clifford, with a laugh.

'Why haven't you come, then?'

'Well, because I am afraid of getting shut up in that back room.'

Eugenia kept looking at him. 'I should think you would like that.'

'Like it!' cried Clifford.

'I should, if I were a young man calling upon a charming woman.'

'A charming woman isn't much use to me when I am shut up in that back room!'

'I am afraid I am not of much use to you anywhere!' said Madame Münster. 'And yet you know how I have offered to be.'

'Well,' observed Clifford, by way of response, 'there comes the buggy.'

'Never mind the buggy. Do you know I am going away?'

'Do you mean now?'

'I mean in a few days. I leave this place.'

'You are going back to Europe?'

'To Europe, where you are to come and see me.'

'Oh, yes, I'll come out there,' said Clifford.

'But before that,' Eugenia declared, 'you must come and see me here.'

'Well, I shall keep clear of that back room!' rejoined her simple young kinsman.

The Baroness was silent a moment. 'Yes, you must come frankly – boldly. That will be very much better. I see that now.'

'I see it!' said Clifford. And then, in an instant, 'What's the matter with that buggy?' His practised ear had apparently detected an unnatural creak in the wheels of the light vehicle which had been brought to the portico, and he hurried away to investigate so grave an anomaly.

The Baroness walked homeward, alone, in the starlight, asking herself a question. Was she to have gained nothing – was she to have gained nothing?

Gertrude Wentworth had held a silent place in the little circle gathered about the two gentlemen from Boston. She was not interested in the visitors; she was watching Madame Münster, as she constantly watched her. She knew that Eugenia also was not interested – that she was bored; and Gertrude was absorbed in study of the problem how, in spite of her indifference and her absent attention, she managed to have such a charming manner. That was the manner Gertrude would have liked to have; she determined to cultivate it, and she wished that – to give her the charm – she might in future very often be bored. While she was engaged in these researches, Felix Young was looking for Charlotte, to whom he had something to say. For some time, now, he had had something to say to Charlotte, and this evening his sense of the propriety of holding some special conversation with her had reached the motive-point – resolved itself into acute and delightful desire. He wandered through the empty rooms on the large ground-floor of the house, and found her at last in a small apartment denominated, for reasons not immediately apparent, Mr. Wentworth's 'office': an extremely neat and well-dusted room, with an array of law-books, in time-darkened sheep-skin, on one of the walls; a large map of the United States on the other, flanked on either side by an old steel engraving of one of Raphael's[1] Madonnas; and on the third several glass cases containing specimens of butterflies and beetles. Charlotte was sitting by a lamp, embroidering a slipper. Felix did not ask for whom the slipper was destined; he saw it was very large.

He moved a chair toward her and sat down, smiling as usual, but, at first, not speaking. She watched him, with her needle poised, and with a certain shy, fluttered look which she always wore when he approached her. There was something in Felix's manner that quickened her modesty, her self-consciousness; if absolute choice had been given her she would have preferred never to find herself alone with him; and in fact, though she thought him a most brilliant, distinguished, and well-meaning person, she had exercised a much larger amount of tremulous tact than he had ever suspected, to circumvent the accident of *tête-à-tête*. Poor Charlotte could have given no account of the matter that would not have seemed unjust both to herself and to her foreign kinsman; she could only have said – or rather, she would never have said it – that she did not like so much gentleman's society at once. She was not reassured, accordingly, when he began, emphasizing his words with a kind of admiring radiance, 'My dear cousin, I am enchanted at finding you alone.'

'I am very often alone,' Charlotte observed. Then she quickly added, 'I don't mean I am lonely!'

'So clever a woman as you is never lonely,' said Felix. 'You have company in your beautiful work.' And he glanced at the big slipper.

'I like to work,' declared Charlotte, simply.

'So do I!' said her companion. 'And I like to idle too. But it is not to idle that I have come in search of you. I want to tell you something very particular.'

'Well,' murmured Charlotte; 'of course, if you must –'

'My dear cousin,' said Felix, 'it's nothing that a young lady may not listen to. At least I suppose it isn't. But *voyons*; you shall judge. I am terribly in love.'

'Well, Felix,' began Miss Wentworth, gravely. But her very gravity appeared to check the development of her phrase.

'I am in love with your sister; but in love, Charlotte – in love!' the young man pursued. Charlotte had laid her work in her lap; her hands were tightly folded on top of it; she was staring at the carpet. 'In short, I'm in love, dear lady,' said Felix. 'Now I want you to help me.'

'To help you?' asked Charlotte, with a tremor.

'I don't mean with Gertrude; she and I have a perfect understanding; and oh, how well she understands one! I mean with your father and with the world in general, including Mr. Brand.'

'Poor Mr. Brand!' said Charlotte, slowly, but with a simplicity which made it evident to Felix that the young minister had not repeated to Miss Wentworth the talk that had lately occurred between them.

'Ah, now, don't say "poor" Mr. Brand! I don't pity Mr. Brand at all. But I pity your father a little, and I don't want to displease him. Therefore, you see, I want you to plead for me. You don't think me very shabby, eh?'

'Shabby?' exclaimed Charlotte softly, for whom Felix represented the most polished and iridescent qualities of mankind.

'I don't mean in my appearance,' rejoined Felix, laughing; for Charlotte was looking at his boots. 'I mean in my conduct. You don't think it's an abuse of hospitality?'

'To – to care for Gertrude?' asked Charlotte.

'To have really expressed one's self. Because I *have* expressed myself, Charlotte; I must tell you the whole truth – I have! Of course I want to marry her – and here is the difficulty. I held off as long as I could; but she is such a terribly fascinating person! She's a strange creature, Charlotte; I don't believe you really know her.' Charlotte took up her tapestry again, and again she laid it down. 'I know your father has had higher views,' Felix continued; 'and I think you have shared them. You have wanted to marry her to Mr. Brand.'

'Oh, no,' said Charlotte, very earnestly. 'Mr. Brand has always admired her. But we did not want anything of that kind.'

Felix stared. 'Surely, marriage was what you proposed.'

'Yes; but we didn't wish to force her.'

'A la bonne heure! That's very unsafe you know. With these arranged marriages there is often the deuce to pay.'

'Oh, Felix,' said Charlotte, 'we didn't want to "arrange".'

'I am delighted to hear that. Because in such cases – even when the woman is a thoroughly good creature – she can't help looking for a compensation. A charming fellow comes along – and *voilà*!' Charlotte sat mutely staring at the floor, and Felix presently added, 'Do go on with your slipper, I like to see you work.'

Charlotte took up her variegated canvas, and began to draw vague blue stitches in a big round rose. 'If Gertrude is so – so strange,' she said, 'why do you want to marry her?'

'Ah, that's it, dear Charlotte! I like strange women; I always have liked them. Ask Eugenia! And Gertrude is wonderful; she says the most beautiful things!'

Charlotte looked at him, almost for the first time, as if her meaning required to be severely pointed. 'You have a great influence over her.'

'Yes – and no!' said Felix. 'I had at first, I think; but now it is six of one and half-a-dozen of the other; it is reciprocal. She affects me strongly – for she is so strong. I don't believe you know her; it's a beautiful nature.'

'Oh, yes, Felix; I have always thought Gertrude's nature beautiful.'

'Well, if you think so now,' cried the young man, 'wait and see! She's a folded flower. Let me pluck her from the parent tree and you will see her expand. I'm sure you will enjoy it.'

'I don't understand you,' murmured Charlotte. 'I *can't*, Felix.'

'Well, you can understand this – that I beg you to say a good word for me to your father. He regards me, I naturally believe, as a very light fellow, a Bohemian, an irregular character. Tell him I am not all this; if I ever was, I have forgotten it. I am fond of pleasure – yes; but of innocent pleasure. Pain is all one; but in pleasure, you know, there are tremendous distinctions. Say to him that Gertrude is a folded flower and that I am a serious man!'

Charlotte got up from her chair slowly rolling up her work. 'We know you are very kind to every one, Felix,' she said. 'But we are extremely sorry for Mr. Brand.'

'Of course you are – you especially! Because,' added Felix hastily, 'you are a woman. But I don't pity him. It ought to be enough for any man that you take an interest in him.'

'It is not enough for Mr. Brand,' said Charlotte, simply. And she stood there a moment, as if waiting conscientiously for anything more that Felix might have to say.

'Mr. Brand is not so keen about his marriage as he was,' he presently said. 'He is afraid of your sister. He begins to think she is wicked.'

Charlotte looked at him now with beautiful, appealing eyes – eyes into which he saw the tears rising. 'Oh, Felix, Felix,' she cried, 'what have you done to her?'

'I think she was asleep; I have waked her up!'

But Charlotte, apparently, was really crying, she walked straight out of the room. And Felix, standing there and meditating, had the apparent brutality to take satisfaction in her tears.

Late that night Gertrude, silent and serious, came to him in the garden; it was a kind of appointment. Gertrude seemed to like appointments. She plucked a handful of heliotrope and stuck it into the front of her dress, but she said nothing. They walked together along one of the paths, and Felix looked at the great, square, hospitable house, massing itself vaguely in the starlight, with all its windows darkened.

'I have a little of a bad conscience,' he said. 'I oughtn't to meet you this way till I have got your father's consent.'

Gertrude looked at him for some time. 'I don't understand you.'

'You very often say that,' he said. 'Considering how little we understand each other, it is a wonder how well we get on!'

'We have done nothing but meet since you came here – but meet alone. The first time I ever saw you we were alone,' Gertrude went on. 'What is the difference now? Is it because it is at night?'

'The difference, Gertrude,' said Felix, stopping in the path, 'the difference is that I love you more – more than before!' And then they stood there, talking, in the warm stillness and in front of the closed dark house. 'I have been talking to Charlotte – been trying to bespeak her interest with your father. She has a kind of sublime perversity; was ever a woman so bent upon cutting off her own head?'

'You are too careful,' said Gertrude; 'you are too diplomatic.'

'Well,' cried the young man, 'I didn't come here to make any one unhappy!'

Gertrude looked round her awhile in the odorous darkness. 'I will do anything you please,' she said.

'For instance?' asked Felix, smiling.

'I will go away. I will do anything you please.'

Felix looked at her in solemn admiration. 'Yes, we will go away,' he said. 'But we will make peace first.'

Gertrude looked about her again, and then she broke out,

passionately, 'Why do they try to make one feel guilty? Why do they make it so difficult? Why can't they understand?'

'I will make them understand!' said Felix. He drew her hand into his arm, and they wandered about in the garden, talking, for an hour.

XII

Felix allowed Charlotte time to plead his cause; and then, on the third day, he sought an interview with his uncle. It was in the morning; Mr. Wentworth was in his office; and, on going in, Felix found that Charlotte was at that moment in conference with her father. She had, in fact, been constantly near him since her interview with Felix; she had made up her mind that it was her duty to repeat very literally her cousin's passionate plea. She had accordingly followed Mr. Wentworth about like a shadow, in order to find him at hand when she should have mustered sufficient composure to speak. For poor Charlotte, in this matter, naturally lacked composure; especially when she meditated upon some of Felix's intimations. It was not cheerful work, at the best, to keep giving small hammer-taps to the coffin in which one had laid away, for burial, the poor little unacknowledged offspring of one's own misbehaving heart; and the occupation was not rendered more agreeable by the fact that the ghost of one's stifled dream had been summoned from the shades by the strange, bold words of a talkative young foreigner. What had Felix meant by saying that Mr. Brand was not so keen? To herself her sister's justly depressed suitor had shown no sign of faltering. Charlotte trembled all over when she allowed herself to believe for an instant now and then that, privately, Mr. Brand might have faltered; and as it seemed to give more force to Felix's words to repeat them to her father, she was waiting until she should have taught herself to be very calm. But she had now begun to tell Mr. Wentworth that she was extremely anxious. She was proceeding to develop this idea, to enumerate the objects of her anxiety, when Felix came in.

Mr. Wentworth sat there, with his legs crossed, lifting his dry, pure countenance from the Boston 'Advertiser'.[1] Felix entered smiling, as if he had something particular to say, and his uncle looked at him as if he both expected and deprecated this event. Felix vividly expressing himself had come to be a formidable figure to his uncle, who had not yet arrived at definite views as to a proper tone. For the first time in his life, as I have said, Mr. Wentworth shirked a responsibility; he earnestly desired that it might not be laid upon him to determine how his nephew's lighter propositions should be treated. He lived under an apprehension that Felix might yet beguile him into assent to doubtful inductions, and his conscience instructed him that the best form of vigilance was the avoidance of discussion. He hoped that the pleasant episode of his nephew's visit would pass away without a further lapse of consistency.

Felix looked at Charlotte with an air of understanding, and then at Mr. Wentworth, and then at Charlotte again. Mr. Wentworth bent his refined eyebrows upon his nephew and stroked down the first page of the 'Advertiser'. 'I ought to have brought a bouquet,' said Felix, laughing. 'In France they always do.'

'We are not in France,' observed Mr. Wentworth, gravely, while Charlotte earnestly gazed at him.

'No, luckily, we are not in France, where I am afraid I should have a harder time of it. My dear Charlotte, have you rendered me that delightful service?' And Felix bent toward her as if some one had been presenting him.

Charlotte looked at him with almost frightened eyes; and Mr. Wentworth thought this might be the beginning of a discussion. 'What is the bouquet for?' he inquired, by way of turning it off.

Felix gazed at him, smiling. 'Pour la demande!' And then, drawing up a chair, he seated himself, hat in hand, with a kind of conscious solemnity.

Presently he turned to Charlotte again. 'My good Charlotte, my admirable Charlotte,' he murmured, 'you have not played me false – you have not sided against me?'

Charlotte got up, trembling extremely, though imperceptibly. 'You must speak to my father yourself,' she said. 'I think you are clever enough.'

But Felix, rising too, begged her to remain. 'I can speak better to an audience!' he declared.

'I hope it is nothing disagreeable,' said Mr. Wentworth.

'It's something delightful, for me!' And Felix, laying down his hat, clasped his hands a little between his knees. 'My dear uncle,' he said, 'I desire, very earnestly, to marry your daughter Gertrude.' Charlotte sank slowly into her chair again, and Mr. Wentworth sat staring, with a light in his face that might have been flashed back from an iceberg. He stared and stared; he said nothing. Felix fell back, with his hands still clasped. 'Ah – you don't like it. I was afraid!' He blushed deeply, and Charlotte noticed it – remarking to herself that it was the first time she had ever seen him blush. She began to blush herself and to reflect that he might be much in love.

'This is very abrupt,' said Mr. Wentworth, at last.

'Have you never suspected it, dear uncle?' Felix inquired. 'Well, that proves how discreet I have been. Yes, I thought you wouldn't like it.'

'It is very serious, Felix,' said Mr. Wentworth.

'You think it's an abuse of hospitality!' exclaimed Felix, smiling again.

'Of hospitality? – an abuse?' his uncle repeated very slowly.

'That is what Felix said to me,' said Charlotte, conscientiously.

'Of course you think so; don't defend yourself!' Felix pursued. 'It *is* an abuse, obviously; the most I can claim is that it is perhaps a pardonable one. I simply fell head over heels in love; one can hardly help that. Though you are Gertrude's progenitor I don't believe you know how attractive she is. Dear uncle, she contains the elements of a singularly – I may say a strangely – charming woman!'

'She has always been to me an object of extreme concern,' said Mr. Wentworth. 'We have always desired her happiness.'

'Well, here it is!' Felix declared. 'I will make her happy. She believes it, too. Now hadn't you noticed that?'

'I had noticed that she was much changed,' Mr. Wentworth declared, in a tone whose unexpressive, unimpassioned quality appeared to Felix to reveal a profundity of opposition. 'It may be that she is only becoming what you call a charming woman.'

'Gertrude, at heart, is so earnest, so true,' said Charlotte, very softly, fastening her eyes upon her father.

'I delight to hear you praise her!' cried Felix.

'She has a very peculiar temperament,' said Mr. Wentworth.

'Eh, even that is praise!' Felix rejoined. 'I know I am not the man you might have looked for. I have no position and no fortune; I can give Gertrude no place in the world. A place in the world – that's what she ought to have; that would bring her out.'

'A place to do her duty!' remarked Mr. Wentworth.

'Ah, how charmingly she does it – her duty!' Felix exclaimed, with a radiant face. 'What an exquisite conception she has of it! But she comes honestly by that, dear uncle.' Mr. Wentworth and Charlotte both looked at him as if they were watching a greyhound doubling. 'Of course with me she will hide her light under a bushel,' he continued; 'I being the bushel! Now I know you like me – you have certainly proved it. But you think I am frivolous and penniless and shabby! Granted – granted – a thousand times granted. I have been a loose fish – a fiddler, a painter, an actor. But there is this to be said: In the first place, I fancy you exaggerate; you lend me qualities I haven't had. I have been a Bohemian – yes; but in Bohemia I always passed for a gentleman. I wish you could see some of my old *camarades* – they would tell you! It was the liberty I liked, but not the opportunities! My sins were all peccadilloes; I always respected my neighbour's property – my neighbour's wife. Do you see, dear uncle?' Mr. Wentworth ought to have seen; his cold blue eyes were intently fixed. 'And then, *c'est fini*! It's all over. Je me range. I have settled down to a jogtrot. I find I can earn my living – a very fair one – by going about the world and painting bad portraits. It's not a glorious profession, but it is a perfectly respectable one. You won't deny that, eh? Going about the world, I say? I must not deny that, for that I am afraid I shall always do – in quest of agreeable sitters. When I say agreeable, I mean susceptible of delicate flattery and prompt of payment. Gertrude declares she is willing to share my wanderings and help to pose my models. She even thinks it will be charming; and that brings me to my third point. Gertrude likes me. Encourage her a little and she will tell you so.'

Felix's tongue obviously moved much faster than the imagination of his auditors; his eloquence, like the rocking of a boat in a deep, smooth lake, made long eddies of silence. And he seemed to be pleading and chattering still, with his brightly eager smile, his uplifted eyebrows, his expressive mouth, after he had ceased speaking, and while, with his glance quickly turning from the father to the daughter, he sat waiting for the effect of his appeal. 'It is not your want of means,' said Mr. Wentworth, after a period of severe reticence.

'Now it's delightful of you to say that! Only don't say it's my want of character. Because I have a character – I assure you I have; a small one, a little slip of a thing, but still something tangible.'

'Ought you not to tell Felix that it is Mr. Brand, father?' Charlotte asked, with infinite mildness.

'It is not only Mr. Brand,' Mr. Wentworth solemnly declared. And he looked at his knee for a long time. 'It is difficult to explain,' he said. He wished, evidently, to be very just. 'It rests on moral grounds, as Mr. Brand says. It is the question whether it is the best thing for Gertrude.'

'What is better – what is better, dear uncle?' Felix rejoined urgently, rising in his urgency and standing before Mr. Wentworth. His uncle had been looking at his knee; but when Felix moved he transferred his gaze to the handle of the door which faced him. 'It is usually a fairly good thing for a girl to marry the man she loves!' cried Felix.

While he spoke, Mr. Wentworth saw the handle of the door begin to turn; the door opened and remained slightly ajar, until Felix had delivered himself of the cheerful axiom just quoted. Then it opened altogether and Gertrude stood there. She looked excited; there was a spark in her sweet, dull eyes. She came in slowly, but with an air of resolution, and, closing the door softly, looked round at the three persons present. Felix went to her with tender gallantry, holding out his hand, and Charlotte made a place for her on the sofa. But Gertrude put her hands behind her and made no motion to sit down.

'We are talking of you!' said Felix.

'I know it,' she answered. 'That's why I came.' And she

fastened her eyes on her father, who returned her gaze very fixedly. In his own cold blue eyes there was a kind of pleading, reasoning light.

'It is better you should be present,' said Mr. Wentworth. 'We are discussing your future.'

'Why discuss it?' asked Gertrude. 'Leave it to me.'

'That is, to me!' cried Felix.

'I leave it, in the last resort, to a greater wisdom than ours,' said the old man.

Felix rubbed his forehead gently. 'But *en attendant* the last resort, your father lacks confidence,' he said to Gertrude.

'Haven't you confidence in Felix?' Gertrude was frowning; there was something about her that her father and Charlotte had never seen. Charlotte got up and came to her, as if to put her arm round her; but suddenly, she seemed afraid to touch her.

Mr. Wentworth, however, was not afraid. 'I have had more confidence in Felix than in you,' he said.

'Yes, you have never had confidence in me – never, never! I don't know why.'

'Oh sister, sister!' murmured Charlotte.

'You have always needed advice,' Mr. Wentworth declared. 'You have had a difficult temperament.'

'Why do you call it difficult? It might have been easy, if you had allowed it. You wouldn't let me be natural. I don't know what you wanted to make of me. Mr. Brand was the worst.'

Charlotte at last took hold of her sister. She laid her two hands upon Gertrude's arm. 'He cares so much for you,' she almost whispered.

Gertrude looked at her intently an instant; then kissed her. 'No, he does not,' she said.

'I have never seen you so passionate,' observed Mr. Wentworth, with an air of indignation mitigated by high principles.

'I am sorry if I offend you,' said Gertrude.

'You offend me, but I don't think you are sorry.'

'Yes, father, she is sorry,' said Charlotte.

'I would even go further, dear uncle,' Felix interposed. 'I would question whether she really offends you. How can she offend you?'

To this Mr. Wentworth made no immediate answer. Then, in a moment, 'She has not profited as we hoped.'

'Profited? Ah *voilà*!' Felix exclaimed.

Gertrude was very pale; she stood looking down. 'I have told Felix I would go away with him,' she presently said.

'Ah, you have said some admirable things!' cried the young man.

'Go away, sister?' asked Charlotte.

'Away – away; to some strange country.'

'That is to frighten you,' said Felix, smiling at Charlotte.

'To – what do you call it?' asked Gertrude, turning an instant to Felix. 'To Bohemia.'

'Do you propose to dispense with preliminaries?' asked Mr. Wentworth, getting up.

'Dear uncle, *vous plaisantez*!' cried Felix. 'It seems to me that these are preliminaries.'

Gertrude turned to her father. 'I *have* profited,' she said. 'You wanted to form my character. Well, my character is formed – for my age. I know what I want; I have chosen. I am determined to marry this gentleman.'

'You had better consent, sir,' said Felix very gently.

'Yes, sir, you had better consent,' added a very different voice.

Charlotte gave a little jump, and the others turned to the direction from which it had come. It was the voice of Mr. Brand, who had stepped through the long window which stood open to the piazza. He stood patting his forehead with his pocket-handkerchief; he was very much flushed; his face wore a singular expression.

'Yes, sir, you had better consent,' Mr. Brand repeated, coming forward. 'I know what Miss Gertrude means.'

'My dear friend!' murmured Felix, laying his hand caressingly on the young minister's arm.

Mr. Brand looked at him; then at Mr. Wentworth; lastly at Gertrude. He did not look at Charlotte. But Charlotte's earnest eyes were fastened to his own countenance; they were asking an immense question of it. The answer to this question could not come all at once; but some of the elements of it were there.

It was one of the elements of it that Mr. Brand was very red, that he held his head very high, that he had a bright, excited eye and an air of embarrassed boldness – the air of a man who has taken a resolve, in the execution of which he apprehends the failure, not of his moral, but of his personal, resources. Charlotte thought he looked very grand; and it is incontestable that Mr. Brand felt very grand. This, in fact, was the grandest moment of his life; and it was natural that such a moment should contain opportunities of awkwardness for a large, stout, modest young man.

'Come in, sir,' said Mr. Wentworth, with an angular wave of his hand. 'It is very proper that you should be present.'

'I know what you are talking about,' Mr. Brand rejoined. 'I heard what your nephew said.'

'And he heard what you said!' exclaimed Felix, patting him again on the arm.

'I am not sure that I understood,' said Mr. Wentworth, who had angularity in his voice as well as in his gestures.

Gertrude had been looking hard at her former suitor. She had been puzzled, like her sister; but her imagination moved more quickly than Charlotte's. 'Mr. Brand asked you to let Felix take me away,' she said to her father.

The young minister gave her a strange look. 'It is not because I don't want to see you any more,' he declared, in a tone intended as it were for publicity.

'I shouldn't think you would want to see me any more,' Gertrude answered, gently.

Mr. Wentworth stood staring. 'Isn't this rather a change, sir?' he inquired.

'Yes, sir.' And Mr. Brand looked anywhere; only still not at Charlotte. 'Yes, sir,' he repeated. And he held his handkerchief a few moments to his lips.

'Where are our moral grounds?' demanded Mr. Wentworth, who had always thought Mr. Brand would be just the thing for a younger daughter with a peculiar temperament.

'It is sometimes very moral to change, you know,' suggested Felix.

Charlotte had softly left her sister's side. She had edged gently toward her father, and now her hand found its way into his arm. Mr. Wentworth had folded up the 'Advertiser' into a surprisingly small compass, and, holding the roll with one hand, he earnestly clasped it with the other. Mr. Brand was looking at him; and yet, though Charlotte was so near, his eyes failed to meet her own. Gertrude watched her sister.

'It is better not to speak of change,' said Mr. Brand. 'In one sense there is no change. There was something I desired – something I asked of you; I desire something still – I ask it of you.' And he paused a moment; Mr. Wentworth looked bewildered. 'I should like, in my ministerial capacity, to unite this young couple.'

Gertrude, watching her sister, saw Charlotte flushing intensely, and Mr. Wentworth felt her pressing upon his arm. 'Heavenly Powers!' murmured Mr. Wentworth. And it was the nearest approach to profanity he had ever made.

'That is very nice; that is very handsome!' Felix exclaimed.

'I don't understand,' said Mr. Wentworth; though it was plain that every one else did.

'That is very beautiful, Mr. Brand,' said Gertrude, emulating Felix.

'I should like to marry you. It will give me great pleasure.'

'As Gertrude says, it's a beautiful idea,' said Felix.

Felix was smiling, but Mr. Brand was not even trying to. He himself treated his proposition very seriously. 'I have thought of it, and I should like to do it,' he affirmed.

Charlotte, meanwhile, was staring with expanded eyes. Her imagination, as I have said, was not so rapid as her sister's, but now it had taken several little jumps. 'Father,' she murmured, 'consent!'

Mr. Brand heard her; he looked away. Mr. Wentworth, evidently, had no imagination at all. 'I have always thought,' he began, slowly, 'that Gertrude's character required a special line of development.'

'Father,' repeated Charlotte, '*consent.*'

Then, at last, Mr. Brand looked at her. Her father felt her leaning more heavily upon his folded arm than she had ever done before; and this, with a certain sweet faintness in her voice, made him wonder what was the matter. He looked down at her and saw the encounter of her gaze with the young theologian's; but even this told him nothing, and he continued to be bewildered. Nevertheless, 'I consent,' he said at last, 'since Mr. Brand recommends it.'

'I should like to perform the ceremony very soon,' observed Mr. Brand, with a sort of solemn simplicity.

'Come, come, that's charming!' cried Felix, profanely.

Mr. Wentworth sank into his chair. 'Doubtless, when you understand it,' he said, with a certain judicial asperity.

Gertrude went to her sister and led her away, and Felix having passed his arm into Mr. Brand's and stepped out of the long window with him, the old man was left sitting there in unillumined perplexity.

Felix did no work that day. In the afternoon, with Gertrude, he got into one of the boats and floated about with idly-dipping oars. They talked a good deal of Mr. Brand – though not exclusively.

'That was a fine stroke,' said Felix. 'It was really heroic.'

Gertrude sat musing, with her eyes upon the ripples. 'That was what he wanted to be; he wanted to do something fine.'

'He won't be comfortable till he has married us,' said Felix. 'So much the better.'

'He wanted to be magnanimous; he wanted to have a fine moral pleasure. I know him so well,' Gertrude went on. Felix looked at her; she spoke slowly, gazing at the clear water. 'He thought of it a great deal, night and day. He thought it would be beautiful. At last he made up his mind that it was his duty, his duty to do just that – nothing less than that. He felt exalted; he felt sublime. That's how he likes to feel. It is better for him than if I had listened to him.'

'It's better for me,' smiled Felix. 'But do you know, as regards the sacrifice, that I don't believe he admired you when this decision was taken quite so much as he had done a fortnight before?'

'He never admired me. He admires Charlotte; he pitied me. I know him so well.'

'Well, then, he didn't pity you so much.'

Gertrude looked at Felix a little, smiling. 'You shouldn't permit yourself,' she said, 'to diminish the splendour of his action. He admires Charlotte,' she repeated.

'That's capital!' said Felix laughingly, and dipping his oars. I cannot say exactly to which member of Gertrude's phrase he alluded; but he dipped his oars again, and they kept floating about.

Neither Felix nor his sister, on that day, was present at Mr. Wentworth's at the evening repast. The two occupants of the chalet dined together, and the young man informed his companion that his marriage was now an assured fact. Eugenia congratulated him, and replied that if he were as reasonable a husband as he had been, on the whole, a brother, his wife would have nothing to complain of.

Felix looked at her a moment, smiling. 'I hope,' he said, 'not to be thrown back on my reason.'

'It is very true,' Eugenia rejoined, 'that one's reason is dismally flat. It's a bed with the mattress removed.'

But the brother and sister, later in the evening, crossed over to the larger house, the Baroness desiring to compliment her prospective sister-in-law. They found the usual circle upon the piazza, with the exception of Clifford Wentworth and Lizzie Acton; and as every one stood up as usual to welcome the Baroness, Eugenia had an admiring audience for her compliment to Gertrude.

Robert Acton stood on the edge of the piazza, leaning against one of the white columns, so that he found himself next to Eugenia while she acquitted herself of a neat little discourse of congratulation.

'I shall be so glad to know you better,' she said; 'I have seen so much less of you than I should have liked. Naturally; now I see the reason why! You will love me a little, won't you? I think I may say I gain on being known.' And terminating these observations with the softest cadence of her voice, the Baroness imprinted a sort of grand official kiss upon Gertrude's forehead.

Increased familiarity had not, to Gertrude's imagination,

diminished the mysterious impressiveness of Eugenia's personality, and she felt flattered and transported by this little ceremony. Robert Acton also seemed to admire it, as he admired so many of the gracious manifestations of Madame Münster's wit.

They had the privilege of making him restless, and on this occasion he walked away, suddenly, with his hands in his pockets, and then came back and leaned against his column. Eugenia was now complimenting her uncle upon his daughter's engagement, and Mr. Wentworth was listening with his usual plain yet refined politeness. It is to be supposed that by this time his perception of the mutual relations of the young people who surrounded him had become more acute; but he still took the matter very seriously, and he was not at all exhilarated.

'Felix will make her a good husband,' said Eugenia. 'He will be a charming companion; he has a great quality – indestructible gaiety.'

'You think that's a great quality?' asked the old man.

Eugenia meditated, with her eyes upon his. 'You think one gets tired of it, eh?'

'I don't know that I am prepared to say that,' said Mr. Wentworth.

'Well, we will say, then, that it is tiresome for others but delightful for one's self. A woman's husband, you know, is supposed to be her second self; so that, for Felix and Gertrude, gaiety will be a common property.'

'Gertrude was always very gay,' said Mr. Wentworth. He was trying to follow this argument.

Robert Acton took his hands out of his pockets and came a little nearer to the Baroness. 'You say you gain by being known,' he said. 'One certainly gains by knowing you.'

'What have *you* gained?' asked Eugenia.

'An immense amount of wisdom.'

'That's a questionable advantage for a man who was already so wise!'

Acton shook his head. 'No, I was a great fool before I knew you!'

'And being a fool you made my acquaintance? You are very complimentary.'

'Let me keep it up,' said Acton, laughing. 'I hope, for our pleasure, that your brother's marriage will detain you.'

'Why should I stop for my brother's marriage when I would not stop for my own?' asked the Baroness.

'Why shouldn't you stop in either case, now that, as you say, you have dissolved that mechanical tie that bound you to Europe?'

The Baroness looked at him a moment. 'As I say? You look as if you doubted it.'

'Ah,' said Acton, returning her glance, 'that is a remnant of my old folly! We have other attractions,' he added. 'We are to have another marriage.'

But she seemed not to hear him; she was looking at him still. 'My word was never doubted before,' she said.

'We are to have another marriage,' Acton repeated, smiling.

Then she appeared to understand. 'Another marriage?' And she looked at the others. Felix was chattering to Gertrude; Charlotte, at a distance, was watching them; and Mr. Brand, in quite another quarter, was turning his back to them, and, with his hands under his coat-tails and his large head on one side, was looking at the small, tender crescent of a young moon. 'It ought to be Mr. Brand and Charlotte,' said Eugenia, 'but it doesn't look like it.'

'There,' Acton answered, 'you must judge just now by contraries. There is more than there looks to be. I expect that combination one of these days; but that is not what I meant.'

'Well,' said the Baroness, 'I never guess my own lovers; so I can't guess other people's.'

Acton gave a loud laugh, and he was about to add a rejoinder when Mr. Wentworth approached his niece. 'You will be interested to hear,' the old man said, with a momentary aspiration toward jocosity, 'of another matrimonial venture in our little circle.'

'I was just telling the Baroness,' Acton observed.

'Mr. Acton was apparently about to announce his own engagement,' said Eugenia.

Mr. Wentworth's jocosity increased. 'It is not exactly that; but it is in the family. Clifford, hearing this morning that Mr.

Brand had expressed a desire to tie the nuptial knot for his sister, took it into his head to arrange that, while his hand was in, our good friend should perform a like ceremony for himself and Lizzie Acton.'

The Baroness threw back her head and smiled at her uncle; then turning, with an intenser radiance, to Robert Acton, 'I am certainly very stupid not to have thought of that,' she said. Acton looked down at his boots, as if he thought he had perhaps reached the limits of legitimate experimentation, and for a moment Eugenia said nothing more. It had been, in fact, a sharp knock, and she needed to recover herself. This was done, however, promptly enough. 'Where are the young people?' she asked.

'They are spending the evening with my mother.'

'Is not the thing very sudden?'

Acton looked up. 'Extremely sudden. There had been a tacit understanding; but within a day or two Clifford appears to have received some mysterious impulse to precipitate the affair.'

'The impulse,' said the Baroness, 'was the charms of your very pretty sister.'

'But my sister's charms were an old story; he had always known her.' Acton had begun to experiment again.

Here, however, it was evident the Baroness would not help him. 'Ah, one can't say! Clifford is very young; but he is a nice boy.'

'He's a likeable sort of boy, and he will be a rich man.' This was Acton's last experiment. Madame Münster turned away.

She made but a short visit and Felix took her home. In her little drawing-room she went almost straight to the mirror over the chimney-piece, and, with a candle uplifted, stood looking into it. 'I shall not wait for your marriage,' she said to her brother. 'To-morrow my maid shall pack up.'

'My dear sister,' Felix exclaimed, 'we are to be married immediately! Mr. Brand is too uncomfortable.'

But Eugenia, turning and still holding her candle aloft, only looked about the little sitting-room at her gimcracks and curtains and cushions. 'My maid shall pack up,' she repeated. '*Bonté divine*, what rubbish! I feel like a strolling actress; these are my "properties".'

'Is the play over, Eugenia?' asked Felix.

She gave him a sharp glance. 'I have spoken my part.'

'With great applause!' said her brother.

'Oh, applause – applause!' she murmured. And she gathered up two or three of her dispersed draperies. She glanced at the beautiful brocade, and then, 'I don't see how I can have endured it!' she said.

'Endure it a little longer. Come to my wedding.'

'Thank you; that's your affair. My affairs are elsewhere.'

'Where are you going?'

'To Germany – by the first ship.'

'You have decided not to marry Mr. Acton?'

'I have refused him,' said Eugenia.

Her brother looked at her in silence. 'I am sorry,' he rejoined at last. 'But I was very discreet, as you asked me to be. I said nothing.'

'Please continue, then, not to allude to the matter,' said Eugenia.

Felix inclined himself gravely. 'You shall be obeyed. But your position in Germany?' he pursued.

'Please to make no observations upon it.'

'I was only going to say that I supposed it was altered.'

'You are mistaken.'

'But I thought you had signed –'

'I have not signed!' said the Baroness.

Felix urged her no further, and it was arranged that he should immediately assist her to embark.

Mr. Brand was indeed, it appeared, very impatient to consummate his sacrifice and deliver the nuptial benediction which would set it off so handsomely; but Eugenia's impatience to withdraw from a country in which she had not found the fortune she had come to seek was even less to be mistaken. It is true she had not made any very various exertion; but she appeared to feel justified in generalizing – in deciding that the conditions of action on this provincial continent were not favourable to really superior women. The elder world was, after all, their natural field. The unembarrassed directness with which she proceeded to apply these intelligent conclusions appeared to the little circle of spectators who have figured in our narrative but the supreme exhibition of a character to which the experience of life had imparted an inimitable pliancy. It had a distinct effect upon Robert Acton, who, for the two days preceding her departure, was a very restless and irritated mortal. She passed her last evening at her uncle's, where she had never been more charming; and in parting with Clifford Wentworth's affianced bride she drew from her own finger a curious old ring and presented it to her with the prettiest speech and kiss. Gertrude, who as an affianced bride was also indebted to her gracious bounty, admired this little incident extremely, and Robert Acton almost wondered whether it did not give him the right, as Lizzie's brother and guardian, to offer in return a handsome present to the Baroness. It would have made him extremely happy to be able to offer a handsome present to the Baroness; but he abstained from this expression of his sentiments, and they were in consequence, at the very last, by so much the less comfortable. It was almost at the very last that he saw her – late the night before she went to Boston to embark.

'For myself, I wish you might have stayed,' he said. 'But not for your own sake.'

'I don't make so many differences,' said the Baroness. 'I am simply sorry to be going.'

'That's a much deeper difference than mine,' Acton declared; 'for you mean you are simply glad!'

Felix parted with her on the deck of the ship. 'We shall often meet over there,' he said.

'I don't know,' she answered. 'Europe seems to me much larger than America.'

Mr. Brand, of course, in the days that immediately followed, was not the only impatient spirit; but it may be said that of all the young spirits interested in the event none rose more eagerly to the level of the occasion. Gertrude left her father's house with Felix Young; they were imperturbably happy and they went far away. Clifford and his young wife sought their felicity in a narrower circle, and the latter's influence upon her husband was such as to justify, strikingly, that theory of the elevating effect of easy intercourse with clever women which Felix had

propounded to Mr. Wentworth. Gertrude was for a good while
a distant figure, but she came back when Charlotte married
Mr. Brand. She was present at the wedding feast, where Felix's
gaiety confessed to no change. Then she disappeared, and the
echo of a gaiety of her own, mingled with that of her husband, often came back to the home of her earlier years. Mr.
Wentworth at last found himself listening for it; and Robert
Acton, after his mother's death, married a particularly nice
young girl.

Glossary of French Words and Expressions

affreux	dreadful
aisance	affluence
à la bonne heure	all in good time
beau cousin	handsome cousin
beau vieillard	handsome old man
bon	good
bonté divine	good heavens
cachette	hiding place
camarades	friends
ce sera clair, au moins	that will be clear, at least
c'est bien vague	that's very vague
c'est de son âge	it's appropriate for his years
c'est fini	it's over
chaussures	shoes
chinoiseries	objects and furniture from China, or decorated in a Chinese fashion
comme c'est bariolé	how multi-coloured it is
comme c'est bien	how nice it is
comme il faut	correct, proper
comme vous devez avoir raison	how right you are
cousine	cousin (female)
dame	indeed
dans cette galère	in that situation (literally, 'in that ship', a reference to a line from a play by Molière (1622–73))
désagréments	annoyances
en attendant	while waiting for
en famille	as part of the family

en l'air	up in the air, unsettled
ennui	boredom
galant homme	gentleman
habitués	regular visitors
il faudra lui faire un peu de toilette	we will have to dress it up a little
intime	intimate
je me range	I'm settling down
je ne la crains pas	I'm not afraid of it/her
je n'en suis pas là	I'm not in such a bad state
je n'y comprends rien	I don't understand anything
la cour, [faire]	to pay attention to, court
la main heureuse	delicate touch
les beaux jours sont passés	the fine days are over
les yeux doux	sheep's eyes
mais entrez donc	but do come in
mal-élevée	badly brought up
mise en scène	staging (of a play)
nous n'avons qu'a nous tenir	we only have to do the right thing
nous n'en sommes pas là	we're not at that stage
par exemple	for example
pas de zèle	curb your enthusiasm
plans reculés	(in art criticism) background
porte à porte	directly next door
portières	door hangings
pour la demande	for the proposal
quatrième	fourth floor of an apartment building
qu'en savez vous?	what do you know about it?
que voulez vous?	what do you mean?
salon	drawing room; also, in European society, a regular gathering of literary or artistic people at the house of a leading personage
soubrette	maid
tête à tête	private/intimate conversation
ton	tone, mood
tu vas voir	you'll see
visite d'adieux	farewell visit
voilà	there it is

voix du sang	ties of blood
vous plaisantez	you are joking
vous serez de la partie	you'll be one of us
vous vous y prenez mal	you are setting about it the wrong way
voyons	let's see
vrai monde	social mainstream (literally, 'real world')

Notes

I

1. *upwards of thirty years since*: The most extensive account we have of the genesis of *The Europeans* is in a letter from James to William Dean Howells in 1877, in which he writes of his intention to set his story in some 'imaginary locality in New England 1830'. A few lines later, however, he tells Howells that 'I shall play havoc with the New England background!' (*Letters*, vol. II, p. 106). As I suggest in the Introduction, James constructs a narrative structured around contrasts that are prone to unravelling. His lack of concern with documenting the co-ordinates of a precise social history (see note 2 below) contributes to the 'havoc' that allows him to evoke an American mood, often for comic effect.

2. *huge, low omnibus . . . small horses*: One contemporary review of the novel, by the Boston critic Thomas Wentworth Higginson, criticized James for placing horse-cars in the Boston of the 1840s. They were not introduced to the city until the 1850s. See F. W. Dupee, ed., *The Question of Henry James: A Collection of Critical Essays* (1945; New York: Octagon Books, 1973).

3. *Hebe . . . wine-cup*: Daughter of Zeus and Hera, and wife of Hercules, Hebe was the cup-bearer of the gods; her name in Greek means 'young maturity', a combination suited to James's complex representation of Eugenia, who is being described here.

4. *Mid-May's Eldest Child*: The reference is to John Keats (1795–1821), 'Ode to a Nightingale' (1820): 'And Mid-May's eldest child / The coming musk-rose, full of dewy wine, / The murmurous haunt of flies on summer eves.'

5. *Reigning Prince*: See II, note 4.

6. *Bohemian*: The use of this word for a struggling artist was still quite new in the 1840s; see V, note 4.

7. *Mahometan*: An alternative, and now rarely used, term for a

Muslim; the *Oxford English Dictionary* cites its continued presence in the nineteenth century.

II

1. *Prince Camaralzaman and the Princess Badoura*: Characters from *The Arabian Nights*, a collection of stories that first appeared in Arabic around 650 AD, and became popular with non-Middle Eastern readers in the eighteenth and nineteenth centuries through translations. James was familiar with the 1847 edition of *The Arabian Nights*, edited by Edward Forster and published in four volumes in New York and Boston. Princess Badoura is the daughter of the King of the Interior Islands, in China; Prince Camaralzaman is the son of the King of Khalidan. The prince and princess are alike as twins and decide to exchange clothes. When magically separated, the princess rules in his place and marries as a man. In the end, order is returned when the prince returns and marries both the princess and her queen.
2. *refection*: Refreshment.
3. *as the Queen of Sheba came to Solomon*: 1 Kings 10:1–13. Like Eugenia, Sheba arrives at the court of King Solomon bearing the traces of exotic difference: 'with a very great train, with camels that bare spices, and very much gold, and precious stones' (v.2, Authorized version of the Bible).
4. *Silberstadt-Schreckenstein*: The name is a combination of the German words for 'silver', 'town', 'fright' and 'stone', suggestive of a location both attractive and alienating. The paradoxical nature of this combination is perfectly suited to Eugenia's unsettled state, as revealed in Felix's next remarks. The younger sons of royal princes in Germany automatically bore the title of prince; hence the need to distinguish the Reigning Prince from his brother or brothers. Morganatic marriages were a legal device to ensure that, when a prince contracted a marriage with someone of lesser rank, no hereditary titles or possessions devolved to the children of the marriage, or to the spouse.

III

1. *killed the fatted calf*: A reference to the biblical parable of the prodigal son (Luke 15:11–32), in which the dissolute son's return is celebrated by his father.
2. *it looks like a magnified Nüremberg toy*: Nuremberg, in

Germany, has been a centre of toy production for more than six hundred years. Charles Dickens (1812–70) had earlier used the same analogy as Felix when describing the suburbs of Boston: 'the small churches and chapels are so prim, and bright, and highly varnished; that I almost believed the whole affair could be taken up piecemeal like a child's toy, and crammed into a little box' (*American Notes for General Circulation* (1842), ed. Patricia Ingham (London: Penguin Books, 2000), pp. 34–5).

3. *Deborah and Hephzibah*: Eugenia's references here are to ridicule the Puritan practice of naming children after biblical characters. Deborah is referred to in Judges 4:4; Hephzibah appears in 2 Kings 21:1.

4. *barouche*: A fashionable type of horse-drawn four-wheeled carriage.

5. *Empress Josephine*: Marie-Josèphe-Rose Tascher de la Pagerie (1763–1814), the first wife of Napoleon I. This is perhaps a strange item on display in the Wentworth household. Josephine's regal status and her liberal sexuality would seem to sit uneasily with a Puritan ethos. Yet, in addition to supporting my contention in the Introduction that James deliberately sets out to disrupt the expected cultural markers in the novel, Josephine's ambiguous marital status is akin to Eugenia's morganatic relationship. Josephine married Napoleon in a civil ceremony in 1796, and again in a religious service in 1804, before the marriage was annulled by her husband in 1809.

6. *Unitarian*: Unitarianism, a Christian denomination with its origins in Reformation Europe, was well established in New England by the 1840s. It rejected the doctrine of the Trinity and advocated instead a liberal theology of reason and 'self-culture'. Major figures in the history of American Unitarianism include William Ellery Channing (1780–1842) and Ralph Waldo Emerson (see VI, note 6.) Eugenia, thoroughly Europeanized and married into European aristocracy, is presumably a Catholic, like her mother, hence her close questioning of Mr Brand's status here.

IV

1. *court-plaster*: Patch of adhesive fabric, often silk, used for covering small cuts and abrasions.

2. *soubrette*: The character of the *soubrette*, or maid, in popular French drama was usually coquettish or intriguing. The use of

the word here highlights the relationship between identity and forms of theatrical performance that James plays with throughout the novel.

3. *bombazine*: Corded material, either of silk or, more likely in this context, cotton.

4. *Quakerism*: Quakers, members of a Christian sect founded in England in the mid-seventeenth century, first arrived at Boston in 1656; the Quaker colony of Pennsylvania was founded in 1682. For much of its early history in America, the sect was viewed as dangerously heretical and its members often persecuted. By the mid-nineteenth-century, Quakerism was one of many Protestant denominations on the east coast. Eugenia's reference to it in association with the Wentworths here is nothing more than a form of cultural shorthand for her perception of her cousins' simplicity and apparent lack of artifice.

5. *eleemosynary*: From the Latin for alms, eleemosynary here reminds us that Eugenia was living in the cottage through her uncle's charity.

6. *quarter-day*: One of four fixed days in the year when payment of rent and other quarterly charges is made.

7. *of Madame de Staël, of Madame Récamier*: Anne-Louise Germaine Necker, Madame de Staël (1766–1817) and Jeanne-Françoise-Julie-Adelaide, Madame Récamier (1777–1849), two notable French conversationalists and hostesses of *salons*. Madame de Staël was also an important author, whose novel *Corinne* (1807), in part an examination of national differences, was widely read and admired in the United States.

V

1. *peccadilloes*: Small faults or trifling offences.

2. *daguerreotype*: An early form of photography developed in the 1830s by Louis Jacques Mandé Daguerre (1789–1851) in France. In the United States, daguerreotypes began to appear in 1839, and one of the earliest commercial portrait studios was opened by Robert Cornelius in Boston in 1840.

3. *Their name is legion*: Refers to Mark 5:9: 'My name is Legion, for we are many.'

4. *A Bohemian*: Gertrude's confusion over the meaning of the word here is understandable. The *Oxford English Dictionary* cites 1848 as the earliest use of 'bohemian' in the sense meant by Felix, the same year that Henri Murger (1822–61) published in

France *Scènes de la vie de bohème* (*Scenes from Bohemian Life*).
5. '*Nicholas Nickleby*': A novel by Dickens, published in 1839, whose hero similarly spends time with a theatrical troupe.

VI

1. *Schloss*: Castle (German).
2. *pension*: Allowance paid as part of her marriage settlement.
3. *putting your trust in princes*: Echoes Psalm 146, v. 2: 'put not your trust in princes'.
4. *Celestial Empire*: China.
5. *Emerson's Essays*: Ralph Waldo Emerson (1803–82), Transcendentalist philosopher, poet and lecturer, was arguably the most important nineteenth-century American intellectual. His first series of *Essays* was published in 1841, the second in 1844. The provincial nature of antebellum New England culture, James thought, was particularly suited to the 'early newness' of Emerson's thought: 'In the light, fresh American air, unthickened and undarkened by customs and institutions established, these things, as the phrase is, told' (*Hawthorne*, in *Literary Criticism*, vol. II, pp. 383, 384).

VII

1. *house-thief*: The Osgood edition has 'horse-thief'. James's manuscript reads, more plausibly, 'house-thief', and the text has been changed accordingly.
2. *Philistine*: In the Old Testament, the Philistines were the traditional enemies of Israel, but by the mid-nineteenth century the word had come to signify someone deficient in culture and civilized values. Mr Wentworth's startled repetition may suggest he is thinking of the original meaning.
3. *Sicurissimo*: Most certainly (Italian).
4. *Leghorn hats*: Stiff straw hats with a flat crown.
5. *epithalamium*: A song or poem composed in praise of a bride and groom.

VIII

1. *the Common*: At the heart of Boston, the Common is the oldest public park in the United States. The area was designated common pasture land in 1634. It was also used for military

purposes and public hangings. From 1830 the grazing of cattle was forbidden.

IX

1. *Newport*: In the nineteenth century, a fashionable holiday resort on Rhode Island, fifty miles from Boston. The James family lived in Newport between 1858 and 1859, and again between 1860 and 1864. In chapter six of his travel book *The American Scene* (1907), James writes of his sense of contrast between the Newport of his childhood – 'a whole world that called out to the long afternoons of youth, a world with its scale so measured and intended and happy' – and that which he encountered in 1904 – 'it now bristles with . . . monuments of pecuniary power' (New York: Penguin Books, 1994), p. 158).

2. *'North American Review'*: An important literary and cultural journal that began publishing in Boston in 1815, and continued to be based there until 1940. James's essays and reviews regularly appeared in its pages, the first appearing in 1864 and the last in 1912.

X

1. *Andiamo*: Let's go (Italian).

XI

1. *Raphael's*: Raffaello Sanzio (1483–1520), Italian painter of the Renaissance.

XII

1. *Boston 'Advertiser'*: The *Boston Daily Advertiser* (1813–1929), Boston's most successful daily newspaper in the nineteenth century.

PENGUIN CLASSICS

WASHINGTON SQUARE
HENRY JAMES

'Why, you must take me or leave me ... You can't please your father and me both; you must choose between us'

When timid and plain Catherine Sloper acquires a dashing and determined suitor, her father, convinced that the young man is nothing more than a fortune-hunter, decides to put a stop to their romance. Torn between a desire to win her father's approval and passion for the first man who has ever declared his love for her, Catherine faces an agonizing choice, and eventually becomes all too aware of the restrictions that others seek to place on her freedom. James's masterly novel deftly interweaves the public and private faces of nineteenth-century New York society, and is also a moving study of innocence destroyed.

Part of a series of new Penguin Classics editions of Henry James's works, this edition contains a chronology, suggested reading, notes and an introduction discussing the novel's lasting influence and James's depiction of the quiet strength of his heroine.

'Perhaps the only novel in which a man has successfully invaded the feminine field and produced a work comparable to Jane Austen's' Graham Greene

Edited with an introduction and notes by Martha Banta
Series editor Philip Horne

PENGUIN CLASSICS

THE GARDEN PARTY AND OTHER STORIES
KATHERINE MANSFIELD

'Kisses, voices, tinkling spoons, laughter, the smell of crushed grass'

Innovative, startlingly perceptive and aglow with colour, these fifteen stories were written towards the end of Katherine Mansfield's tragically short life. Many are set in the author's native New Zealand, others in England and the French Riviera. All are revelations of the unspoken, half-understood emotions that make up everyday experience – from the blackly comic 'The Daughers of the Late Colonel', and the short, sharp sketch 'Miss Brill', in which a lonely woman's precarious sense of self is brutally destroyed, to the vivid, impressionistic evocation of family life in 'At the Bay' and the poignant, haunting miniature masterpiece 'The Garden Party'.

This edition contains an introduction by novelist Lorna Sage discussing Katherine Mansfield's life and her mastery of the short story form, with further reading and notes.

'One of the great modernist writers' Lorna Sage

Edited with an introduction and notes by Lorna Sage

THE STORY OF PENGUIN CLASSICS

Before 1946 ... 'Classics' are mainly the domain of academics and students; readable editions for everyone else are almost unheard of. This all changes when a little-known classicist, E. V. Rieu, presents Penguin founder Allen Lane with the translation of Homer's *Odyssey* that he has been working on in his spare time.

1946 Penguin Classics debuts with *The Odyssey*, which promptly sells three million copies. Suddenly, classics are no longer for the privileged few.

1950s Rieu, now series editor, turns to professional writers for the best modern, readable translations, including Dorothy L. Sayers's *Inferno* and Robert Graves's unexpurgated *Twelve Caesars*.

1960s The Classics are given the distinctive black covers that have remained a constant throughout the life of the series. Rieu retires in 1964, hailing the Penguin Classics list as 'the greatest educative force of the twentieth century.'

1970s A new generation of translators swells the Penguin Classics ranks, introducing readers of English to classics of world literature from more than twenty languages. The list grows to encompass more history, philosophy, science, religion and politics.

1980s The Penguin American Library launches with titles such as *Uncle Tom's Cabin*, and joins forces with Penguin Classics to provide the most comprehensive library of world literature available from any paperback publisher.

1990s The launch of Penguin Audiobooks brings the classics to a listening audience for the first time, and in 1999 the worldwide launch of the Penguin Classics website extends their reach to the global online community.

The 21st Century Penguin Classics are completely redesigned for the first time in nearly twenty years. This world-famous series now consists of more than 1300 titles, making the widest range of the best books ever written available to millions – and constantly redefining what makes a 'classic'.

The Odyssey continues ...

The best books ever written

PENGUIN CLASSICS

SINCE 1946

Find out more at www.penguinclassics.com